Forget Batman and Robin! This dynamic duo will blow your mind!

— JANET, BARNES AND NOBLE REVIEWER

Frost, Eva and their Aunt Maggie are wonderfully drawn, feisty women.

— IND'TALE MAGAZINE

With ghostly legends, mystery, heartbreak, murder, and possession—this book will keep you flipping the pages desperate to find out what happens next.

— VANESSA, BOUND AND BREWED

Fans of Sam and Dean Winchester will definitely get a kick out of this book.

— CLAIRE, THE COFEEHOLIC BOOKWORM

The bond between the sisters felt genuine and just seemed natural.

— BOB, PLATYPIRE

Thrilling and captivating.

Once you start reading this book you will not want to put it down even for a minute.

I will definitely be getting the sequels. I like the different twist on ghost mythology in the story, the teenagers are authentic, and the humor is sly to add a little fun, the occasional smirk.

A good blend of mystery, paranormal, and romance. It is a clean read, nothing crude in it. I feel good about recommending it to my friends – a quality that many books in this genre don't possess.

I love the way each chapter is from a sister's point of view.

Totally fun and imaginative read. The sisters are relatable, the supernatural is thrilling, and the settings are true-to-life. I am so excited to have a new series!!!

SLEEP, DON'T FRET

Sisters of Bloodcreek #2

MARY GRAY, CAMMIE LARSEN

MONSTER IVY
PUBLISHING

Cover Design by Cammie Larsen

Read a FREE short story prequel about our favorite Blurred One turned hunter friend, Leo, by visiting BookHip.com/PWSHNX.

ISBN (ePub): 978-1-948095-14-3
ISBN (Paperback): 978-1-948095-15-0
ISBN (Audio): 978-1-948095-16-7

To Travis, for making us do this.

The transmigration of souls is no fable.

— RALPH WALDO EMERSON

CHAPTER 1 - EVA

Clutching the steering wheel like a purple-haired granny, I slam on the brakes. I narrowly avoid hitting a rusty delivery truck that's just decided it owns this tiny road. "Come on, New Orleans!" I wail. "You're supposed to be better than this."

So many one-way streets. And people. Drunk people. Walking every which way to dodge piles of trash. I guess I'm not sure what I expected, but I think it has something to do with being somewhat . . . classier? Bigger? Definitely a little cleaner.

"You said it was the best yesterday," Frost argues, all sassy with her chin tucked into her plaid collar. I stick my tongue out at her, but through the corner of my mouth so I can focus on this monstrosity of a neighborhood.

"That's because yesterday was awesome," I concede. "City Park was awesome—and we had the boys and Mags with us." Those big ace trees, friendly people, a gorgeous gazebo to cuddle with Raylan in? Those were all hard to be mad at. "But this French Quarter is madness."

Some dude in the debonair mixture of a beret and

Hooters shirt steps right in front of Betsy. I brace myself and slam on the brakes again, as I had finally reached the speed of like five miles an hour. "Really, dude?"

Frost holds her hands up like I've somehow blamed her.

"Tell me it gets better," I demand, but lightly. She's taken on so much responsibility since Dad died, I try to remember to not need anything from her.

It's true we've been in the French Quarter for a whole three minutes, so I probably shouldn't be making such definitive accusations about the place, but still. Give me potholes and roadkill to dodge, not drunk pedestrians and speeding trucks. It's enough to make me, the usual designated calm driver, spaz.

"Google says to turn left up here," Frost says. "Two more minutes to your love-ah." She lets me vent about driving conditions, so I assume for now that she agrees with me. "Saint Mary. Turn."

"Yes'm. Here we go, because I cannot see anythi—" I end in a shriek and slam on the brakes again as a taxi speeds down Saint Mary street. "This is the worst." But I risk glancing up for a half-second, and I'm digging the intricate green and black iron work on hundreds of balconies. And the different blue, green, white and red stucco, even if it's all mossy and faded. "Cool architecture, though."

Frost gives a dainty snort as she tucks a gorgeous strand of blonde hair behind her ear. "The worst, with cool architecture." She looks back at her phone for directions. "Got it."

"Oh, hush up your mouth." I wink at her sideways, not really caring if she sees. She knows I love to play on Mom's way of saying "shut up," and she knows I sound way more irritated than I am. It's still an adventure in a new city, and she actually took two days off work to be here. No way I'd actually be mad. "Two more minutes till we're re-u-ni-ted!" I sing like a hairband singer from the eighties.

"And we test out our hunting skills," Frost sings less dramatically, but the fact she's singing back at all proves she's almost as excited, even if we're both still a smidge nervous.

"Watch out, world!" I hold my ringed fist out for her to bump.

"Darn straight," she agrees while bumping my fist.

I reach a stop sign and glance at my sister. My heart feels good when I see her self-satisfied grin instead of the usual weight-of-the-world emptiness she carries most days. She must be getting into the excitement of the hunt.

"Now pull into this parking lot. Grab a ticket over there." She points to a ticket machine across the lot. "We better hurry, it's getting dark."

"Look at you, getting better at directions, Sacajawea." She has enough she can tease me about, but I'll never let her live down how she forgot her way to chemistry class five times in our two-hallway school.

Finally able to see that this road is free of taxis and renegade pedestrians, I gun it across the street to the parking lot. "Yeah, we just need some handsome men and our dear friend Mags back to enjoy this city." I roll down my window to grab a parking pass and take a breath of the Deep Southern air but end with a cough, like my body has sampled this air and rejected it as poison. "Ugh! It smells like puke, pee, and poop put together! For crying out loud."

Frost gets a wicked grin on her face that I usually see in the mirror. "All the better to hunt down evil, my sister."

———

I peek around Maggie's worse-for-wear Buick and squint through the foggy New Orleans night. Here, behind the gorgeous, towering St. Louis Cathedral, we've set our trap. The cathedral's shadow looms even in the dark, making this a quiet street with plenty of room for us novice hunters to mess up. Thankfully, the smell has changed from that of excrement to red pepper and garlic. We must celebrate with Cajun food after this.

Our target is a renegade witch doctor, Monsieur Avi, who's been granting wishes of love. What he fails to inform his clients is that once they are happily coupled up, the spelled lover goes nuts and kills everyone their new boyfriend or girlfriend has ever loved, including family. Mags guesses he's killed at least fifty people.

Now, we wait for Avi to fall into our trap. I'm happy to get to hang with Raylan for a second and tell him my latest insane nightmare. He's crouched next to me behind the Buick.

"I was surrounded by cannibals," I whisper. "They were tiny little creatures, but they were going to eat me alive. I begged them to let me die first, but they weren't having it."

Old iron groans from the other side of the car where Frost places a nasty bear trap on the old cobblestone street.

"I was able to get my gun and shoot myself in the head, but I didn't die right away." I grimace and tug my black tee down for reassurance. "Instead, I just felt my head fill up with blood while the little effers started gnawing on my hands."

Raylan looks equal parts mortified and amused, and with his hair messed up in the back like usual, my heart palpitates a bit. He gives me a quick peck on the lips before asking, "Why are your dreams so violent?"

I give him my most angelic look. "So I can be so perfectly sweet in real life?"

Maggie growls from behind a giant Cypress, where she's promised to wait while we attempt to prove ourselves. "Focus, Eva. Beau should be showing up any second."

Beau. Poor, dumb Beau. He's handsome enough, but he's a ginger, and that's really not my thing. I think he's related to Wade somehow and moved to Bloodcreek a couple months ago, which has kept Frost distracted since Leo left her to go get born. But talk about a step down. She seems happy enough though, and right now, he makes the perfect bait for our witch doctor trap.

Beau's twangy voice carries through the humidity like a steamboat on the Mississippi. "I've got the cash in my car."

There it is. The signal he's just around the corner. My heart pounds, adrenaline surging, and I pray my sweat doesn't soak through my shirt. Though I can't hold back an inch of a grin when I turn to Raylan.

"My turn." I get to take out the baddie. Frost is going to get him in the bear trap, then all I gotta do is grab his cane and recite the spell that blocks his magic before he can get himself out of the trap. Plenty of backup, but this time, the Abram sisters got this.

Not like the time we were supposed to stab that fugly shape-shifter in St. Louis with the silver dagger I somehow left in Maggie's car. So this is the night I redeem myself and call myself a bonafide hunter. Then maybe we can celebrate with some beignets and that fried whatever deliciousness I smell.

"Take care of him, babe," Raylan whispers. "Beau probably secretly wants the love spell to work so Frost'll go crazy for him, and I can't have anything happening to you." He nudges my knee with his. "And Beau? You know any guy that confident must be compensating for something." We snicker quietly together, but footsteps scrape on the deserted pavement, and I tighten my grip on my baseball bat. A telltale click of a cane. They're here.

"Do not worry, young friend." The witch doctor, Avi's, melodic voice rasps through the murky air. After seeing the pictures of these witch doctor dudes in Mag's library, I can't wait to see what sort of get-up he's got on.

"Well, I can't wait to have this beauty fall in love with

me." Beau's voice booms, and I'm pretty sure all of New Orleans can hear him. "Her name may be Frost, but she sure is a hottie."

Raylan and I exchange matching grimaces. They're so close, I can smell the herbs radiating from our target.

"She'll be *all mine*," Beau says. The last signal.

Frost whips the bear trap out by its chain from under the car with a lightning-fast, tearing rattle and a *snap*. The trap's snagged its target, Avi's foot.

Howling curses from the witch doctor have me sprinting around the car. He's tall and powerfully built, his arms and chest all mountains and curves under his thin velvet vest. With the confidence of weeks of practice with Raylan, I club the "doctor" on the head with my bat, knocking his top hat to the cobblestone. His salt and pepper dreadlocks streak with blood. His eyes roll to the back of his skull, and his whole body drops like a sack of potatoes.

But then he's rolling on the street toward his cane like he just woke up from a tiny snooze, so I snatch his bird-head skeleton cane, just like Mags told me, and recite the spell before he starts working some of his hoodoo magic. He can't do nearly as much without his bewitched cane.

"*Ultra magicae. Nolite malum hoc.*" The Latin still feels weird to say, but I do like the sound of it, even if Leo did it so much better.

Avi hisses, then spits at me. I dodge in time, but if this is gonna be a thing, I'll wear waders next time instead of my cute, perfectly ripped jeans I scored at the thrift shop.

"Stupid children." He heaves, and his voice is darker somehow. And way creepier. Like I should whack him twice as hard.

He lunges for his cane, super fast, but howls again as the bear trap bites further into his thick ankle.

"We will come for you," he says, "and you will wish you

had more than your little bag of tricks." His face morphs into a twisted smirk. I'm gonna ignore that little voice in my head, reminding me that if *Monsieur Avi's* spell did happen, it would be me and my loved ones meeting an early end. We'll have none of that.

"How about you stop while you've got a head?" I wink at the man and stomp on his cane, snapping it in half.

Frost, Maggie, and Raylan all emerge from their hiding places. Maggie's looking stalwart as always with her Reaper and fanny pack. Raylan cocks his .45, but Frost puts a finger to her lips. She gives a quick finger jab behind her, toward the square, where drunk tourists meander by. They're pointing to the hundreds of purple, pink, green, and gold Mardi Gras beads dangling from an oak trees' branches like a newer, tackier Spanish moss. Don't need them getting involved.

The now-impotent witch doctor spews what I have to assume are all sorts of damning curses. I consider covering his mouth to quiet him, but the tourists are stumbling away, and to be honest, this dude looks real germy. Like he should maybe spend less time getting innocent people killed and more time bathing? Not in a hurry to touch that. Still, he's trapped, so Frost holds out her fist to me, and we follow a triumphant fist bump with hip bumps. Hers is as bony as ever.

"Great job, girls." Mags beams with pride as she lowers her Reaper. "But how about next time, you don't antagonize the target?"

The man continues writhing in the trap, trying to pry it open with his fingers.

His voice rises to a scream. "You little bi—"

Raylan bolts to his side and *POP*, shoots him in the head, cutting off Avi's less eloquent curse. The witch doctor slumps to the ground.

"Told you he needed to die." Raylan shoots a know-it-all wink at Maggie.

Well, that escalated quickly . . . We didn't plan on killing him, just taking away his magic, but with his body count, I suppose Raylan just did a favor to the human race by disposing of him directly.

"You and your trigger-happy sister," Maggie says, finger jabbing at Raylan.

"He was a murderer," Raylan scoffs. "He'd just find another way to kill."

Beau prods Avi's limp body with his foot. "Muscles has got a point."

"Yeah, but we ain't murderers," Maggie says, like this isn't the first time.

Frost slides up to Beau, who grabs her in a gorilla hug. Her eyes are blank when she lightly hugs him back.

After a ten-second staring match with Raylan, Mags huffs and turns to Frost. "Y'all done good," she says, nodding in assurance. "Real good, my little huntin' darlin's."

CHAPTER 2 - FROST

*W*e should be training, but I can handle a celebratory float down the bayou.

As Eva said on the drive from New Orleans to the boonies and through marshy lands and cattails, "What's the point of fighting if we never enjoy the win?"

Yes, this little adventure shall be good. I can buy into that. And, with the sun dipping below the horizon, making the sky a hazy orange, cicadas blaring as if through a megaphone, I figure I can live in the moment.

"You sure did know how to trap that witch doctor," Beau teases as we heave our canoe over flattened weeds and mud that squishes beneath our boots. His twangy drawl's a little too "Bloodcreek" for my taste, but even I can admit it's a little endearing. Like he's part Luke Bryan.

His Wranglers hug his spindly legs, and the massive hunting knife he personally forged is a badge of honor, clipped to the side of the belt made of some hide he skinned himself. His boots, though large, are surprisingly attractive, and he washes my half of the dishes at Lindy's without pay, so I let him lurk around.

While Mom's been faithfully turning in resumes, day after day, I've decided to provide for us all. Bills, the mortgage. All the fun stuff. Sometimes, I think I see Dad or Leo lurking in the trees or in the shadows. Approving or disapproving of a hunt. I don't blame them if they're quasi-critical. My fingers itch to grab the dagger stashed in my boot, but we can practice later. I can accept that.

As Beau and I hoist our canoe over fallen reeds and marshy grasses, it's like we've entered a new, fairytale-type of land. Where the only thing that matters is mosquitos flying around my nose and smelling the moisture in the air and dankness.

Spanish moss drips from tree limbs like they've taken on the part of being fairies themselves. And as I stare at them, they're bowing, curtseying—all of them, draped in a sheer fabric.

Locusts applaud the dancers in a low, distant hum, and white-winged herons flap their wings like an eerie percussion.

"I've never seen a bayou before," I murmur softly to Beau. I almost wish I could wrap the view of this place in the hollow of my hand.

He glances back and shoots me a wink. "It's one of my favorite places to go."

When we meet a moss-covered boulder, in tandem we lift the canoe, and when we make it to the water, Beau says, "We made it, girlie girl."

Placing his end of the canoe into the river, he waits for me to follow suit. Maggie roars from her already floating canoe, "Raylan!"

He and my sister are only a few paces behind Beau and me.

Maggie's confident, alto voice squashes any hint of wildlife from tarrying close. "Your sister's a little more this way downriver?"

Raylan cheerfully marches like he's part S.W.A.T. team officer. "Yes, ma'am!"

When Eva accidentally smashes her end of the canoe into the boulder, Raylan catches my eye, and the softness in his gaze reminds me all over again that he's absolutely smitten with my sister. Gently, he takes the whole canoe and carries it like it weighs nothing at all.

Maggie's voice continues to boom from the murky water. "Well, hello, little fella."

Wary, I turn to find a one-eyed alligator. Scales and horns transversely line the creature's face and back like he's part dinosaur. A single fold of skin droops over the hole that used to house his eyeball, and a primal raptor-like growl curls from his currently closed mouth.

Maggie glides even closer to the alligator, and she must have a death wish. She's always taking in injured animals and nursing them back to health.

"Be careful," I murmur.

Beau uses his oar to splash me with a little water, as I haven't gotten much farther than the water washing over my rain boots' ankles.

"Aren't ya comin'?" Beau calls.

He's already thigh-high in that gator-infested water, readying our canoe, soaking his Wranglers. But I'm not so sure I want to go on this canoe trip now. I'd forgotten about all the gators in the water.

"Don't be like that," Beau chides in his low drawl. "He's scareder of you than you of him."

I roll my eyes at his framing of words.

Casually, Maggie plops a pale hotdog into the water and coos at the animal like she thinks it's cute.

Raylan cries, "I should have brought my fishing pole!" as the scaly beast swallows its fourth hotdog in one white-mouthed gulp.

"I think," Maggie says, "I shall name her Eleanor."

"And now she's named her," I complain to Beau.

As we push off in our canoe, he shoots me a devilish grin. "Doesn't she name all her creatures?"

He has a point. There was the time Maggie put a cast on a stray cat's arm. Or the time she actually fastened wheels to a squirrel missing its front legs.

Quickly, I scramble into our canoe, and the fact that Beau knows this about Maggie proves he's been paying attention to my little world. It's a little flattering. A little disarming. I'm not sure whether to be glad or regretful that I let him tag along.

Not wanting to be Maggie's new pet's *hors d'oeuvres*, I quickly seize the wooden paddle waiting for me in the middle of the boat and paddle real quick to make it past Eleanor's razor-sharp mouth. We're just veering around a large floating piece of driftwood when Raylan authoritatively instructs, "Dip your oars a little deeper into the water."

I glance back to find that Eva's oar is barely dipped an inch into the water, so she shoots him a dirty look.

Raylan holds up his one free hand. "Or sit. And float."

We round water-submerged, bald cypress trees covered with alabaster mushrooms and a hairy hand-sized wolf spider Eva doesn't need to know about.

As Maggie paddles past us with her super muscular arms, Beau steers from the back of our canoe. "Wonder what she's like," Beau says. "Raylan's sister, the female Raylan Wilks."

It's something I've been wondering a lot about myself. It's not like I'd ever say anything, but it *is* a little odd, making introductions via rowboat—but Eva's never been more delighted. Or scared. What will this mean for their relationship? Will the sister be great... or awful?

Beau pokes my back with the tip of his oar and says all playfully, "Come on! Get back here!"

As if I'm going to crawl back to snuggle with him like we're an item. Like we're a pair.

I roll my eyes because he has a lot of brass.

A bright red maple rustles in a gust of wind, and I swear it's Leo, watching my reaction to him even now. What would Leo say about Beau, anyway? That he's nothing but a cliche of a cowboy, replete with the truck and hat?

Eva clambers over her own canoe to join Raylan at the back of their boat, and I would do anything for that ease, that comfort. But Beau is just a friend—who also happens to be teaching me how to throw knives. Really well.

The rustle of that maple's leaves warns me Leo doesn't exactly approve.

"Froster." Beau pleads like I might change my mind about cuddling up with him even now.

So I give a swift shake of the head. *Nope.*

"Why you avoidin' me?" he asks. "It's like you don't remember the time I cooked a whole *pack* o' hot dogs for you."

"On your radiator."

"Hey! I'm as resourceful as they come."

I sigh, really wishing he'd take the hint. "Not going to happen."

I don't mention the fact that I'm not the only girl who's gained the attention of Beau Jones. In the few short months he's been in Bloodcreek, he's gained the reputation of quite the womanizer. The fact that I've never let him kiss me has only cemented the fact that he only wants a girl who poses a challenge.

"Up here!" Maggie calls, swiftly dipping and rowing with her oar.

Beau's lazy voice curls toward me from the back of the boat. "Good thing I'm a patient fella."

More scaly fungus lines gum trees' bark and elephant ears

drip over the bank, and I swear I can hear Leo laughing at my dismissal of Beau.

A raccoon clutches a white-barked gum tree growing horizontally out of the water. I'm just about to point him out when a throng of reeds only partially obscures the scene of a dozen women dressed in long-sleeved, high-necked white dresses, holding miniature candles in the water.

Maggie pulls up her wooden oar. As do Beau and I.

When "Reva"'s boat bumps into ours, Eva shrieks and I very nearly do, too.

"Sorry." Eva sounds a little short of breath as she pries herself out of Raylan's arms.

I laugh as Eva and I lock eyes, and in that brief second, I can see her watching me with concern. She's not the one who's supposed to be worried—about food money, about how to afford the next tank of gas in our car. But she can't know how all that stuff weighs on me, so I shoot her a playful smile. *Too much kissing, girl.*

She flashes me a matching grin. She does her best to fix the wispies of her hair, and I'm reminded all over again of how I once caught her and Raylan kissing after Eva had just finished changing the oil of our car. She had grease on her face and oil dousing her shirt, but Raylan looked at her like she was the most beautiful girl he'd seen in all the world.

"So." Eva raises her eyebrows at the old-timer dressed women chanting in the water. If we'd happened upon this scene in Texas or even in Bloodcreek, we'd be freaking out, but this just about sums up the oddity and reverence of the Cajun-Creole cultures.

In the middle of the group, though, sits a tall, perfectly proportioned girl in an almost-sinking canoe. Her legs are folded in front of her, and she's wearing *a lot* of makeup and eyeliner.

There's also this predatorial way she holds herself. Like,

even though she's sitting absolutely still, at the slightest hint of a threat, she'd quickly and efficiently slit her attacker's throat.

Eva's demeanor shifts a little as she takes in the girl. She whispers, "She's. . . "

She doesn't even have to finish. "I know."

Because I *do* know. She's beautiful, but in such a way that she obviously spends months in the salon getting her nails done and whatever else. Eva and I've always been in the camp of *au naturale*, but Raylan's sister looks like she models for a supernatural hunting magazine before giving interviews for the news.

All traces of humor fall away from Maggie's face, as she'd just as soon line her own face with peanut butter than allow someone to con her into using cosmetics. Maggie casually rests her hand on her fanny pack the way she does when she's ready to defend our group.

Eva pulls her hair up into a knot, showing she's in high-stress mode, so I murmur, "You're *way* hotter."

She laughs nervously as the chanting of the women grows louder. "Not that he'd ever be attracted to his sister."

I shrug. "It's just nice to know when one's the hottest girl in the bayou."

Eva whisper-laughs, "I love you."

Raylan's sister—Tess—takes in our somewhat untidy group. The slightest narrowing of her eyes and faux relaxation of her shoulders tells me I'm being assessed for my value. She takes in Beau's collar-length red hair and the home-forged knife strapped to his leg like she's a seasoned auctioneer and she's assessing his worth.

"You found us," Tess says, her voice both articulate and congenial. Gracefully, she holds out her arms to the women chanting waist-deep in the water. Their white aprons float, and none of them look at us in the eyes. I've a feeling they're in the middle of a ritual.

"What language is that?" Eva asks.

"They are speaking Creole," Tess explains like she's the higher authority now. She wordlessly surveys Maggie and the fanny pack still wrapped around her middle when Raylan holds out an oar.

"Here."

Tess stretches her full lips into what I suppose is a smile, but it doesn't match what's registering in her eyes. She settles her gaze on the miniature spot between Raylan and Eva in their canoe and says, "There's something I want to show you first."

A case, maybe?

Raylan perks up as he lowers his oar, though Maggie, to his right, watches, a fly on the wall.

One of the mob-capped women dramatically dips her hand into the water—like she's reaching for something—and all the women continue chanting their minor-keyed tune. The candles in the water bob in time with their song.

Eva makes a face like she means to say, *Ease off the creepiness, girls,* when all at once, that one mob-capped woman heaves what looks to be a twelve-foot rope out of the water.

A snake.

Unghhh.

A diamond-shaped head slithers out a forked tongue, and the creature curls its lithe, slender shape into half a circle.

Like she's going to eat the creature whole, Tess eagerly leans forward. She reaches out to pet the olive-green reptile when the snake suddenly lunges at her.

Tess jerks back with her Swedish Swim Team smile, and if the girl didn't give me the heebie-jeebies before, she sure does now.

Murmuring in that foreign language—Creole—Tess says

something to the woman with the snake before turning to us. "Since we took out their rogue witch doctor, the women want to present this gift to us. Of course we accept. Rejecting it would be rude."

She says "we" like she was there.

Extending her hand toward the snake, Tess murmurs that old language, coaxing the olive creature to come toward her. It lifts its head and cocks it to the side, and I glance at Raylan, who's looking as concerned as when Beau actually beat him at a knife-throwing contest—a first for him, for sure.

The twelve-foot water moccasin slinks toward her.

Tess wraps the creature in her arms like she's putting on a shawl, and a not-too carefully veiled look of disgust flickers on Maggie's face.

The chanting waxes and grows. A heated crescendo. The women caress the snake one by one like they worship it. Like they're sad to see it leave before they wade out of the water.

When the final woman brushes her bony fingers along the water moccasin's scales, Tess angles toward us like she's the leader of our group now.

"They've imbued her with enough poison to kill a Blurred One," she informs us all.

"What?" Maggie's heavy voice blasts over the group. Not that permanently killing a Blurred One isn't something Maggie wants, but whenever we've asked if we should dig up Knox and find a way to kill him for good, she's always said to let sleeping dogs lie.

To leave him alone.

Tess gently lifts the snake like Maggie never even spoke. "Think of the damage she'll do. She'll end Knox the way *you* should have, brother."

Raylan's cheeks darken, but he doesn't so much as get defensive now.

"Is that Marie Laveau's snake?" he asks, and I recognize the name of another witch doctor. One of the most famous practitioners of hoodoo. Mom (and Dad) would freak if they knew we were having anything to do with that sort of dark magic.

"Her name is Zombi," Tess purrs as Maggie's worried eyes narrow. "Legend goes, Marie Laveau struck a deal with the devil. She wanted her first husband dead, so the devil gave Zombi magic for killing Blurred Ones—as long as Marie Laveau forfeited her soul."

"How very sentimental," Maggie grumbles.

I expect Maggie to tell Tess to take a flying leap back to wherever she came from, but something makes Maggie clamp her jaw shut. Maybe it's because she knows what this moment means to Raylan—reconvening with his sister after all these years.

Lifting a studded, expensive-looking boot into the spot right between Raylan and my sister, Tess marks her territory in the boat.

This is so very different than how I imagined this reunion would go.

Eva ducks her head before scooting over.

"We need to dig up Knox," Tess says as she settles herself between the pair. "It only makes sense to let Zombi finish him off for good."

Raylan shifts uncomfortably, gently rocking their canoe. "Is it really necessary?"

Tess cuts a glance at Maggie, and it's like she already knows how to undermine her. "Would you really risk him getting out?" Tess asks.

The silence that stretches over the bayou is so awkward that even Beau doesn't say a word. He scratches the side of his leg as a crow caws somewhere behind the bearded, mossy cypresses and gums.

Wordlessly, Maggie sticks her oar into the river.

She doesn't mutter anything as we pass a group of green elephant ears.

She doesn't utter one syllable when we row past a throng of showy red maples.

It isn't until Eva, Raylan, and Tess are pulling up to shore and lifting their canoe that Maggie floats up next to me and says in her lowest mama bear warning, "That girl's got to go."

CHAPTER 3 - EVA

There's nothing like a little Queen, powdered donuts, and mechanic work to settle us back home after our road trip. About thirty seconds after we docked our canoes, Mags suddenly had "urgent business." Tess didn't seem very happy with our speedy exit, but at least I got to meet her, even if it didn't go quite as I'd pictured. Raylan keeps saying it went well, though, so there's that.

No one really seems to know what to say about it. Well, except Maggie. She knows exactly how she feels, and it ain't good, and I have a feeling she's taking her frustration out on Betsy here, the way she's clanging around under my car.

I've been helping her put in the radiator we found at the dump for over an hour, and it's completely unlike us to tiptoe around these things. I want to understand where Maggie's coming from, but heck if I know why she feels so strongly about this. Tess did seem a little bossy, but also seriously skilled, so maybe there's just too many chefs in this here chicken. I personally think killing Knox permanently sounds amazing. Maybe then I could quit having dreams of Mr.

Grease Lightning eating my soul. So, I try again. "*Why* don't you want to kill Knox?"

Mags coasts on her belly-up scooter before rifling through her toolbox. "You should let sleeping dogs lie."

"You keep saying that." I hold out a socket wrench for her, because radiators are way out of my automobile know-how. "But why? This isn't like killing a magic-less witch doctor. This is Knox."

It's like I've hit a nerve—no, not a nerve. A chord. Mags stops her scootin' around and shakes her short brown curls, not ready to accept the socket wrench from me. Sitting up with a groan, she says, "Did I ever tell you about the ancient Greek mythical creature, Lamia?"

Oh goodness. This is probably gonna take awhile, so I lean against her shed and slide to the ground. "Doesn't ring a bell."

"That's because I show you Willy Wonka, and you dream Oompa-Loompas wanna eat your brains."

I cringe, shaking away the memory of the dream from my shoulders and everything else in my body, because that was one awful nightmare.

"Lamia was one of Zeus' mistresses. Hera was Zeus' wife, so she was obviously jealous of Lamia." Mags leans over without looking me in the eye and holds her knees. "And rightly so. But Hera was so jealous of ol' Zeus stepping out, she thought to make Lamia pay."

I adjust my position so a twig isn't digging into my butt. "Seems legit. What'd she do?"

"Hera killed all of Lamia's children—out of spite."

"Oooh." Way to ruin a good revenge story. "That's awful."

"That's what I keep telling you!" Maggie finally grabs the socket wrench from me. Wheeling under Betsy again, she clicks and twists to get the radiator in place.

"What's that got to do with Knox? It's not like Tess is some kind of scorned lover."

Mags wheels out from under the car, sits up, and sets her sights straight on me. "Lamia couldn't leave it there." She wags the wrench at me. "Lamia decided to hunt and eat unsuspecting children all the rest of her days."

I stare at Mags, trying to make sense of what she's telling me and coming up short. "Seriously messed up. But what the heck does this have to do with Knox?" I do my best to keep my voice from getting snappy. "He's going to somehow come back from the dead and eat kids? Mags, come on."

Maggie grabs a roll of duct tape and flings it straight at my face.

I duck, but just in time. "Hey!"

"Knox isn't going to eat kids, you knothead!" She falls back and rolls under Betsy again. "But there's no saying what his other Blurred friends will do if you step over that line. It ain't been done before," Mags grumbles for the third time. "If you ask me, we oughta let what was done stay done. Don't go kickin' the hornet's nest."

She makes a good point, obviously. We've been really lucky that the Despairity haven't come back, that no other Blurred Ones seem to care that we exist. But every once in a while, I feel phantom fingers around my throat, squeezing harder and harder till I die of asphyxiation, or Knox straight-up breaks my neck. Like he's just one magic spell away from getting back here to finish the job.

"I don't know, Mags."

The clanging stops, and the driveway is awfully quiet, like we're on opposite sides of some prison-style plexiglass. "I'm almost done here," she says, her voice way too calm. "You go on in."

"But you're helping me—"

"I said, 'go on in,'" she says with a tone I've only heard her use against her old freezer that likes to form ice cubes on the walls instead of in the ice cube tray.

Well, okay then. I don't need someone being that cranky with me.

I get up and dust myself off. I feel heavy, but surely she's just overreacting. Either way, I'm ready for some space from her for a bit. "Well, thanks a lot, Mags," I say with just enough tone so she can wonder if I'm being genuine or sarcastic.

I stalk inside, heading for the bedroom I always stay in, but for the hundredth time, the second I get to the room, those phantom fingers are scratching at my throat. I veer back to the couch. I'm already regretting my tone, half ready to head back out and apologize, but the suddenly extra loud clanging of metal keeps me holed up inside.

CHAPTER 4 - FROST

*B*alancing a plate of chicken fried steak in one hand, I daintily grab a wine glass with the other, careful to not let the steak's gravy dribble down the front of my shirt.

I can deliver it in one piece. I can do this. I'm getting better.

I veer around a newly-installed Cadillac couch and tiptoe around a squirrelly boy who won't stay in his chair. I duck, too, just in time, when he tosses a ketchup-covered fork in the air.

Creeping past a guy shouting obscenities at the TV, I make it past a cowboy who's still wearing spurs over his boots.

"Now that looks real good," says a bearded guy with a pot belly and overalls, so I lower the plate to that tricky spot between the knife and fork.

Frost, don't spill the gravy on his arm.

I'm just settling his wine glass on the tablecloth when his voice comes out really sharp. "That ain't for Orval, honey."

I gawk at the elegant wine glass that I actually safely

brought over here. Slowly, I turn my eyes to his yellowed fingers, up his large, oil-stained shoulders, all the way up to his aged, yellow eyes.

But *Orval* . . . I thought that was wine.

"Sorry." I reach to remove the wine glass, but an arm with flashy ropin' muscles swoops in and plucks up the stem like he was waiting for this moment all along.

In its place, Beau sets down an already frothy-filled jar.

"Here ya go, Sammy!" says Beau. He flashes his most brazen smile. He used to use that on the girls who'd stop by in nothing but Daisy Dukes and spaghetti-strapped shirts—until he hired me for his mom.

Still trying to figure that one out.

But I can't *believe* he's rescuing me on yet another faux pas. Once, I gave a ticket to a man before I'd even delivered his food.

Beau gave the guy a meal on the house.

Last week, I completely forgot to turn a ticket into the kitchen, only to learn that the man waited for his food for two *hours*.

Beau gave him free drinks and made him a sign for his hotel that reads "PLEASE DO NOT SHOOT DEER FROM MOTEL," because apparently, that's how we smooth things over in this town.

It all comes down to the fact that I make a terrible waitress. But it's the only job close enough to home that can pay the bills. Plus, upping our security measures back home doesn't come cheap. That holy water well I've been eyeing will cost seven grand at least.

"Orval sounded like a *wine* name," I murmur to Beau as we make our way back to the kitchen and the clanging of pots and pans where his mom, Lindy, works.

Beau fixes a stray tassel on the shoulder of my uniform. "Jus' give it a few more weeks." He has to sound all comforting now. He reaches up and slips a piece of hair behind my ear, and I bristle.

"Waitressin'," he adds, "is growin' on you."

I think he's going to erode even more of my layers when he goes one too far. He curls an over-confident arm around my waist—like we're "goin' steady" now.

I shove off his arm, fighting the urge to go for the daggers in my boots.

Daggers he taught me to throw.

So I say through gritted teeth, "Watch your boundaries, Beau."

I don't spell out the reasons why I stay—because Mom hasn't exactly nailed down how to interview. She begins by telling potential bosses that she's still in mourning, and it takes all her energy to even leave the house. She's still processing, and Eva and I both know it'll be awhile before she figures out how to cope in the real world.

Beyond that, our home needs to be a real defensive fort. The sort of place a Blurred One, or any other monster, could *never* find its way through. I don't know what's going to happen between Tess and Maggie, with Tess wanting to use her snake to permanently take Knox out, but if you ask me, the idea doesn't sound so terrible.

We'd never run the risk of Knox getting out.

Mom and Eva would have the protection and stability they deserve.

Beau leans down like he plans on planting a kiss on me now, his country-boy cologne hitting me like it has tentacles, so I shove him on the chest, hard.

I *still* can't believe I work in this place. "You are unbelievable!"

Wade, of all people, saunters into the diner, the curls on his neck lifting as he walks. He and Beau wave at each other like they're best pals, and *how in the heck is this my group now?*

I seize the nearest plate of food at the yellow laminate counter. It's loaded with French fries, and Eva would be insisting I bring her a plate if she showed. Leo would be eyeing them like he's never tasted a fry in his life, and I'm stalking across the diner because I'm not supposed to be thinking about Leo.

By the time I make it to the center of the room, fork-throwing boy has now gone onto drawing on the table, and I glance around, trying to remember who ordered this food.

Beau juts his thumb at a frizzy-haired lady with blue eyeshadow.

I deliver the plate before skulking back to Beau.

"I have something for you." He good-naturedly grabs a plate of hush puppies, catfish, and cream o' corn. He delivers the plate without so much as knocking into a chair.

"You'll like it," he says when he comes back to me.

I can't think of a single thing I would want from Beau Jones. Except for maybe salt bags? I'd take a couple of those.

Gripping me by the suede gracing my shoulders, he levels his muddy brown eyes on me, and I try not to see the care and concern. Do my best to ignore the soul who helped Raylan and Maggie repair the front porch, the guy who helped me repair the weed wacker when I was running late for work.

Beau says he's always known about hunting. His mom, not exactly my favorite person in the world, has hunted creatures his entire life, and they've never stayed in one place for long. Until now. Apparently, she wants to put down roots.

If Beau says he has a gift for me, I should be impressed. Grateful. But what if I'm not ready to move on from the past? Forget Leo?

CHAPTER 5 - EVA

I stare down the dark abyss of the old abandoned mine shaft like it's some ancient pit in *Lord of the Rings*. Sighing to calm my nerves, I appreciate the mixture of cedar, gasoline, and dirt in the air.

I feel like I'm being pulled in like five different ways. Nostalgia—*Aw, this is where Raylan confessed that I'd grown on him like a good-looking fungus!* Another— *Shoot, I'm going to see the guy who wanted to use me as his personal Energizer Bunny for eternity!* And, *Don't show Tess I'm actually so scared I may just wet myself.* Oh yeah, and definitely, *You're totally choosing Tess over Maggie, and she's probably gonna take fifty years to forgive you.*

But I'm gonna choose to focus on, *Let's kill Knox 'cause he deserves it. We won't run the risk of him getting out and hunting us down, and Tess and I will bond.* Yes.

"So." I tie a knot in my hair while watching Raylan pull the winch line from Tess' crazy-nice truck. Lifted quad cab with custom rims and whatnot nice. "He's not going to send out some kind of magical homing beacon when he dies that sends all the Blurred Ones across the world here to avenge his death?" Mags' voice is still kinda rattling around in my brain.

But Raylan trusts Tess, and she's his only family, so I *kinda* need to be earning some brownie points here. Although, still not sure why we had to come up here while Frost and Beau were at work. New family bonding?

"Whenever you're ready, Raylan," Tess says. She stands on the other side of the giant hole, holding the giant snake, Zombi, all wrapped around her like she's Britney Spears.

"Yes, ma'am," he says. With his sexy sideways grin, he switches the winch's cable release, so it slowly descends down the shaft where Knox has been rotting for these five months. I see him keeping one eye on me, though. "Eva, you sure you're okay with this?"

My heart calms, taking comfort in his presence. I nod, knowing he'll pick up on my doubt. If he's on the fence, maybe he'll change his mind. If he doesn't, this must be the right call.

But before he can say anything, Tess interjects. "She knows it's the right thing to do."

We stare down the infinite black hole for what seems like an eternity, and Tess says something about buying the best cable out there because it's so long, but I can't look away or respond.

Finally, I hear the clang of the hook hitting the metal cage. Raylan swings and prods the cable till it's snagged. He looks at me again, and his brow raises just a bit in question, in a silent, *You ready?*

I don't trust my voice or even my face right now, so I go back to staring at the pit. I hear the crunch of his boots as he strides back to the mega truck. He reverses the cable.

"Here we go," I whisper to myself, and I steel my nerves as best as I can. The winch groans and winds, the cable rubbing against the metal grate covering the mine. The scraping sound reminds me of the feeling of the ropes when Knox tied me to Maggie's bed. "Just breathe," I whisper again, like this talking to myself is becoming a thing.

The cage emerges into view below the grate. My lungs aren't sure they want to work right now.

It's Knox, but just barely. He's splayed across the cage's bottom, his skin in patches of green, yellow, and gray. His eyes are so sunken that they're basically craters in his face. Almost like his time in purgatory has turned him into the Despairity he so desperately didn't want to become.

Oh, man, I made out with that—I choke on a gag.

He gives a wry smile, which used to make all us ladies weak in the knees, but now he looks a lot like Gollum, teeth all nasty shades of black and gray. That's all the movement he gives, though. Guess five months in absolute darkness with no food or water is rough on the complexion. He just lays there, staring at me like I'm just a token reminder of a life he once lived.

"I did," he says, taking a raspy breath between words, "enjoy," a breath, "killing," another, "your dad."

All right, we made the right choice.

I do my best to feign boredom, determined to not give him an ounce of satisfaction.

"Shut your trap, Knox," Raylan growls like he'd enjoy nothing more than to dropkick Knox's head into the ocean.

Knox weakly lifts his head toward Raylan and gives some sort of cough-slash-laugh before his head drops back down. Whatever. Tess is going to take care of him soon enough.

I help the winch wedge the cage back through the hole in the grate, satisfied Knox is way too weak to do anything to me. Once it's free, I let the cage fall to the grate with a giant *clang*.

Tess saunters over like she's the star of the show and we were her opening performers. Zombi's green scales slither around her arms, giving me shivers. Who's threatening now?

She plants herself by me like a tribal warrior, and Knox can finally see her.

Knox's eyes widen, and he begins breathing faster, wheezing and shuddering. "I remember—"

"Funny how," Tess interrupts with a decidedly humorless face, "being bound to a vessel is all you Blurred Ones want, and yet that's the very thing that makes it possible to kill you." She casually cocks her perfectly dark chocolate-colored hair to the side, but her cheekbones and lips are rigid while she's studying him. She's either a way better actor than me, or she has very random reactions to things.

After a long, high-noon type of moment, complete with a hawk screeching somewhere, she throws Zombi onto the cage.

The giant snake slips inside effortlessly with Knox barely able to scoot six inches away from her. It only takes about five seconds before she sinks her teeth into his throat. There are no screams, no flashes of light or evaporating smoke. As she wraps herself around Knox's frail, disgusting body, he lays limp, with no reaction except maybe a bit of amusement on his face as he locks eyes with me and fades even more. Maybe this is actually the humane thing to do?

Tess pulls her Kimber handgun and aims between the cage's bars. She holds it for a minute, studying Knox. Then, abruptly, holsters her gun. I feel my heart relax and tighten at the same time. "Change of plans," she says. "Bullet's too good for you."

She marches to the back of her truck and pulls out a gas can.

"Tess," Raylan calls. "We don't need to do that."

My eyes widen as I realize what she intends to do. I don't know if I can stomach it, even for this horrible soul.

"Zombi weakened him, and the gun might finish it, but fire is the sure-fire way." She coughs a laugh. "Get it?"

Raylan's jaw pulses, and he holds his hand subtly up to me, signaling me to stay out of it. Happy to oblige. "It's just a really bad way to go," he says, and I can't help but think he sounds a bit like an experienced hostage negotiator. Like this isn't the first time he's had to mediate things within his family. "You sure it's necessary?"

Tess shrugs mechanically, like she's trying really hard to look like she doesn't care. "Definitely."

"Where'd you learn about all this?" Raylan's voice softens.

Tess' eyes pierce him, but to his credit, he doesn't flinch. "I have many sources." She marches back to Knox and immediately unscrews the gas cap. She starts pouring it on his face, the gasoline splashing where the screw remains in his philtrum. "A small price to pay for each of your victims."

I appreciate the thought, really, but to be here, watching this man about to be set on fire? It doesn't feel right, no matter how evil he is. He's helpless now. I almost summon the courage to say so, but the defeated look on Raylan's face scares me off. Why does she have such a hold on him? He's never been one to be told what to do. He finally meets my eyes, and like we both find the courage we need, we turn to her. "Stop," I say, at the same time he says, "Tess."

She acts like she doesn't hear us. Deliberately tosses the gas can back onto the ground. Raylan storms toward her like she's a semi-tamed jaguar. "Tess," he says again. "This is pretty messed up."

Again, she ignores him and pulls a shiny lighter from her pocket, like she's planned this all along. "Pupils, this is how it's done." While he tries to reach for her arm, she lights her flame and tosses it onto Knox.

My hand flies to my mouth in surprise while Raylan yells something at his sister, his face red. She calls Zombi back to her and congratulates the snake with a kiss on the head. Eesh.

Knox screams as he's enveloped in flames. My throat

tightens like a giant marble is in it, and my stomach churns. A breeze catches the smoke, and I grimace at the stench. He stops moving within a few seconds and moans. Within a minute, he's silent.

I only peek at him. A charred, black mess.

He's gone.

"We did it, kids." Tess beams with a *you will be happy* intensity at Raylan and me. Then, with a swagger that may even beat Beau's, she practically bounces back to her truck, calling to me. "I'll make you into my mini-me, and we'll be unstoppable."

Raylan slowly walks to me and wraps his arms around me. "Sorry," he murmurs in my ear. "She can take things too far sometimes. Ever since our parents died."

I bury my face in his chest and inhale deeply to get the smell of Knox out of my system. "That was . . ." I can't even form the words.

"I know." He squeezes tighter, and I pull myself as deep as I can before letting go.

"It's not like he didn't deserve it." I manage a small grin. "He needed the school of *hard Knox*." I grunt at my own terrible pun, but Raylan groans loudly, shaking his head.

He rests his forehead on mine, and it's all gonna be okay.

CHAPTER 6 - FROST

*T*he porch creaks as Beau and I mount the steps leading to my front door. Holes in the yard from when Eva and I chopped stumps are now landmines chock full of rock salt should any supernatural creatures try to pay us a visit.

Our sycamore jingles from the silver jewelry we hung in its lower branches for taking out shapeshifters and were-wolves. The wind chime near our porch swing is adorned with so many wingnuts, a hundred Blurred Ones could be trapped in their vessels.

Every Celtic sigil Maggie could find is carved and spray-painted on our door, along with Native American, Greek, and Roman. Knox may have had the power to wear them down, but not every Blurred One will have his level of power, so it's worth the effort.

Down in the storage room, we've stuffed so much fire-power that we could fill twenty AR-15s and keep shooting for days after. Courtesy of Raylan.

Maggie yearns to help out, do more, but she's not the one

who took out Dad, so my job is to make sure we're taken care of.

Eva and I set up the shooting range around back. When we first wake up in the morning, we make sure we're packing a full array of silver bullets—or jewelry, if Eva's off to school— wingnuts, holy water, and rock salt.

Maggie got us these tiny battery-operated screwdrivers we keep in our front pockets at all times.

We've ditched all pocketless pants from our wardrobe.

Sometimes Eva complains that I'm going a overboard, but there must be something a little terrible in my eyes, because once she looks at my face, she drops the subject.

It's good for her to worry. For her to be scared.

The new swing Eva and Raylan built squeaks as it sways in the wind, and I close my eyes against the memory of Leo primly standing in front of it, reading his Latin.

Beau and I tramp over the wood that now smells of new stain—also, courtesy of Raylan. He, Maggie, and Beau spent hours carrying lumber and hammering nails while Eva and I helped Mom come out of her room again.

Work-wise, Mom would do great at any doctor's office. She's great at answering phones and is super organized. But no one's called, and I won't sign up for classes until she's found the *right* job.

Beau taps an errant nail with the toe of his boot. "Need to hammer this ol' do-dad in." I don't know how, but he's sort of becoming the person I both want to push away and need to keep around.

I'll never forget the moment he realized Eva and I were also hunters. He'd given me a ride home from work one day, and when he saw the porch blown to bits, he asked what happened with this wide look of excitement on his face. I told him the septic guy accidentally crashed into it while pulling out of the driveway, but when Beau caught sight of the spray-painted devil's trap, he laughed in his lazy way and told us his mom's a former hunter. Turns out he's the best knife-thrower Maggie and Raylan have ever seen. So, we let him in our group.

It's the best worst decision we've ever made.

Pulling the key I always keep 'round my neck, I unlock the first of the locks on the front door. I chant a spell Maggie taught me to release the threshold blockade charm and splash a bit of holy water on the handle in case it sizzles—an indicator that a Blurred One or other supernatural being has been here.

There aren't any red flags. Nothing stands out, so I wrap my hand around the cool handle and cautiously open the door.

The flat silence of the house hits me like it always does, like a socked foot to the throat. Cicadas no longer hum outdoors. The weather's turned too cool. No Dad, treading up quietly in his evening slippers...

After we're inside, Beau tugs the door closed. "Think your mama's sleepin'?" He stealthily pulls off his fancy cowboy boots with the lizard skin and square toes. "Want some pie?" He strolls through the living room like he owns that, too.

I pull off my tasseled boots—another part of Lindy's non-negotiable uniform—and place them in my cubby, grateful for the sense of order Mom's gotten back to keeping up in our home. Fresh vacuum lines mark the carpet, and not a speck of dust lines the Nutcrackers on the shelves.

Slipping my knife from the inside strap of my boot, I secure it on my forearm via a metal and leather clasp and pull down my sleeve to not alarm Mom. Gone are the days when I go anywhere without being armed. Took me long enough, but it's a lesson I've learned.

"I'm cravin' razzleberry." Beau moseys past the digital piano.

I tread past the Clavinova—Dad bought the instrument for me even though it cost thousands of dollars—and straighten one of the doilies on top, spotting Eva's pink and silver glitter-cased phone. She must be training outside, so I check for messages in case Maggie called.

Not finding anything, I run my fingers along the ivory keys, which, despite their weighted plastic composition, don't make a sound. It almost makes me want to pull out the bench, push the power button, and stick the headphones on. But Beau is here, and the last thing I need is for him to fall in love with me because of my Chopin.

By the time I make my way into the kitchen, Beau has a nearly-empty pie plate in his hands. A purple smudge of berry lines the corner of his mouth, and he looks at me with so much guilt that I place my hand on my hip, pretending I'm Lindy, his "mama." "Caught you red-handed."

He slips what's left of the last piece on the counter. "I'll grab ya a plate. Here."

I sigh as he opens the cupboard, not exactly feeling hungry.

"You really should eat somethin', Froster."

Too tired from our shift, I lift myself up on the Formica counter, and he's always been one to keep the peace, so he lets it go, pulling himself up, as well.

Our legs swing side-by-side in comfortable silence, and this teensy part of me almost enjoys the companionship, but then he's placing his hand on mine, and I'm pulling my hand away from his because the only person who's supposed to touch me like that is Leo.

"*You* are a womanizer," I grumble.

His smile's as wide as the nearby watering hole. "Not anymore."

I roll my eyes. "How many girlfriends have you had, Beau?" At least I know I've been the only girl for Leo.

Delicately, he toys with the shoulder fringe of my Western shirt. I don't slap his hand away, because he seems to need to keep his hands busy, like a four-year-old. "Doesn't it help," he says, "that I want to be with you now?"

I slip down to the tile, which kisses my socked feet. "Nope."

Beau slips from the counter, looking equal parts rejected and hopeful. "You're so pretty, I'd eat the corn outta your sh—"

I knock him upside the head. "You are not helping yourself."

He tries wrapping his arms around my waist. "Can we just live in the moment?"

Laughter tears like an infestation from my throat. Here he knows of my deep and abiding relationship with Leo, and yet he keeps pushing me too far. He claims he's okay with just being friends, but he's obviously not.

I grab the cool glass pie plate and stuff it in the fridge before I decide to use my new stabbing skills. "I never should have let you come to New Orleans."

The hurt on his face is enough to wash away some of the crust surrounding my heart. "Sorry. I'm sorry." I think about touching his hand, but I can't actually bring myself to do it, so I leave it at that.

He rubs his hand over his face, suddenly old and tired, and the frightening truth of the matter is he's been the one person to suture the broken pieces of Frost Abram back together. When I finally started eating real food, and my stomach couldn't handle it, *he* was the one who followed me out to the parking lot and held my hair. Anytime Chastity and Charity come strolling into work, he avoids the notorious flirts, pretending Lindy needs him to get something from the refrigerator.

Beau may have been a player for eons, but, apparently, ever since meeting me, he's sung a different tune.

"I'm sorry," I say for the second time.

He shakes his head, causing the bottom of his hair to tickle his collar. "I really do want there to be a 'me an' you.'"

"You and me." I nearly smile, and then I laugh because it's all become so tedious—boys and caring for my family and barricading my home. I shouldn't even *be* mildly attracted to Beau, but the fact that he's still here means I appreciate him. Either that, or I'm desperate.

"Thanks for helping me." I nod to the curio cabinet and a few other odds and ends he helped me piece back together from last spring's Knox encounter.

"You're doin' a great job."

I wish he'd hold back the compliments. What he doesn't say is, I killed my own Dad, and because of my carelessness, Eva got captured by Knox. Twice.

"We should go outside and practice," I say, but the gunfire suddenly going off from the backyard warns me that Eva and Raylan might want to be alone.

Beau reaches out a gentle hand to toy with my hair. "You should write in page six o' your journal that Beauregard is a complete and utter dipsh—"

"Now *there's* an idea."

He curls a finger around my front belt loop. "You know I'm always here for you." He lowers his head like that's the spell I needed to hear to lower my guard.

With the palm of my hand, I push back his meaty and freckled forehead. "Go home, Beau."

He plants his hands on his hips like a scorned woman. "I sorta think you don' want me to go."

"All you ever think about is—" I avert my eyes away from his lips.

"'Cause I *like* you." He tugs on the dagger I've hidden up the sleeve of my shirt. And this heartbreaking look of hopefulness flashes over Beau's eyes. But I can't have him getting ideas, so I snatch up his keys from the counter and hand them over.

As he accepts them from me, thoughts hit me like a typhoon.

If Beau wanted me to confess the complete and utter truth, he'd let me talk about the fact that I still keep Leo's teacup on my dresser.

I still visit the big oak on Maggie's property where we looked at the stars. I even researched Japanese samurais because he was one for a while.

Seeing the resolve in my eyes for him to leave, Beau lowers his hand from my sleeve. "Maybe I should go."

His shoulders droop, and this stupid twinge of guilt churns through my stomach when I suddenly remember what he said before. "Wait. You said you had a gift?"

A smile of almost-missed opportunities flashes over his lips when the sound of electronic music suddenly blares from the direction of the piano—Eva's phone.

Heart ratcheting up to double time, I scamper from the kitchen, knowing the call could mean anything—Maggie telling us she's grabbing Bavarian creams to a sighting of werewolves.

Short of breath, I lift the phone. "Hello?"

"Eva?" The confident yet scared voice sounds familiar.

"This isn't E—"

"They're *here*." The curtness of her voice tells me I'm speaking with Tess, her breath coming out in short gasps. The fear in her voice is so unlike what she sounded like when we met up in the bayou.

"The Despairity!" she wails as an array of gunshots burst on the other side of the phone.

More frantic breathing.

"I can't," she says. "Get them out—"

Something crashes as the other side of the line falls dead.

I lock eyes with Beau.

CHAPTER 7 - EVA

*R*aylan—my *boyfriend*—and I trample down the back deck's wooden stairs to head to our shooting area. We just finished giving Mom a decent pep talk for her next job interview, while pretty much polishing off Frost's amazing razzleberry pie. We've got a pistol in one hand, holding hands with the other.

I carry my favorite gun of Dad's that I've pretty much made my own, my Glock 9mm, and Raylan totes his "more manly" XD .45. I prefer my gun to not leave my hands sore and bruised just from shooting a few rounds.

To say it's been five months of complete and utter bliss might be a bit of an overstatement, but it's been pretty dang close. We never even had a real talk to make things official, but ever since we tossed Knox down that hole the first time, we've basically been inseparable. Sure, he may be a bit head-strong, and I have been a little rollercoastery lately, but no fight lasts longer than a couple of hours. And he always kisses any hurt all better.

Let's just say I haven't even thought about another boy since this man walked into my life. It feels kinda weird that

I've been in a relationship longer than Frost, but she really didn't lose a whole lotta time before heating things up with Mr. Beauregard and his man-bun. At least he helps her remember she's nineteen and not forty-five.

I get to have Raylan in his smoky blue T-shirt that matches his eyes, trudging through the woods with me, even though he could be anywhere. He pretty much only hangs out with me, or Maggie, or goes hunting. He and Maggie are supposed to take us to hunt down some banshees in South Dakota during Christmas break. I don't know if that will happen now, though, since Maggie seems to still be cranky about this Tess drama.

I suppress a twinge of guilt at going behind her back to kill Knox. She hasn't been over since our little argument, and I'm sure she knows about Tess' little bonfire by now. I make a mental promise to go over and smooth things over after we're done shooting.

Target practice used to be Dad's and my thing. We spent so many afternoons out here with the smell of the wood and hay baking in the sun that I got pretty good. I even earned the nickname "Eagle Eye" from him after a particularly solid day. I can hardly believe he'll never be here with me again.

Raylan understands what it's like. He lost both his parents, plus Leo. I don't think he's ever been close with anyone else, besides Tess. Makes me feel pretty dang special. He did practice throwing knives out here once with Beau, but that hasn't lead to any kind of bromance. We have such a small circle, we should really all try to get along better. Next mental note, be nicer to Beau and try harder to figure out Tess. Plus, Tess certainly has a different set of hunting skills and point of view from Mags. I'm sure I could learn a ton from her, too. Like how she can afford different pairs of Tony Lamas for every day of the week. She certainly took off fast after we took care of Knox, though.

She claimed she had another gang of monsters to tend to back home.

"You think she likes me?" I don't bother clarifying. Raylan knows there's only one woman I would be feeling insecure about.

"How could she not?" He looks me up and down, at my snug purple T-shirt, joking but appreciative. I can't help but giggle a little.

"It's true." I wink, but can't help but push. "It's hard to read her."

"She's not warm and fuzzy, but she's got a big heart." He holds my gaze with those wide open oceans he's got for eyes, and their depth makes me forget to breathe. "She's always looked out for me. Even if it had to be from far away." He holds out a hand for me to give him my gun so I can put on my ear protectors.

I shake myself out of the trance he so easily puts me in.

"All right, babe, you ready?" he hollers through the clunky plastic now on my head. That's right, he calls me babe. Among other things.

"Dang right, I'm ready," I say, squaring my shoulders. "Dad's been teaching me for years. He's going to let me try his AR soon." I realize what I'm saying but can't stop the words before they've hit the air. Raylan flashes those tumultuous eyes back to me. I stare at the ground, trying to straighten my brain once again. How did I forget? Even for a second?

"What?" I challenge softly, squeezing my eyes shut against the memory of Dad's proud grin and breathy chuckle that day when I nailed the bulls-eye six times.

Raylan gives a slight shake of his head. Thank goodness he seems to get it. Patient, this boy. He picks up the cardboard we're using for a target, but I grab it from him to buy myself some time to chill. I stomp off toward the hay bales a few yards off. Looking around for a nice chunk of clay, I pick one up and scrawl in giant letters over the entire target, "HITLER." Nothing like killing Nazis to lighten the mood.

Dropping the clay and brushing the remnants from my hands, I feel how tight and brittle the clay leaves my palms.

The sun is sinking into the trees, their shadows snatching at us. It'll be dark soon. I hurry back to Raylan, gently shoo a ladybug from my arm, and grab my gun. Raylan nods that he's ready, so I square myself with the target, the way Dad always taught me. I raise my gun, ready to land these bulls-eyes. I relax my shoulders, aim, and fire. I don't even hit the target. I try again and miss. I fire five, six rounds and miss every one. One lands a good three feet wide.

"Seriously?" I hiss. I lower the gun and shake out my body. Pretend I can't still smell Knox's burnt remains if I stop moving for even a second. "Hitler's got nine lives, apparently," I joke, but my delivery is flat. Raylan just watches me struggle, but gives me a courtesy smile, fingers rubbing his beard in thought. I shove the gun into his hands so I can stop humiliating myself and pout, but he grabs my hand instead, and then his strong fingers grip my arm. Gentle, but firm.

"Stop." His voice is muffled through the ear protectors, but I can still hear his command. His face is a mixture of his usual mask and something new—a kind determination. Hands low on my hips, he guides me back to my perfectly-worn dirt patch in front of the target, with me fighting the urge to screw this whole practice and just turn around and kiss him. But I have to admit I do kind of like this kind of manhandling.

"Get in your stance." He speaks loudly so I can hear. I oblige, but somehow, his understanding and misplaced faith in me chokes me up, making the target dance before my eyes. He reaches his sturdy arms around my shoulders and takes my left hand and places it under the gun, so it's cupping the grip and my right hand instead of the gun in the back.

"Tess actually taught me this." He half shouts into my protected ear. "It will make you steadier and will keep you from needing stitches. The action is barely missing your skin. Now try again."

I know this. Why am I making such a rookie mistake?

I blink and shake so any renegade moisture in my eyes can fall to the ground, not my face. I shoot. I hit the target, top right. Better. I let myself have a small grin, but hide it from my trainer. I let the gun down for a second to breathe, and he reaches one hand up and lightly rubs my neck.

It's kind of weird, but it makes me think of something Dad would always say when Frost and I were little and would walk on his back to help massage it out. "I'll give you just one hour to stop doing that," he'd joke, making us laugh and never want to stop.

I put the gun down on the nearest hay bale, avoiding looking at Raylan. I'm feeling way more vulnerable than I care for anyone to witness.

"Let's go do something else," I say, and I'm already walking back toward the house. "Get Frost to make more pie?" Before I can get more than two steps, though, Raylan snatches my arm and pulls me to him, wrapping his strong arms around me, into the most perfect hug. There is no lust in me. Instead, he's like a charger for my soul. I'm so drained. I just let him hold me.

I don't even cry but bury my face into his neck, smelling his maple-meets-apples skin. He's always keeping me from falling apart. The ear protectors are in the way and probably digging into his shoulder, so he takes them off with one hand, throws them onto the ground, and then holds me all the tighter because he knows just how much this helps.

After a few long, long minutes, my heart relaxes, and I

think I can tuck the rest of the sadness away to deal with another day. But now I need to de-serious this moment, so I reach down to Raylan's back pocket. He starts to straighten, unsure how to handle this, because we haven't really gone there. Instead, though, I grab the knife he keeps in his pocket, open it quickly, and dash back just enough so I can slide it up and over his chest, Norman Bates style.

His eyes crinkle the way that makes my heart race. "Nice."

I laugh a high, sing-song laugh to show I am done with the vulnerability. "Yeah, I would have held it to your throat like in the movies, but I don't know how to without accidentally slicing it."

"Yeah, that wouldn't be very helpful." He locks his fingers behind my lower back and pulls me closer. I bask in his sweet attention for a moment, and then lean in to kiss my favorite lips on the planet. The lust is definitely back.

His lips part just enough for them to completely envelope mine, and I delicately lick just inside his mouth. Now commencing experiment to see if one can replace food with kissing.

He pulls me tighter with one hand and runs the other up my back, drawing a trail of shivers, until it's tangled in my hair.

Footsteps run through the woods, and we jump apart. We're both grabbing our guns when a slender figure emerges at a sprint. It's Frost, and her face—it's what I saw the day our family changed forever.

"Raylan, hurry." She puts her hands on her knees, trying to catch her breath. I shudder, despite the heat. "Tess needs help."

*R*aylan floors his truck. Frost may have to stay behind for the dollar bills, but I *can* call Maggie.

I dial her number for the millionth time, but my finger still hovers over Send, sure Mags won't be too ecstatic to run to Tess' rescue. I could have Frost call her. Not that I love being passive-aggressive, but that seems like the easiest route at the moment. I shoot Frost a quick text.

Tell Mags.

Silence. But she'll respond as soon as she can.

"How did they find her?" Raylan asks for the third time, but he knows I've got no clue. It's seven-hundred miles to New Orleans. Too far. If they want misery to feed on, Tess does seem to have an abundance of that under her perfect surface.

"She's strong," I whisper, since the truck is silent. Turning on music seems wrong. "She'll hang on."

He stares at the darkening road, grips the wheel harder. "Sounds like someone else is gonna burn." He pushes the truck impossibly faster.

CHAPTER 8 - FROST

I hate that I'm not already headed back to New Orleans with Raylan and Eva, but I texted Maggie, just like Eva asked, and as soon as I explain things to Lindy, I'll be on my way. I tried calling her like thirty times to see if I could get work off, but Lindy's notorious for never picking up. And Beau hasn't been answering, either, ever since he said he had to take care of a few things before we could hit the road.

I'd already be halfway to Arkansas if Lindy would simply give me the green light.

I try wiggling the key in Lindy's front door lock for the hundredth time, a few of the sun's rays shining on the aged, squatty downtown stores of Bloodcreek—Miss B's Anteeks, Hair Cuts 4 U, and Ranch Reef-flections. People here like phonetics.

The crisp autumn breeze is teasing the ends of my hair when the sound of heels clipping pavement nearly makes me drop my keys.

A spray of light highlights the tint to Lindy's red hair, and I don't know why, but she creeps me out.

Drat. I do drop the keys.

I shoot Lindy a guilty grin before leaning down to the cement and scooping up the metal keyring.

I shouldn't be terrified of Lindy, but she's kind of threatening, the way she pounds those defenseless chicken steaks. The way she talks to her children. Beau's the eldest of seven.

Lindy looks at me primly, with this quizzical tilt to her eyebrows. It's like she thinks she's this great Southern lady, but this is Bloodcreek, and there's nothing spectacular about her diner.

A tasseled blouse fits much too snugly around her torso, and her high-heeled boots and big hair would make me fall over.

She waits for me to blink, to prove that she intimidates me by looking away, but I won't give her the satisfaction, so I jut out my chin, recalling *exactly* what I need to tell her.

"I need a little time off."

Her misleading, delicate nature is the exact antithesis of Beau's. "Do I detect a lazy girl who wishes to be let go?"

The jab is not unlike something Dad would say, so I state, "A friend of ours needs help."

Barely any emotion at all registers on her face. How is it that some people grab, hold onto, and flaunt even the smallest smidgen of power?

"I gathered from my son that your sister took off with her boyfriend without so much as a backward glance back home."

I can't tell whether she intends to insult me or Eva more. Maybe we should have let that witch doctor we took out in New Orleans—Avi—do a little bit of his magic on her.

As the wind tousles Lindy's paprika curls, I think I'll tell her to leave Eva out of this—demand she treat Beau and his siblings with more decency, as well—but the clock is ticking. Eva's on the hunt and needs backup now.

"You do realize," Lindy says, "that I've wasted time and

resources training you." It's a slap in the face, but there's so little emotion in her words.

"And I appreciate it." Perhaps she, too, was repressed as a child.

Lindy's cheekbones shoot so high, it's like someone took a giant nail file to either side of her face when she was a bad girl. Her stance, so imperial, is like she owns all of Bloodcreek, not just this stretch of the strip mall.

Lindy rests her hand on the tassels of her bag. "You study, you hunt, you flirt. However do you have the time to waitress at all?"

I flare my nostrils as the heady scent of stale French fries flits over the road.

"You are young," she adds. "You should focus on work. And your schooling, because we wouldn't want your pretty mind to go to the gutter."

What does she want from me? A *thank you*? I'm the one who keeps track of all that's in her cash register. I may not be too great at taking down orders and delivering food, but if it weren't for me, Beau would be hitting up every girl from here to Tennessee—and I'm not too sure it would be ending there.

"I sure do enjoy spending time with Beauregard," I say, because I know it's the last thing she wants to hear.

"He enjoys dating." Her eyes stitch into mine like embroidery needles.

My mind flits back to the throng of girls that used to wait around for Beau to finish closing up the diner. After the fourth time it happened, he grabbed my hand, and we snuck out the back door. He asked me if I wouldn't mind driving to Rolla with him to pick up some new chairs, and I remember being surprised that he never mentioned the girls' attention to him at all.

In his own way, Beau's a gentleman of sorts. He may be

like a pet, and annoying as all get-out, but he can also be pretty amazing, considering his roots.

The sun flits across the face of my watch, reminding me of what's at stake, so I jump to the point. "Raylan's sister is in trouble. I'm going to need a few days off so I can help out."

Beau's mother tilts her head to the side like she's a bloody aristocrat defending the social hierarchy in a Regency-era novel. "That seems like Raylan's sister's problem, not yours." She grips the long tassels of her purse. "You will not have a job if you go."

CHAPTER 9 - EVA

We've talked about what we would do if the Despairity, those ultra-depraved Blurred Ones, ever came back, heaven forbid. We never came up with a great plan, seeing that our resident expert on Blurred Ones is now shaking a baby rattle and hasn't learned to talk yet, but we had a pretty decent plan of action. But, dang, if an experienced hunter like Tess could get taken by them . . . I shudder at the thought of what they would have done to our already-broken family.

So for the last two hundred miles, we've been strategizing what to do. Raylan's understandably freaked out, since he's the type to pack a machine gun to kill a mosquito "just in case." He's about to blow a gasket at the inadequacy of our power against the Despairity, especially since they basically just seem like crazed hyena ghosts that suck the life out of you. For now, all we know to use is lots and lots of rock salt and holy water. With any luck at all, we'll have time to paint devils' traps.

But surely Tess had all those?

On the one stop we make for gas, I buy every grain of salt

the gas station has, ten cans of spray paint, and eight gallons of water to bless into holy water.

My phone tells us we're two minutes away, but the way Raylan is driving, that's more like thirty seconds. I strain to see much of anything in this black night, but lights from houses on stilts stab through trees. Can Tess seriously afford to live in a beach house?

"I go in." Raylan repeats the plan yet again. "You wait a full minute before you come in." He shoots his steely eyes at me, and I know better than to argue. "A full minute, Eva. We don't know if these chicks actually have brains, but we're not taking the chance they remember you if we can help it."

"I get it, babe." I give his leg a squeeze as he peels into the long, windy driveway with tall, spindly trees blocking the little bit of moonlight. "You got this."

Without even a glance over at me, he throws the truck into park and bolts out the door. He hasn't gotten two steps before his shotgun is cocked and loaded with rock salt. It's too dark to see much, but his dark form leaps up some steps, and he's a shadow as he disappears through the front door. I set my timer for sixty seconds.

During the first ten seconds, I stare at the black hole where he disappeared, willing him all the luck and power in the world.

The next ten seconds, I catch a whiff of sea air. This shouldn't be the way our first trip to the beach together should go down. It's supposed to be sunlight, junk food, and the tangy smell of sunscreen.

A loud pop throws a flash of light from a window farther into the house, and I focus again. Then another pop. A scream, followed by Raylan's unmistakable voice yelling. It's only been thirty-six seconds. I'm out the door and across the yard before forty.

CHAPTER 10 - FROST

I stuff the foreclosure notice in my backpack, ready to scream.

Once again, I've allowed myself too many distractions—conversations with Beau, hunting trips before we're even really ready.

Maggie and I go back and forth on this all the time. I say we really need to buckle down and secure our home, giving me more time to work. Maggie says the only way she can keep us girls sharp is if we're exposed to new foes.

Ever since she realized she was suffocating Eva and me with all her protective ideas, she's gone the other extreme, letting us go to any town with a moving target within a day or two's drive. Eva's all about it, claiming that her teachers let her get away with pretty much anything ever since Dad died.

Dad.

Whoever thought I would miss his knee-length skirt inspections and proclamation that we wouldn't go anywhere since we needed more "down time" at home?

Mom's absolutely lost without him. I thought I liked her cleaning, but this morning she vacuumed the living room twice. When I passed her in the hall, she was looking for cobwebs in the ceilings, and she'd already removed them last night.

From the edge of my bed, I text Maggie for the twentieth time. Why does it feel like I keep doing the same thing over and over without ever making any progress?

Where are you?? Did you follow Eva, or are you waiting for me?

Maybe she left a day or two ago to pry that snake away from Tess. Gosh, I haven't even seriously thought about the fact that Tess has found a way to permanently kill a Blurred One. Eva mentioned something about her and Raylan going back to the mine to permanently finish off Knox, but was that just Tess' idea? I don't think Maggie would ever condone that.

Beau's fourth message in the last hour flashes on the screen of my phone.

Mama said the both of you talked. Meet me??? I'm at the gazebo.

Like I have time for lazy strolls in the park. I grab another shirt and stuff it in my backpack.

I know how you can keep your job AND go to New Orleans.

A tingling sensation scurries across my shoulders as I stare at the latest text from Beau. If he's serious—if he knows of a way I can keep an eye on my sister *and* keep the house—then this deserves a response. It may be the best option I've got.

Glancing at the teacup resting on my bookshelf, I fight back the urge to pick it up and inspect the gold leafing and tiny pink flowers.

My fingers are flying across the screen of my phone before I have time to second-guess myself.

How?

I shift Betsy into park and shimmy out of my seat, my faux-leather jacket slipping and sliding as I go. I've settled into a pair of cargo pants that don't exactly go with the jacket, but they have enough pockets that I'm able to lug about thirteen different weapons.

Salt spray, holy water, battery-operated screwdriver, brass knuckles. . . .

I glance at the brown-gray river, fog clinging to the trees, reminding me slightly of the bayou at night. A cream-tailed squirrel darts up an oak tree, telling me to hurry up and get out of here.

Slamming Betsy's door, I try not to think about the fact that her fuel tank is low. Beau's old, scratched-up, green pickup is parked a few spaces over, and I'm just rounding it when I spot *rose petals,* of all things, dotting a path through the orange-leafed woods.

Part of me says I should jump back into the car and take off for New Orleans now, but the other part is reminding me that he had a way for me to keep my job.

Stuffing Mom's keys into my clunky purse—which doesn't exactly go with my outfit, either, but is large enough to house Leo's old-school revolver—I take off for the woods. Beau had better have a darned good excuse for stalling me if he wants to keep me around.

The heels of my boots squish the rose petals, the silver handle of my dagger comfortingly grazing my ankle with every step. I resolve that I'll give him three, four minutes, tops. If he doesn't divulge anything of use, I'll bite the bullet and quit Lindy's. I'll find something else.

Swerving around a trio of rose bushes, I hurry past a statue of a girl with a fishing pole to find Beau. He's working over a rectangular table laid out with food inside the gazebo.

His collar-length red hair is pulled back into a high pony,

and a white-flowered garland is wrapping a little too picturesquely around the pillars. A skinny tie runs down the front of his shirt, and he actually looks good. My heart shouldn't be spinning in somersaults.

"What are you doing?" I clutch my revolver-laden purse.

Beau looks down at the food like his answer lies there. Salmon and rice adorn white china plates, and I do believe that's violin music playing from a speaker.

Bits of Beau's fire-colored hair flaps in the breeze, and I shoot him a look that says, *Watch yourself, Beau.*

He laughs and keeps on laughing far longer than is normal before loosening his tie with shaking hands. "Thanks for meetin' me, Froster."

I stomp up the steps of the gazebo.

Looking a little paler than usual, Beau slides into a folding chair. He extends an arm, like he wants me to follow suit. When his eyes flutter to the food on the table, I follow his gaze and find lemon slices, artfully arranged on the salmon and wild rice.

I always told Beau that salmon was my favorite food, but I could never afford the price.

He's chipping away at my ironclad heart. Not fair.

As I perch on the end of my chair, the nail in the coffin comes when I spot a silver box wrapped in red ribbon. Nestled between twin taper candles.

I start standing up when he holds up his hands.

"I just need you to hear me out." He raises his eyebrows.

I should turn tail and go right now, but what of these past three months? He's the one who infused my lawn with salt mines. He's the one who taught me how to raise my dagger's aim a little higher. When Lindy kept making me stay long after closing while not increasing my pay, Beau threatened to report her to the Better Business Bureau.

He reaches for a fluted glass, which looks to be filled with sparkling cider, before throwing back a drink.

I could wait for him to spill, but we're wasting time. I lean forward as my chair squawks. "How do I keep my job and still go?"

After a beat, he rises to his feet before sitting once more. With unsteady hands, he pours himself another drink and moves as if to pour me more, but mine's still full.

He sets down the bottle of cider.

He's just opening his mouth to tell me what's on his mind when a little boy about half my height toddles out from under the table. He nearly pulls off the tablecloth.

A deep maroon flush creeps up Beau's neck, flowering across the width of his jaw. "You're jumpin' the gun!" He reaches for the waistband of the boy, but the boy darts away with a giggle.

A pair of ponytailed twins hop down from a rather tall slide nearby, and Beau lets out a shaky breath, wiping his brow with the back of his hand.

A freckle-faced boy jumps out from behind a trash can, nearly causing me to fling a dagger, but these are Beau's siblings, I'm sure.

Two more boys crawl out from under the table, hair sticking up in static as I scamper to my feet just to look at them all.

Six. Boys and girls.

Six miniature human beings who all have the same red hair and curl to the nose as Beau.

All dressed to the nines. Skinny. Skin's taken on a yellowish pallor.

"Beau . . ." I mumble, because I don't want to come right out and say this isn't the time to meet so many boys and girls, but Lindy always treats them like crap, so I linger. Besides, with their sickly faces and sad little eyes, they look terrible. Two of the kids actually have scratches on their arms. Another has black eyes and looks like it's been weeks since he washed his hair.

"It ain't as bad as it looks." Beau must see the concern in my eyes. He holds out his arms. But then drops them and ducks his head. "Actually, it's far worse than you'd ever suppose."

The fact that this is the first time I've seen Beau's siblings is yet another reminder that Lindy keeps them all under lock and key above the diner.

"I don't *usually* introduce my brothers and sisters to my girls." Beau smiles like I just caught him with a hand in the cookie jar. "But desperate circumstances, desperate times. Ain't that right, Tater?"

He's talking to one of the ponytailed twins who hopped from the slide. She springs into a cartwheel, and her dress flies down, revealing a pair of pink underwear.

Beau's cheeks flare bright pink. I think he's going to scold his younger sister when he suddenly says way too fast, "I sorta need you to marry me, Froster."

I stare at the dimple that flashes in his embarrassed cheek, too confounded for words. I want to help him, I do, but *marry* him?

The two oldest boys begin poking at each other.

Beau nervously scratches the back of his neck like he wants nothing more than to rip off his confining shirt. When one brother flicks another brother in the ear, Beau pushes them apart and apologetically says, "But I, uh, can't exactly tell you why, though."

The boys start complaining that Beau's being unfair.

Seeing there's absolutely nothing I can do—I can't marry him; that would be absurd—I jump away from my chair. It tips over with a clatter.

I don't know why his siblings look like they do or why

Beau thinks marrying him will help things at all, but if I've learned anything, it's to stick with the plan.

Protect Eva before something bad happens. And Mom.

"I'm sorry." I seize my bulky purse.

But Beau moves to grab the silver box with the red bow, and we very nearly knock heads. He groans. "You're fixin' to leave . . ."

He looks so sad and downtrodden, I almost don't go, but I scamper down the gazebo steps.

"Say you'll marry me, Froster!"

CHAPTER 11 - EVA

I tear up the stairs three at a time—flying with desperation to get to Raylan and Tess. Terrified that *I* am the backup.

Bursting through the door, I don't even try to be quiet. With my pistol cocked and ready to fill those Despairity witches with massive amounts of salt, I fumble through the open room. A streetlight filters in, making the curtains on Tess' windows look like swinging ghosts.

I bang into bulky couches, searching for Raylan and Tess. It smells like a mixture of oregano and pee in here, and sweat's already trickling down my back. A muffled noise like a splash comes from behind the curtains. With a quick wipe of my face on my shirt sleeve, I dash around a sofa table and dodge a tipped-over barstool.

I spot a bit of light reflecting off what looks like a back door. A gust of wind slams it wide open, and I'm hit by the silty smell of the Gulf's water, but I run to it, crunching glass under my boots.

Bursting onto a large wooden deck, I slam into a wall of freezing cold air. My lungs spasm at the sudden change. I cough for breath, and I'm hit with the feeling that I *never* should have come here. I just make things worse, always charging in, overly confident. They're probably dead already.

Um, no. That would be the Despairity talking. I shove the panic grappling for control of my throat way, way down.

Peering across the deck to the ground below, I can finally see the situation. In the moonlight, Tess floats face-down in her swimming pool, her inky hair spilling around her like a mythical creature. Creeping forward, I almost trip over something long and metallic in my path. Raylan's shotgun lays right in front of me, abandoned. I hear him grunt and curse down below, mixed with the freaky heaving, screeching sounds of the Despairity. He's trying to army crawl to Tess, but they're on him like vultures.

I don't stop to think or plan. I holster my gun, grab his shotgun, and bolt down the stairs to the pool.

The instant my feet hit the stone surrounding the pool, I blast all five shells into the Despairity, barely noting the pain of the thing slamming into my shoulder.

They waiver but don't disappear. They turn to me, their faces even more hideous than I remember from my nightmares, like they've recently decided to add the bloated-slash-rotten look to their usual smudged faces. I toss the shotgun to the side and pull my Glock out again, but it's so cold, I almost drop it. My hands shake as I grip it as tightly as I can, fighting the feeling that this was inevitable. I should just let it be, and go peacefully.

But Raylan. I will not let him go that easily. They're blocking my view of him. Good. Let him go grab Tess. I unload my entire clip into them, and they seem to fade a bit more with each blast.

The tallest one groans like she's about to eat her favorite tasty treat. "*Ehhhhvaaa, always delicious.*"

The sound of my name coming from her messed-up face is revolting. I fake a giant flinch and gag.

"Witch, please," I say as I fumble to reload my gun, despite the freezing metal. "I'm delicious, you're nasty. I don't blame you for being angry."

A splash tells me Raylan must almost have Tess, but it also makes the spirits glance at him. My voice wavers, but I'm fairly good at acting way tougher than I feel. Too bad I have no idea what to do if they don't disappear. . . . And I left the holy water in the car. Nice move, Eves.

I finally succeed in loading the modified bullets and snap the clip back in place. "Seems you've been working out," I say, "but how much more can y'all take?" Hopefully not many, 'cause now I've stopped planning my own funeral, and I'm thinking about Knox with his rope, tying me to the bed. Of Dad's arm landing on me. Of Dad's funeral. What a vicious weapon they have.

I let the kick of the gun keep me grounded. One bang, breath. Two. The smell of sulfur keeps me focused. They're fading, but just thirteen more rounds might not be enough for three of these things. Surely Raylan has Tess by now?

The middle smudge of a girl holds back a bit and starts to turn back to the pool. "*Almost gone*," she breathes and raises her arm toward Raylan.

"Yep, you are." I shoot a prayer to the Man upstairs and unload the rest of the rounds into them, and they're gone.

I sag with relief, already feeling the weight of their power disappear. Forty degrees warmer, fifty pounds lighter.

I'm ready to celebrate and hug my boyfriend and my future sister-in-law, but—Tess' hair still spools around her body in the water. "Tess?" I cry, then my knees buckle when I can't see Raylan. I run to the pool's edge to pull Tess out while searching frantically through the dark for Raylan.

I'm able to grab her boot and lug her out of the water,

drenching myself and the area with the saltwater. But still, no Raylan, and Tess isn't breathing.

"Dammit." I sob and try to remember the CPR I learned at girl's camp. Turn her head to the side, check for breathing, check pulse . . . in what order? Call 911? There's no pulse, and she's totally not breathing, but *where is he?* I start compressions. Try not to get my panic-drooly-snot all over her as I give her mouth-to-mouth.

A truck rumbles by the front of the house, and the headlights give just enough light that I see a darker shape on the bottom of the pool. My heart plummets down there with it. Tess coughs up water, but I'm diving into the pool before the truck's sound disappears.

CHAPTER 12 - FROST

I stomp on the gas to push Betsy over a stretch of railroad tracks at the foot of the next winding hill.

Beau has *got* to be kidding me. Marry him? Marry him! I can't even. . . .

It's like I've stepped into this alternate reality where I've given my life to entertaining an over-confident cowboy who wants nothing more than to seduce an unsuspecting filly.

But this isn't even remotely what I want.

I was on my way to becoming something.

The plan was supposed to be me eating ramen three meals a day and studying flashcards until a little after midnight.

Leo was supposed to be here.

We would have co-majored in psychology.

A dead skunk on the road makes me jerk the wheel to the right, and as I realign myself, I fight back the fantastical image of Leo and me mapping out the rest of our lives together. We'd go on nature walks and take part in Civil War reenactments with him whispering about the parts that never really happened in history. Maggie would find a way to cure him of being a Blurred One. We'd raise a family.

I pound the wheel, wishing I'd been born another day. A place where I never met Leo.

While I pass shrubby autumn forests hunching in the moonlight, I let the truth of what I need to do resettle inside me like an anvil.

I need to take care of Eva and Mom. Forget about boys and make amends for what I did to our family.

I glance down at my phone, which is strewn on the far side of the passenger seat, but it doesn't blink. No messages or notifications from Maggie. I should call Mom, but I'll wait till I stop for gas and tell her I'm headed back to New Orleans.

My pleather jacket is all but suffocating, so I rip it off and crank up the AC. The lukewarm air reminds me that Eva told me that we need a new part, and I smack the steering wheel again because it *all* comes back to money.

I roll down my window, indulging in the somewhat brisker air splashing against my face, when a green, rusted-out truck comes lumbering up beside Betsy.

The fumes coming off the green monster could pollute the entire South. The cab lights are lit up like Christmas, and Beau rolls down his window and gestures wildly at me.

"Pull over!" he yells. The wind's whipping some of his red hair out of his pony, like he belongs in some country rock star magazine. "I need to explain!"

I gun the accelerator. "Nuh-uh." And I roll up my window, because he is trouble.

He lays on his horn like he wants the attention of every cop from here all the way to Abilene. He better quit that if he doesn't want me to tell Mr. Harris to pass along to every hunter he knows that Beau's really a banshee.

He continues honking.

"WHAT?" I cry.

Beau holds out his hands like I'm his princess in the pea.

Blurred Ones be darned, he is *looney*.

Regardless, my hands loosen around the steering wheel, and I find myself avoiding his eyes. Mostly because I know he'll never stop. Not unless I talk to him. So I ease up on the accelerator and pull over to the shoulder. The last thing I need is to explain my situation to the highway patrol.

I flip on the emergency lights and pat my trusty dagger in my boot. Just in case.

Without the squealing of tires, Beau follows suit and, thankfully, he doesn't honk to announce his victory. He checks his rearview mirror once for oncoming traffic before flinging open his truck door and clomping over in his lizard boots to the other side of Betsy.

When he takes a seat inside, his eyes gleam. "Thanks. I was fixin' to dive between our windows if you didn't pull over."

A train horn blares in the distance, and I think maybe I should suggest he make himself useful if he's going to cause so many problems—Eva and Raylan could be in danger, and he's as good a hunter as any.

"You need to marry me," Beau says, rubbing a sweaty palm down the length of his pant leg, "for the good of humanity."

I scoot away from him on my cloth seat.

"My brothers and sisters are *beggin'* me."

"They don't even know who I am!"

"Don' you worry your pretty little mind. I've told them everything."

I'm not entirely sure what "everything" involves, and I'm pretty sure it paints him as the fearless warrior who frequently swoops in to rescue the grieving honey of Bloodcreek.

The idea makes my blood steam. It reminds me of the boys in the psychiatric ward who used to think they could call in favors if they offered me their canned peas. "Do you always claim 'rescuing the innocent' to fulfill your current endgame?"

His eyes stretch open wide. "Huh?"

"The beer mugs! When I thought that Orval was wine!"

"That's not—" Beau rubs the back of his neck so hard it's like he's stretching out a cowhide. "Don' be—"

I click off the emergency light. Obviously, he's not here to molest me. If I were Eva, I'd say something akin to *Speak now, or forever I'll break your face,* but she's not here, and the faster we get this over with, the sooner we get to New Orleans.

Beau loosens his tie and wipes the sweat building up on his brow like I really am an affliction for him, and he'd like nothing more than to break free.

Maybe his mom asked him to do this. Maybe she's the reason why he's acting so crazy, although that would be insane, because she absolutely hates me.

He rubs the freckles on his forehead like he's trying to concentrate, and I'm tired of beating around the bush, so I summarize.

"You expect me to marry you just because you brought along your siblings."

He stares down at his long fingers. "Sorry, Froster. I can' explain."

"You do realize I'm not anywhere *near* that point."

His usually self-assured demeanor melts as his shoulders droop, and he won't look me in the eyes. His voice goes all too monotone when he asks, "Don' ya like me?"

My heart compresses. "That's not the point!"

And he turns to face me, his usual teasing face giving way to defeat. He hangs his head, and I hate myself for making him feel pain. He helped me check up on Eva when I was worried she was ditching school, but she was actually in trigonometry. He taught me the difference between skinny and gutting knives. How to remove the handles to increase speed and improve balance. But we can't get engaged, especially since I'm still in love with a Blurred One.

I fight back the image of Leo turning into a butterfly to show me what Knox did. How he admitted it was dangerous for me to stay in room six-six-six, but he was glad I did because it meant he got to see me.

"Go home, Beau." I fight back the tears.

I can't even look up. All I can see is his long fingers lying too flatly on his lap, like he wishes this were all a bad dream.

A semi-truck rumbles past, followed by a minivan with Kentucky plates, and the only time Beau's been this quiet is when he made a dish of split and curled hotdogs he affectionately called "Redneck Sushi." Lindy told him he was as pubescent as his daddy.

"Mama," he says. "She's kinda crazy." With unsteady hands, he reaches into his suit jacket pocket and pulls out the silver box with the red ribbon.

I don't inch toward it, because I don't want anything from him.

Trapping me with his mud-brown puppy dog eyes, Beau says, "That is why I *need* to give you—"

A loud *thump* cuts across the back roof of Betsy. The entire car bounces as the wheel bearings squeak. Something's on the trunk. My hands automatically go to my knives.

It's a little bizarre. Maybe we are actually dreaming, because in the rearview mirror, I suddenly see all four-feet-eleven of a tasseled shirt-wearing Lindy.

Her nostrils flare like she's a dragon, and she's ready to roast her meat.

CHAPTER 13 - EVA

"Y ou did what?" Raylan yells, dripping pool water all over Tess' fancy floor. The veins in his neck bulge like another appendage.

Tess stares at him, defiant, her bloodshot eyes and wet hair the only signs that she just about died out there.

"I was going to trap them, force them into some vessels, and let Zombi help me finish them off for good. So, yeah, I lured them here." She sips the hot chocolate I made for her. She *is* strong, seeing that they fed on her for a good eight hours, yet she's with-it enough to talk.

"*And?*" he presses, less impressed.

"And one of the would-be vessels broke loose and got the drop on me." She picks at a lone speck of lint on the arm of her beach couch, reclines like a queen on her throne. "Didn't realize I'd picked up an escape artist."

"'Would-be vessels'? Let me guess. Giving criminals a chance to redeem themselves?" Raylan slightly narrows his eyes at his sister but keeps his face curiously neutral.

Tess gazes out the window.

"And by yourself. Where was your backup?" He paces past

the white marble island of the kitchen and unsheathes a knife from a butcher block that looks like it could hack a werewolf in half with a flick of the wrist. Girl needs to teach me these hunting skills that buy all these pretty things.

Tess takes a long drink of her hot chocolate. "You know I work better alone." She holds her gold-lined mug out to me. "Now, Eva, please put this in the sink. It's morning. Let's get some sleep."

A sound like air gushing from a balloon comes from Raylan, and with it, his neutral facade vanishes. He looks like he's about to grab her mug and chuck it, but settles for clenching and unclenching his jaw a few hundred times. Looks like he knows to try this battle another day.

Making myself as small and quiet as possible to avoid setting off this powder keg, I take the mug and silently set it in the sink. This ain't my first family drama rodeo. Sleep now, peace, and answers in the morning.

CHAPTER 14 - FROST

A pen rattles in the cup holder. My sunglasses slip from the faux-wood console to the matted floor.

Lindy's grabbing Betsy's trunk and shaking us like we're a rattle.

She's a little too strong.

"*What* is your mom?" I grip the side of my door. Is she a demon? A wicked-strong vampire, maybe?

Beau twists around to shoot his "mama" a look of so much hatred that all I can do is gape at the boy.

He shoves the silver box into my lap. "Open it!"

Just as I reach for it, though, Lindy lifts the car sideways.

I grab the handle above the door, preventing me from tumbling into Beau's arms. Betsy squeaks as the box rattles to my feet, and my seat belt's digging into my neck. Beau braces my legs so I don't kick him in the face.

I'm a suspended icicle, just hanging, as Beau cries, "Are you all right?"

The car swings so abruptly in the other direction that I'm slamming my face into the center console. Nose smashes into my brain.

We rock like Betsy's going to lay back on her left side, but the side of my neck clips my headrest, and I accidentally kick Beau's shoulder. The crown of my head strikes the window on the driver's side.

The air is *cold* with all these splinters of glass embedding in my cheeks, and all I can think is Maggie and Eva will flip out because of all the time they spent fixing up Betsy.

The seat belt's twisted around my neck, and when I wrench it out of the way, Beau throws open his door and flies out of Betsy.

He's nothing but a blur of black, red, and white.

He wraps his arms around his "mama" outside my door and behind me by ten or so feet. She's still all decked out in her Western wear, while veins, black and aggressive, emerge from her pensive face.

A creature I've never seen before.

She grips the long black straps of her leather purse. A whip—connected in several sections by rings and thorns and rocks embedded in the strands. It's *nothing* like the whips back at Maggie's. I would do anything for my fanny pack-wearing friend to show up and pull out any number of her secretive oddities, but I'm grabbing my dagger from my boot and springing from the car.

The metallic clink of the whip tells me any connection with that will be pretty bleak. Lindy's heeled boots are planted casually, shoulder-width apart, and I have a feeling she's used this whip many times.

Placing himself between us, Beau grabs the rocky studs embedded in the whip with his bare hands, and Lindy flings it back, slicing deep wounds into his palms on either side. It's like a bad dream—where I'm rooting for a boy I wish I'd never spoken to today.

"You can't kill her." From the end of his mother's whip, Beau tries to break free.

A single vein erupts from the side of Lindy's face. "*You* should start obeying me." She cracks her whip again, and it releases Beau and curls around my arm like a snake.

The rocks and tiny thorns embed in my flesh, and the metal reminds me of how Lindy is cold and unbending.

My dagger drops with a clatter to the street, and I remember the box Beau tried to give me. It probably houses a weapon. If only I could go back in time.

Lindy elegantly holds her whip with the poise and grace of a horse trainer. "Looks like you cut your face, dear."

I can't believe this is Beau's mom. It's like she was raised in the most upper crust of high society, and he—like she boarded him up and only let him out for train robberies.

If I could just get control of the whip, I could dive back into Betsy and grab the box.

Lindy's boots clip against the asphalt, the tassels on her shoulders fluttering in a puff of wind. It's like she believes she's the heroine in her own novel. She's the martyr, though I can't see why she's fighting.

I grip the whip, its metal and studs digging into my palms. Cuts off all feeling. I think my fingers will be nothing but bits of frayed leather she'll attach to her purse and dye.

"What are you?" I cry.

A far-off look flutters across her eyes. "Someone you should fear to see."

Beau presses his fingers to either side of his face. "Stop this, Mama! You're bein' colder than a banker's heart on foreclosure day."

Softening a little, she says, "Do you think I'm going to just stand by and watch you destroy our lives?"

"Imma tryin' to bridle all the insanity!"

A new emotion flickers across her face. "*You* are trying to thwart me."

From the crumbling side of the street, I connect my one

free hand with the handle of my fallen knife. I've just raised the blade to sever the first of her whip's strings when, quick as a lion tamer, she *yanks* me toward her, so we're chest-to-chest.

I don't know how it happened so fast, and she smells of heated iron. Both electric and earthy. I don't know why I don't expect it, but more black veins emerge from her face. She's lived a tortured past, and she doesn't wish to change her ways.

There's a blur of black—Beau's moving inhumanly fast as he strikes his mother, sending her away from me.

He pins her to the ground.

"Get off of me," she seethes. She throws him off, and he re-tackles her. They roll.

There's this faint crunch as Beau breaks away.

He favors his ankle, and with a grimace, he pops it back in place before spinning around and shoving his "mama" to the dark, veiled spot beneath Betsy.

I take the opportunity to go for the silver box he tried to give me. I scamper for the still-open driver's side door and stoop down to retrieve it, but something grabs me by the ankle and pulls me underneath Betsy.

Air whooshes over my head, and it's like I've been launched from a rollercoaster. I scream.

In the dark, Lindy's thorned and metal whip connects with itty-bitty needles along my hairline. I jolt from a million ccs of aggression and a greedy attempt to make some sort of mind-link. It's like I feel a vacuum in my head sucking away at my spirit, my soul. Suction is set to high.

I grip the handle of my dagger and plunge it into what I suppose to be her hand.

She screams. I must be lucky.

It's like she's never been stabbed before. Like she's only accustomed to winning.

The dainty tentacles of her whip retract from my hairline, but her grunting and sucking noise tells me she's pulling my dagger from her hand. She whispers, "How did you do that?"

Beau calls from outside the underside of my car. "I *told* ya she's mighty tricksy!"

Lindy slaps the whip at the side of my face, and I slice it off with a second dagger.

"Urghh!" she screams. She rolls away from me, and with a simple roll and push-off from the gravel, she climbs out from the underside of Betsy.

Beau's and her boots are separated by only a few feet when she sneers, "Maybe I should finish *you* off for defying me."

I can hear the smile in Beau's voice as he says, "See what the others say."

"*Arghh!*" Lindy snaps her whip to the sky. I don't know whether to laugh or pee that I've made her so angry. "I suppose I'll have to wipe her mind," she says.

All I can smell is dust and road and her creepy iron scent, and I just want to get away from her and drive away.

I look around for my dagger, but when I find it, it's embedded in the heart of one of Betsy's tires.

Dang.

Lindy's boots clip the asphalt as she approaches where I'm hiding. "I want her to see my face," she says, "so the subconscious part of that girl knows to fear me."

Like a tentacle with fangs, her studded whip curls under the car and again embeds along the hairline of my face.

I wake to a killer-bright sun lasering through the blinds and my eyelids.

"Kill me now," I mutter and pull the blanket over my head. I wonder for a half-second what happened to my blackout curtains, but then the fifteen-million thread count sheets remind me where I am. Beach house with Raylan and his scary but awesome only living relative. I jump out of Tess' giant Pottery Barn-style guest bed and slide my capris back on. Didn't exactly have time to pack jammies.

I peek into the hallway to make sure I can dash to the bathroom unseen. Haven't looked in a mirror since yesterday afternoon, and I am probably *scary*. The coast is clear, so I tiptoe down the hall's dark wood floor, careful not to bump the gorgeous glass mosaic hanging on the wall. The blues, reds, and greens capture enough life that they shine little mesmerizing, dancing shapes on the floor.

"No need to sneak around." Tess' cool voice comes from behind me. I spin around to argue that I wasn't sneaking, but her straight face changes to a smile as soon as I see her. She's already dressed in jeans that look like little tailor elves made them for her, and her perfectly arched eyebrows and lined lips remind me to buy makeup from somewhere other than the dollar store someday.

"I just didn't know—"

"You are completely fine, sweetie." She smooths her snug crew cut tee with a quick, stiff smile. "Whenever you're ready, I've got something to show you."

"Awesome, yeah, let me just go pee—er, use the restroom real quick?"

Thankfully, she gives me a tiny wink.

"Of course." She glides past me to the kitchen, leaving a trail of perfume probably made from unicorn sweat behind her. "And no need to wake Raylan." She lifts her chin to a room at the other end of the hall. "He needs his rest."

"Sure thing."

I get ready as quickly as I can. Don't need her thinking I'm high-maintenance, and I'm so curious to see what she wants to show me that all I do is pee, brush my teeth with the new toothbrush left out on the counter, and splash some water on my face. I'm in and out in a flash. I find her in the kitchen, and she's got—yes!—two Diet Cokes in hand. Also looks like she's got magical cleaning powers, because you'd never guess there was a giant fight in here last night.

She hands me one of her perfectly cold sodas. "Raylan said you understand Diet Coke is the only way to go." Yes, the three of us can get along just fine, and I grin bigger than a Gasconade catfish at the thought of Raylan talking about me. I pop open the ice-cold can and enjoy the bite of the first sip of soda, thankful the caffeine will wear away the cobwebs in my brain.

"All right, hon. Let's talk." She slides onto the matching barstool of the one I dodged last night. She crosses one leg over the other, suddenly looking much softer than her usual stoic warrior stance.

Careful not to scratch her floor, I pull out the other stool, surprised at how heavy the wood is. Girl's seriously got expensive tastes. Maybe she's gonna teach me how to make money hunting, although the thought of her knowing our secondhand-only situation makes me want to crawl into her kitchen cabinets and die. But if Raylan trusts her, I can trust her. She watches me, not speaking, so I carefully perch on the stool and make a mental note to not swing my legs.

"I'm in a tough situation, and I need your help," she says.

I try not to let the shock that she could want help from *me* to show on my face. As long as it doesn't involve barbecuing monsters, I'm in.

"While I'm grateful you and Raylan are here, it does make things a little complicated."

Uh. Does Tess have a boyfriend or something? "Oh, I'm sorry."

"Couldn't be helped." She takes a long drink of her soda like she's in a commercial, finally sets it down on her coaster, and licks her ruby lips. Hashtag doesn't-even-burp. "But I want to believe I can trust you."

"Of course you can," I blurt, but she looks at me through the corner of her eye, like I just spoke out of turn. I'm just gonna be quiet.

"It's really hard for me to talk about, but I'm trying to own up to the fact that I failed Raylan." She swivels her seat around to face the opposite kitchen counter. There's a picture in a bright silver frame—definitely not from our favorite dollar store—and, ohmygosh, it's little Raylan! With a woman with Raylan's eyes and a man with a cute little bouffant. They must be his parents. A long, dark mane announces a young Tess in a shirt that's four sizes too big. I have to chomp my lip to keep from squealing at Raylan's little Transformers shirt. So. Freaking. Adorable. *Dang,* we'd make pretty babies.

"I took off to take care of a few things," she says, "and was so happy to be away from our parents' drama that I just left him alone. I didn't know our father had gotten so addicted, because I never asked."

She shakes her head, and it's the first time I notice she has some fine wrinkles around her eyes. "So, long story short, we're both hunters now, and I try my best to look out for him, but it's still so dangerous. There are too many monsters."

She swings her stool back to me and puts her hand on my arm. It's cool and surprisingly soft, but so unexpected, I flinch and immediately feel guilty as she retracts her hand to her lap.

"Eva, I can get rid of Blurred Ones for good." She pauses, watching me with those laser-focused eyes again. I have no idea what to say. "I'm almost there. I know they're just one monster, but it would go a long way to keeping Raylan and us all safe. They're too dangerous and too manipulative."

"Well, of course! That would be amazing." Plus, I don't add, Maggie won't be mad at me anymore if we get rid of them altogether. "How do we do it? Anything you need. I want to keep him safe, too." I try to reflect her calm, business-only attitude. "Trust me."

"I hope I can." She looks at me like Raylan used to do. Eyes locked on me but body leaning away just a bit. Assessing. Once again, I guess I pass the test, because she keeps talking. "You've got to be strong. It's not going to be easy. And you have to promise me you'll keep Raylan out of this. He won't understand." She starts to push off her stool but hesitates. "You haven't known this life very long, but you're smart, and you'll figure it out. Even the worst Blurred Ones can do some good."

I nod more confidently than I feel because I have no idea what she's talking about. She laughs a singsong laugh. She is gorgeous when she's not staring you down with laser eyes.

"You'll catch on, mini-me." She grabs her soda off the counter and waves for me to follow her into the walnut kitchen, which sparkles like a magazine ad in the morning light. Are we cooking up a spell? I linger when she opens a large, heavy door to her pantry, but she lowers her voice and says, "Come check it out."

Inside, beside the broom and mop that hang on heavy-duty iron hooks on the wall, she pulls another hook down, and a wall moves. What the heck, it's a freaking secret passageway!

"Get out of town," I gasp.

She gives a prim huff. "Not yet, hon."

Behind the door to the *secret passageway,* wooden stairs lead down into another room, I guess on the ground between the house's stilts. The cold, stagnant smell of concrete wafts up the stairs. Ah, this must be her weapons room. Nice!

"Watch your step," she says, disappearing into the darkness. "The light's at the bottom."

I'm so flipping excited, I'm starting to breathe kind of loudly, so I cover my mouth. But something rotten reaches my nose, so I filter the air through my fingers. The unmistakable sound of a metal chain comes from the dark below, like she's got Frankenstein's monster down here. I freeze.

"Uh, Tess?"

"Remember, I'm trusting you." I can barely see her grab the string attached to the light. "I can, right? To keep Raylan safe?"

Right, of course. "Yes."

"Good." She pulls the string, and I squint against the sudden light. Chained to the wall, covered in what looks like layers of dried blood, long hair falls over the captive's face.

"Is it another creature that knows how to kill Blurred Ones?" I whisper, because even though it's a monster, it feels weird to talk about it right in front of it.

"It has answers. But it hasn't been talkative yet, even with incentive." Her gaze travels to a workbench behind us. A drill with a filthy bit lays on its side. Just like the one we pushed through Knox's face. The memory makes my knees wobble. Something clicks in my mind. The color of the hair. The lean but strong build of those shoulders.

I peer closer at Tess' captive, and my breath hitches at the sight of hanging suspenders.

Every muscle in my body screams at me to bolt to my friend. "*Leo?*"

CHAPTER 16 - FROST

I glance at my rearview mirror, pretty sure something just shook my car. But we're on a bench seat. It smells like the greased and repaired parts at a hardware store. I take in the large, clunky gear shift and the wider cab.

I'm in Beau's truck.

He's driving?

This look of compassion washes over Beau's face as I pry my face off the dust-covered window and force my eyes to stay open. A tear drips from one of my eyes, and, confused, I wipe it off with the back of my sleeve.

I thought I was in Betsy.

Beau's suit jacket lays protectively on my lap, and his eyes watch the road with a level of seriousness I've rarely seen.

When I spot the red-ribboned box he tried to give me, I find that it's open.

He nods toward me. "I kinda decided to put that on you while you were asleep."

My hand flutters to my throat, and I find a silver chain with a little vial of—something.

Black liquid swirls through the glass, and Beau says, "To keep you safe."

It's like I'm living in a fog. I blink to try to clear my brain. "From what?"

A flash of a memory flares over my eyes, and it's like I can *see* myself being pulled under Betsy. But that's ridiculous. Someone crashed into us. My mind is telling me that now. That's why I'm so disoriented, and my arms, back, and head feel so sore. Like a video recording, I can see the Volkswagen Golf veering out of its lane and smashing into Betsy, rendering me unconscious.

I ask, "Where's Betsy?"

Gently, Beau reaches over and squeezes my hand, and I'm still so confused, I don't pull away.

"She required a lil' tune-up," he says. "I knew you'd wanna hit the road like a gobble o' turkeys."

I must have really hit my head, because I don't remember *anything*. Except that maybe a yellow—red?—car smashed into my window. I press my fingers to my scalp, because now it feels like I've been stabbed with a thousand thorny weeds.

I grab the sun visor and flip open the mirror to find seven or so deep gashes along my hairline.

"I was gonna call the police." Beau smiles guiltily. "But I knew the hurry you'd be in to get to New Orleans."

A sliver of pain shoots through my skull, and I press the back of my head into the headrest of my seat.

"You'll be real sore for a while. Want some Tylenol or Ibuprofen, dumplin'?"

But the memory's shifting in my head. A Volkswagen wasn't plowing into me; I was plowing into *it*.

Like I'd been driving.

But I thought Beau had gotten me to pull over.

"I'm sorry." I grab the crown of my head as the dreamcatcher hanging from Beau's mirror makes me even dizzier. "What happened?"

I'm seeing myself grabbing that ax all over again and thrusting it into Dad's back, and I liked it, but that was Knox lying to me.

I'm saying goodbye to Leo outside the library.

Knox has Eva and me in that fiery circle, and everything spins and spins—

Beau grabs my shoulder and steadies me. Moves me from the nightmare where I almost lost my sister to Knox and the Despairity.

Maybe the Despairity caused the driver to crash into us. I can't put my finger on it, but it feels an awful lot like someone's been messing with my mind.

"How did you say you know about Blurred Ones?" I try to grasp the things that make sense, a hint of normalcy. "You always said it involves your mom, but you glossed over how exactly they came into your life."

A sheen of panic flashes over Beau's muddy eyes, and his fingers tighten around the steering wheel before he reaches out and turns down the volume on the radio.

I hadn't even noticed the music was on. I am completely losing my mind.

It's like his voice is barreling toward me from a tunnel when he says, "Mama don't treat me an' my brothers an' sisters real good."

While he grasps the steering wheel, the skin on his knuckles stretches white.

"She took my pops for all he's worth and got custody of me, Awan, Enoch. Everybody." He taps the steering wheel with his thumb, like he's forcing himself to be brave. "Mama's the type of person who always gets what she wants. We've learned that you have to be prepared if you wanna stand in her way."

I remember how she met me outside the diner, and I have

to agree. But as my gaze settles on a rim of blood on Beau's neck, I find that the top two buttons of his white shirt are unbuttoned, and, earlier, he was wearing a tie. A small piece of glass protrudes from his skin, and I open the glove box to find the wad of napkins I stuck in there last week.

"Why are you bleeding?" I ask, because I swear, *I'm seeing a flash of black, like a whip grappling for my arm*, and I'm going insane.

Looking down, I find that my arm has cuts and looks a little purple. Maybe this necklace is making me see things? I reach for it, clasped around my neck, but Beau traps my hand.

"That necklace is the only thing keepin' you alive."

He's not telling me things.

I stare into his steady, guilty eyes and want to rip off the necklace, but the slackness of his jaw tells me he isn't joking.

"What is it?" I ask.

"A ward 'gainst Mama." He bites the inside of his lip. "I kinda sorta snagged it from Avi."

The witch doctor we took out in New Orleans.

I don't know, but I feel like he's being honest. But he's also hiding something else from me. "Why?"

"Lotsa witches use it to avoid detection from the likes of you an' me. I figured Mama would come after you eventually."

"Your mom's a witch?"

He presses his lips together like he wants to cry, but he shakes his head. "Jus' keep the necklace on, okay?"

My heart—well—it flips sideways. Beau's displaying true concern, and while I can't detect *exactly* what's going on, I can tell that he's trying to protect me. Maybe these flashes mean I have too much on my plate. Eva's always telling me to take a mental health day.

So I click off my seatbelt and scoot over a little on the bench to show that I hear him, I see him, and everything will be okay.

He settles his arm around my shoulders, and I find that I don't even want to push him away. Something scratches in my throat when I ask, "Your mom isn't abusive, is she?"

A rigidity shoots all the way through Beau's shoulder and down his fingers' length, which all but makes the hair on my arms stand up straight.

I think he'll find an easy way to reply, but the raindrops pelting the windshield are the only sound for a stretch.

"The first time I saw Blurred Ones," he eventually says, "consortin' with Mama was right after graduation."

At first, my mind flits back to my graduation day—when Dad was so recently put in the ground, and Leo was gone, and I somehow numbly walked across the stage. But Beau's a full year older than me. He must be referring to his own graduation day.

"I drove over to the diner," he says. "Found 'er choppin'." He shivers. "An' I thought, 'that don' look like chicken.'"

Suddenly, the road bends, and Beau cranks the steering wheel to the right. When we dip down a hill, even more raindrops pelt the glass, and we are in the typhoon of a dangerous story.

"When I asked her what it was," he says, "all she said was the Blurred Ones got her to change sides."

I reach up and hold the pendant at my throat, wondering how dangerous Lindy could really be. Maggie and Eva have always agreed that Lindy gives them the creeps, but we always brushed it off to a serious lack of personality.

Beau pulls me a little tighter as he kisses the top of my head, and it actually almost feels nice to be held that way. "As ya know, I'm a 'glass half full' kinda guy, but when I saw how Mama had it out for you, I knew I needed to up my game."

A layer of cotton fills my throat as I try to figure out what to say. I know what it's like to be under the thumb of a tyrant parent. What I don't mention is the fact that Eva and I used to have to walk on eggshells when Dad was alive. He always mistreated Eva, and I never protected her until it was too late. I don't say any of these things, because I've never talked about that part of my past. All he knows is Dad died.

That simple reminder makes me hungry for someone to get to know me. He may not be Leo, but he has a protective instinct, and it's so nice to see that reflected in somebody.

I curl my hand around Beau's arm, which isn't quite the right length or shape, and I listen to the low purr of the rickety truck until Beau slows down and veers off to the right.

My throat tightens as he pulls onto the shoulder, and I know what he's doing. He shifts his truck into park, and I can *feel* his desire to be with me.

Eyes awash with hope—and some unexplainable grief—he leans down, and his lips are only three inches from mine. He's kind of handsome, and he's kind of dumb, but he's *here* for me.

I shouldn't let it happen. Part of me wants to bash in my brains, but I let those lips brush against my own, and I grab the back of his hair, wide awake.

CHAPTER 17 - EVA

"What is Leo doing here?" I fight to keep my voice even while my mind struggles to catch up. To figure out real fast what my next move should be, 'cause I don't think Tess would think too kindly of my impulse to run to him and comfort him.

As if my words bring him back to life, Leo turns his head just enough to look at me. Behind the hair hanging in his face, I see dark filth and blood, not the youthful yet ancient, kind soul that looks like he should be hanging out with James Dean and Cary Grant at the same time. I feel Tess' laser gaze on me, watching instead of answering why on earth she has him chained up in here like the worst creature in existence. He looks almost as bad as Knox did.

I force my face into a mask, like I'm even slightly impressed, following my gut that screams, *Keep it cool*! "I actually kind of know him. Did you know that?"

"Yep," Tess says with a bored smile. "I know he behaved well around my brother, and he's in love with your sister."

The way she holds herself now—the lightly crossed arms, the placid face—all say she's relaxed, but there's a tidal wave of tension barely peeking out of every muscle. I need to tread *very,* very carefully. Crossing her could mean a disaster of everything from causing problems with Raylan, to, I don't know, her snapping my neck like a dried-out twig.

Suddenly, she launches into movement. Grabbing a rough two-by-four from the floor, she nudges Leo's head up with it, like he's too nasty for her to touch with her hand. His hair falls enough out of his face for me to see him clearly for the first time. And oh my—*no.*

Right there above his lip, where we tested the key to taking down Knox, she's screwed the sigil back into his face.

I remember how stoic Frost cried and the heavy guilt of when he let us put that thing in him before. I have to shove my hands in my pockets to keep from punching her.

He's like a happy Labrador puppy who even gets my jokes. How could she lock him up like a monster?

"He chose the devil's side," she's explaining while I try to conceal my freak-out. "He did. No matter how you try to twist it. He doesn't get to just go and forget."

She moves the board, and his head drops like a macabre bowling ball. "Well?" Her voice is getting choppy with agitation. Her mask is slipping. I need to hold mine. I clear my throat.

"Sorry, just a little shocked to see him." I kneel down in front of him. "But, yeah, how do you want to use him?" Leo, look at me.

A tiny sound escapes the back of her throat, like she's annoyed I haven't figured it out already. "He knows what I need. You can just help get him to tell me." Forthcoming, this one.

I nod back like I'm a doctor concurring. "What can I do to help?"

"Thought maybe since you knew him," she leans back

against a steel pillar, "you could talk some sense into him. You haven't fallen for his lies, have you?"

I force a laugh. "No. And you don't think Raylan would get it?" Leo still won't—can't?—look at me.

She scoffs loudly. "He's made it abundantly clear he doesn't have the stomach for these things. Plus, he's got the wool pulled over his eyes concerning this one." She nods at Leo like he's an old lemon car.

I brusquely swipe the hair from his eyes, trying to sell this. "I told Frost all the time she was crazy." I glance back at Tess and see a gleam in her eye. She's not buying it. Leo, you know me and even knew me in the pre-mortal world, right? I lift his chin and try to scream it with my eyes. His are so dull. Empty like the dead Avi. I'm not sure how much he's taking in right now.

Please forgive me. "I see you found the same tool we used." I grab the screw above his lip with my fingers and twist it like I'm testing a light switch. He only moans, which makes my heart sink even further. *What has she done to you, friend? I will be back for you!*

"Yep. Here." She holds out a rag with a conspiratorial grin. "I think I hear Raylan, so we better scoot, but looking forward to your help, mini-me."

I resist slapping her and instead wipe Leo's blood off my hand onto the rag. Oh, she's not psycho *at all*.

CHAPTER 18 - FROST

The door chimes as Beau and I mosey inside a small Louisiana diner. We were almost to Tess' place when Eva texted me, insisting we meet here. I may have been in a car accident, the details might be a little hazy, but I'm discovering the benefits of seeing a cowboy.

It's about time we got some food, anyway. We haven't eaten since Jonesboro.

Plus, Beau and I can check out the competition—look for any ideas to bring back to Lindy and hopefully redeem my job.

The smell of onions and bell peppers wafts through the diner, and, as we walk past a table, Beau steals a French fry from some stranger's plate.

He grins at me before popping the miniature slice of potato into his mouth, so I swat his fingers—in time to spot Eva's brown hair and rather dark circles under her eyes. She's sitting next to Raylan, and she waves us over.

I think maybe something's wrong, but she smothers whatever weariness she's feeling with an enormous smile, and my heart expands with relief to see her acting like herself.

She raises her menu and says a little too loudly, "I'll bet the hushpuppies are *to die for*."

Raylan, looking as sleep-deprived as Eva, crinkles his brow at her. But there's something underlying his emotions. Doesn't he like hushpuppies?

With those black circles around both of their eyes, the pair probably haven't gotten much sleep since they left Missouri. I'm just glad she's safe. The texts she sent me earlier today were the first I'd heard from her.

Eva searches my face, too, like I'm hiding secrets. I may have used a bit of concealer to hide the cuts in my face from that Volkswagen hitting our car, but one thing at a time. I'll tell her about Betsy getting all smashed up when the time is right. Besides, she's the one who's been on the hunt. Unless the hunt didn't go so well?

My stomach plummets. "Is Tess—?" I don't even know how to broach that topic.

"She's fine," Raylan says, his eyes still on my sister, like he's still waiting for her to, I don't know, divulge some more.

"Have you heard from Maggie?" A wave of panic clutches my chest as I lean closer.

A look of regret passes over Eva's eyes, but then her smile widens. "We used Tess' snake to kill Knox."

"Yeah?" *Good.* The creep will never hurt Eva again.

As a cloud of smoke flutters over the diner, though, I can still detect this layer—this film of undivulged truth Eva isn't saying—and I want to tell her about the day I've had. How I've got a little amnesia from a car crash, and Beau and I finally kissed, but I don't exactly remember all the details.

Plus, something obviously happened with Maggie before they permanently killed Knox. The fact that Maggie was so vehemently against using Zombi to take out Blurred Ones may be why she's not writing back.

But holding grudges isn't Maggie's style.

Raylan skirts another look at Eva—actually chews on the inside of his lip. They're in a fight! That's it. As if to confirm my suspicions, he orders Eva another Diet Coke. Like he's quasi-sucking up, since he doesn't know what's up with her. Or maybe he feels like Eva should have listened to Maggie and left Knox rotting for eternity in that shaft. But something tells me Raylan would always side with Tess. . . .

By the time Beau and I are settled into our shared vinyl seat, the smoke doesn't hang so heavily over our group, and Beau quietly takes my hand.

It shouldn't make me feel guilty.

When we had hit Arkansas, we pulled over and changed into whatever clothes we could find for sale at a truck stop. Beau looks as backcountry as ever in a green camo shirt.

Eva, though, stares at the half-worn letters on my new T-shirt that says, "Roadkill Helper" with a box that's the equivalent of Hamburger Helper. Her gaze finds the necklace Beau gave me, but I'm not sure this is the time to get into the topic of Lindy. Besides, Raylan's never given Eva any jewelry as far as I know, so I boost a shoulder.

Leaning over her ketchup-stained menu, Eva suddenly says between clenched teeth, "We need to *escar-go*."

"But we haven't gotten anythin' to eat!" Beau cheerfully plucks up his menu. He adds in a sing-song voice, "You told us to meet you here."

Catching the dangerous look in my sister's eyes, I give Beau's hand a quick squeeze before letting go. I lay a hand on my sister's arm, but it's *cold*. She actually shivers. What is wrong with her?

"Eves." My voice comes out hushed. "What's going on?"

Her smoky eyes brim with tears, like she *yearns* to tell us but doesn't know how. She starts to say something, but she must think twice because her gaze falls to the pair of rooster salt and pepper shakers on the table.

"Did the Despairity," I murmur, "hurt Tess?" I look to Raylan, who shakes his head, his little cowlick fluttering.

The same Ed Sheeran song we heard back at the Gunter falls over the radio, reminding me of Knox and his cunning ways in that bar. If Eva's found something like him again, I'm going to rip out its throat.

A waitress in a peach uniform appears at the next table, and somewhere outside, a dog yaps. Beau snatches up a fork and scratches the back of his green camo shirt.

Eva's dark eyes flash with disgust. "Were you raised in a barn?"

Beau grins like she just caught us kissing.

Not one to poke the bear, though, he gingerly sets down his fork, only for Eva to slap the table. The action's so out of place for my sister, I wonder if she's encountered the Despairity.

But Maggie made us get permanent tattoos on the inside of our wrists. We felt guilty; Dad never would have approved, but we figured it'd be worth preventing getting possessed.

A pair of bedraggled fishermen mosey through the doorway. Eva raises her hand to trace the condensation that's dripping from her Diet Coke.

"There's something you need to see," she says.

"Creoles," Beau loudly reads from the menu, "are a mixture of African, European, and Louisiana heritage."

"Shhhh!" Eva and I say together.

He pauses mid-thought. "You're kinda sexy when you get all into sisterly mode."

Smoke practically shooting from her ears, Eva says, "Have the two of you been kissing?"

My ears burn, but she shouldn't care if we've been kissing. *She's* the one who pushed me to get into the dating game again. I'd still be holed up in my room and listening to all the best hits of James Horner if I had my way.

I pull a napkin from the sticky, chipped table and dramatically set it on my lap. "Are you done?" I wish she wouldn't spoil a good thing.

Only when her eyes flash with hurt do I remember that it's something Dad used to say when he didn't like a collection of things Eva used to do.

The way he thought she played her music too loud.

The fact that she'd dance while unloading the dishwasher.

Her face turns bright red, and my heart sinks. We're supposed to be the new-and-improved Abram sisters, moving up in ranks, and here am I, tearing her down.

I don't know what to say, so I glance at Beau, and that must be the tipping point.

Because Eva raises her multi-ringed fingers and shoves off from the table.

CHAPTER 19 - EVA

I'm really not one for the dramatic exit. I know they usually do nothing but ratchet up the tension, but nothing else will do right now. I need air. I need to think.

Leo. Tortured. Imprisoned.

I storm past a flaking iron fleur-de-lis sculpture outside the diner and head straight for Raylan's truck. Only I don't have the keys, so I settle for hiding next to it, squatting on the step bar. Not leaning on the door like the many times I've done with Raylan, cuddling, laughing, or kissing. I find myself chewing on my fingernail, and an image of Leo's shredded nails punches me in the gut. I put my hand down in disgust.

I obviously can't leave him in there. But how can I get him out with minimal collateral damage? Frost, just barely moved on . . . after she's elated, she'll probably run to a nunnery out of guilt that she didn't stay single for the rest of her life. And Raylan, knowing his sister did this? He'll be devastated, hate me for being the messenger, and if I somehow don't get murdered by Tess, it'll certainly be a downer at Christmas family dinners.

I trace a groove on a rock, waiting for a revelation that's going to be a miraculous answer to this predicament.

Screw this, I'm calling Maggie. She'll know what to do. My fingers shake as I dial her number, but I totally don't care if she's still mad. We're stronger than that, and I'm sure she'll help.

Meanwhile, Leo's still chained up, covered in his own blood. No one deserves that.

Mags' phone goes to voicemail, ripping the hole in my gut impossibly wider.

Raylan's dark boots appear from around the back of his truck. "Eva," he calls softly, closing the gap between us. "What's wrong?"

I shake my head, not trusting anything I have to say. I've never been good at keeping secrets. . . . How did Tess not know that?

"Eves," he says, a name only he and Frost call me, and gently pulls me off my awkward half-perch, up until he can wrap his solid arms around my waist, making me feel dainty but cared for. "What's going on?" He squeezes me closer. "Are you mad at me?"

I only half-succeed at hiding a snort. "No. Of course not."

"Then what the heck is going on?" He jostles my whole body gently. "Did something happen this morning? Or did seeing the Despairity again scare you?"

I finally look him in his beautiful, stormy eyes. Reaching up, I cradle his face in my hands and kiss his eyelids softly before answering. "I'm just kinda stuck between a rock and a basket case."

He quirks an eyebrow at me. "Well, I know I'm a rock, but who's the basket case? I'll go take care of them right now." *Oh*, he has no idea. I center myself by inspecting a small tear in his gray T-shirt, prodding it a little bit.

"Raylan, you're the best."

"*We're* the best."

Ugh. How does he have so much stupid faith in me? I bury my face in his chest and pull him in as tight as I can.

"Just remember you said that, okay?" My voice is muffled in his shirt, but his sudden stillness tells me he heard. "Tess is gonna be gone hunting till late, right?"

"Mmhmm, why?" I love hearing his voice through his chest. I inhale the apple-maple scent I'll never get tired of as deeply as I can and make myself let go. Time to do the right thing, no matter how much it blows everything up.

"Come on." One more sweet kiss, delicious and warm, for courage. "I've got something to show y'all."

CHAPTER 20 - FROST

*I*t's the simple fact that Eva didn't order any food that I know something's really wrong.

She eventually came back, insisting she wanted to show me something, without so much as a backward glance at Beau. I'm just glad she's okay. If something happened to her again. . .

From Beau's truck, he and I dodge ruts and massive potholes. We swerve around lakes and marshes like the entire state should really be underwater. Eva and Raylan lead the way, and I try not to let the fear that something is really wrong dig like a needle inside my gut, because I've finally found a sliver of happiness.

We veer around a fallen log, and the occasional stilted beach home to the left contrasts with the alligator-hiding reeds lining the bayou to the right.

The GPS and the occasional glimpse between beach houses show we're right next to the gulf, and I roll down my window, eager to smell even a semblance of saltwater.

Tess could be injured. Eva didn't want to admit it to Raylan. She wants me to be there to help sort it all out?

Or Maggie actually came and forgot to turn on her phone. Against all odds, the Despairity got inside her head. That would explain why it's been forever since she texted me back.

When Beau pulls up to a massive three-story beach house with a collection of windmill palms and white-blooming crepe myrtles, I guess that we've made it to the right place. A vehicle for Tess isn't here, but Eva mentioned she'd be gone.

Pink and green caladiums nod at us from the east along with an expensive-looking fountain with sculpted cherubs. They gurgle what I hope to be holy water. Dang, apparently Tess is loaded. It would be nice to have the kind of money where I could afford decent trenches and devil's traps with bags of rock salt. We could hire a technician and line the entire property with laser trip-wires.

Beau hops out of his truck like we're off to kick up our heels at a barn dance. "That sister o' Raylan's got more money than the king o' oil his-self!"

I shoot him a patronizing smile. "Maybe this place is owned by a relative."

Both he and I know that Raylan and Tess are orphans, though. They both hunt as much as they do because they *don't* have anyone.

I examine a pair of kayaks chained to one side of the home, and it occurs to me that maybe Eva, Maggie, and I have it all wrong. If Tess can afford all this nice gear, maybe she knows something about hunting that we have no clue about.

"Maybe she and Raylan got an inheritance." I spot the dings in Raylan's decade-old truck, though, recalling how all his shirts look like he's worn them half his life.

Beau doesn't mention the fact that Lindy's Diner needs a new roof, and how he and his mom simply haven't been able to pool the money.

Tucking an arm around my shoulders, Beau leads me past

a trio of succulents that are so new, they still have tags. Fresh charcoal dirt lines their bases, and I could probably afford new window locks with that kind of cash.

When we make it past their spiky leaves, we meet Raylan and Eva, who're both holding their pistols with a casual wariness.

I reach for the dagger in my boot, and Eva nods.

Her agreement for me to arm myself catches me off guard. "Can we not trust Tess?"

Eva glances at Raylan like there are a million things she hasn't said, and he, in turn, stiffens.

"Just don't let your guard down," she says.

At her failure to defend his sister, a muscle feathers along Raylan's jaw. I like that he's protective of Tess.

It's the pool around back that tells me something is even more wrong. The murky water is green. Brackish. Like it belongs in the bayou on the other side of the street from the house. Judging from Tess' immaculate grounds, it's not something she would typically sidestep.

And the stench—it's like something's decomposing at the bottom of the pool. And I can still feel the pain, the heaviness hanging in the air.

The Despairity's unmistakable thumbprint.

I hold my hand over my mouth as miniature waves crash into the coast several paces off.

When Eva doesn't offer any sort of explanation and Raylan stuffs his hand in his jeans pocket, I grab my dagger from my boot and square off in a fighting position.

"Eva," I say. "What is going on?"

She ducks her head, completely refusing to answer, and starts mounting the house's back steps.

I think she'll pause to turn and tell me, but she mounts stair after stair, completely blocking me out.

Silently pleading for Raylan to tell me what's going on, I

look to him, but he simply shrugs before following Eva up those steps.

So I take Beau's hand, needing the grounding, the confidence. And, mimicking the sound of Raylan and Eva's boots combing the stairway, we mount the staircase.

Wrought iron deck furniture with matching throw pillows greet us at the top. The grouping overlooks a bay of brown water and seagulls flapping their wings in the distance.

An abandoned Diet Coke sits all alone on the table to the left, and the itty-bitty fact that Raylan didn't grab any extra weapons and Eva didn't convene with a planned strike tells me they *don't* have any real knowledge of a threat. But they're prepared. Just like Maggie's always taught us. So I squeeze my fingers around the dagger in my grip.

Unlocking the back door, Raylan lets Eva lead us inside and over a bear rug. It makes Maggie's rug look a little cheap, not to mention the real leather couches. There's an expensive-looking coffee table, and Eva continues trolling through the room to a fancy, stainless steel kitchen.

Somberly turning to face Raylan and me, she lets her jaw go slack, and her shoulders slouch in such a terrible way that I want to wrap her in a big, soft hug.

"I didn't know how to tell you any other way," she says. She avoids my eyes and instead looks to the matte-finished hardwood. And when she opens the pantry door, she reaches inside and pulls something next to a broom and mop —a lever.

The wall inside moves with a rumble.

"No way!" I almost wish we were discovering this together, because I know it must have wigged her out. We've always wanted to experience secret passageways apart from Missouri's caverns and prohibition tunnels.

A sideways glance at Raylan, though, tells me that he had no clue about this secret compartment.

His eyes are guarded, and my stomach flip-flops because it doesn't make sense that he didn't know about this.

Wooden steps snake down like we're entering an oubliette. Maybe Tess has contained the Despairity down here. That would be awesome. It's about time someone stopped them from getting inside my head.

The air's so stagnant, and the space below the stairs is so dark, I have to wonder if there's a new kind of monster down here, at the bottom.

Maybe Tess had to stay behind to keep an eye on it.

"I'll get the light," Eva says, like she's doing chores for Dad.

I'm half-convinced that I'm going to see Maggie—she's going to be holding brownies and readying herself to sing "Happy Birthday" to me, even though it's a few weeks late. I could see this. That would explain why Eva's been avoiding meeting my eyes the last hour.

My breath tenses in my throat, and I do my very best not to trip. This is going to be either really bad or really good, and when Eva pulls a string to turn on the light, I try to make sense of the figure lurking in chains.

It's a lone boy with a widow's peak and screws in his face and hands.

CHAPTER 21 - EVA

"Break me out of here?" Leo's voice is sweet and sad. Frost's face when she realizes it's him . . . I can't believe I doubted even for a minute showing her he's alive.

She sprints to him and falls to her knees, so she's eye level with him, then throws her arms around him like he's the only life preserver in the entire ocean. Feeling a little intrusive at watching this reunion, I look away to Raylan.

Raylan is stone. All except his eyes, which flicker almost imperceptibly, but I've been getting better at deciphering even the tiny movements. A little wider, narrower, bluer— right now he's fluctuating between surprise, horror, and relief until finally, his face drains of color. Shock.

He storms past a deflated Beau to Leo and grabs a metal file the size of my forearm that looks likes it's been used for very unpleasant purposes, judging from the rusty color it's stained. I can't bear to look at Leo's hands. Raylan sets to work breaking the cuffs off Leo. Oh, sweet Leo. Hurting him is like hurting a fluffy panda.

"What are you doing here?" Frost nearly sobs. "Did she

trap you?" Then, scanning his body, her face and neck turn bright fuschia. "Did she torture you?"

"Nothing I couldn't handle." He smiles that sheepish grin we've all missed. Raylan pops the first cuff off Leo's wrist, then grimly takes out the screw there. Leo doesn't waste a single heartbeat before he is holding Frost with his free, bloodied arm. Frost grabs his face and looks like she's going to kiss him, but pulls him close instead. I think I hear Beau choke a little bit, but he stares at the scattered lumber on the floor. He can go sit in the corner with the rest of the discarded tools.

My heart's still heavy but feeling lighter by the second. But Raylan. He's gotten past the shock. The jawbone I love to kiss is pulsing with anger. He reaches for Leo's other hand, still chained, and with grim resolve, he yanks the screw out. I go stand by him for a weak attempt at emotional support and notice for the first time Leo's blood dripping onto Raylan's faded jeans.

Using the file, Raylan pries the second restraint off, and Leo slumps forward, free.

"She'll be back soon." Raylan's usually smooth voice is coarse. "Let's get you out of here, and then me and her are gonna have a talk." This is torture of its own to see his loyalty with his family betrayed. I slide my arms around him. His arms, usually so quick to scoop me into a hug, stay at his sides.

"Yeah, uh." The usually smooth Beau fumbles for words as he juts his thumb toward the ceiling. "I think she's here."

Heavy footsteps come from the main floor above.

All eyes go to Raylan. He drops the giant file onto the concrete with a loud clang.

He twists his head to the side, pulling the tendons of his neck taut, one side, then the other.

"All right, I'll handle it," Raylan says, but as he storms to the stairs, Tess' boots are pounding down them like a loud but crazy-fast ninja. Her silver gun gleams when it appears, clutched like a third hand. Frost and I twist so we're between her and Leo. She surveys us and cocks her gun.

"Guess I can't trust your girlfriend, can I, Raylan?" Tess' entire body radiates with anger, like her once beautiful features exist only to throw ghostly dangers at your face. "I deserve an apology." Every single muscle commanded to act like a good soldier. And yet, in a bizarre paradox, she *looks* calm. The disconnect is terrifying. It takes actual effort to not wilt.

"What are you doing, Tess?" Raylan demands, like he's sure there has to be a twist here to make sense of why his only remaining family would have his best friend locked in her creepy monster chamber.

"He made his choice centuries ago." Tess spits the words, like Leo's very existence is revolting to her. "Think about all the people who have suffered because of him."

"Not really," I argue at the same time Frost shouts, "He deserves a second chance." She's the absolute contrast to Tess —fair hair, skin on fire, muscles trembling with barely-contained rage.

Tess rolls her eyes, and it's like a bank vault rolls between her anger and us. She becomes cold. Robotic. Like she wasn't about to snap all our necks ten seconds ago. "Brother, I'll talk to you privately. I won't stand here and debate with your little friends." She moves to storm right past Frost, I guess to try to chain Leo up again—as if any of us are going to let that happen—and Frost spreads her arms as a human wall. Tess purses her lips for just a second, then aims her gun at Frost.

"What the hell?" I scream and reach for my own gun, but Raylan holds me back. Frost blanches, but within a breath, she sets her jaw and stands her ground.

"You kill me, and you won't be far behind," Frost says softly. I simultaneously want to strangle her and high-five her.

Continuing in her cold voice, Tess keeps her gun leveled on Frost. "Raylan, I am going to rid this world of Blurred Ones. Leonardo is decent *enough* that he is going to help me in the good fight. He just hasn't figured it out yet."

Raylan keeps his voice steady but uses his whole height to tower over his sister. "Leo has saved our lives. He's just a spirit who made a bad choice and wants to do better."

"And this is his chance to do that," she spits. "Because of spirits like him, our parents are dead." Her eyes flick to Leo like she's assessing a carcass at a butcher's shop. "Why aren't you on my side, brother?"

"Of course I'm on your side, but this is crazy." He reaches out like he wants to lower her gun, but stops when she presses the barrel into Frost's forehead.

"You have to trust me." She sounds a little like a pouting five-year-old, but with her shoulders back with confidence that he'll come around.

"Get off your high horse," Frost says. "We're leaving."

"He's not," Tess says about Leo. "But all of you are trespassing. You better be leaving."

But Frost is the embodiment of "still waters run deep." Her eyes are centuries-old granite. Girl's got cajones.

Frost turns her back on Tess like she's just showing her a dance move. Crouches down to help Leo up.

Terrified, I look at Tess. Her eyes are as cold and dark as death. Her hand tightens on the gun, and I swear she is about to pull that trigger.

Raylan moves to help Frost with Leo, I guess 'cause he's crazy-naive about his sister, but he does holler at her, "Put it away, Tess."

Tess doesn't budge. I do see a glimmer of life in her eyes, but they're still so cold. So dark. I tense to launch myself at her, knowing I don't have time to pull my gun, aim, and shoot. I just pray my tackling her doesn't *make* her shoot.

I can't spare time to look, but from the corner of my eye, I see Beau slide toward the stairs like he's about to bolt. *Coward.*

Tess' hand shakes just a bit, ready to shoot my sister right in the back of the head.

Finally, her eyes flicker to her little brother. She slowly lowers her gun—I can almost breathe again. No more funerals for Abrams.

Tess pulls the trigger. A *POP!* blasts so loudly, my ears are ringing as Frost cries out. She's much quieter than I would have imagined. Raylan roars and leaps for his sister while mine crumples to the ground. Frost steals a glance at Tess, face gaping with shock before she even turns to face her wound.

Raylan reaches out to pull Tess to the ground, but Beau's not bolting up the stairs. He gets to Tess first, and with one powerful shove, she flies across the room. Turning around, she charges, every bit as terrifying as a two-ton bull, but Beau's got a two-by-four. With a swipe longer and harder than should be possible, he whacks her across the head with a terrible thud.

I'm at Frost's side before the first blood hits the ground.

CHAPTER 22 - FROST

*L*eo's alive. He was never born.

Head spins. World's a blur.

Wooden stairs swirl around me as strong arms carry me up, up higher.

The pool, green. Like someone's poured sewage in it. A homeless-looking man's handcuffed to the stair railing. Brought here by Tess?

When windmill palm leaves jostle above my head, I know it's Beau carrying me because of his wiry frame and plaid shirt.

He settles me in a truck. Not green. Not Beau's. Diet Coke cans litter the carpet. One of Eva's old Smashing Pumpkins CDs rattles near the door.

Paint fumes wash through my nose.

Someone's shouting an awful lot about blood, and the driver—Leo—peels out of the driveway, and he's such a mess of bruises and cuts.

Tires spin. Wind-up Monster cars. Beside me, Beau's breathing comes out fast and loud.

My leg screams like it's been pounded to death.

Above the knee.

Did Tess shoot me on purpose? If she had shot me any higher, I'd probably have bled out already.

My chest constricts like someone's squeezing my heart, and I just might vomit.

Diet Coke cans rattle as we hit ruts.

Bloody hands grip the steering wheel, and I can't believe Leo is here. Never was born.

Beau's freckled arms cradle my head, and I want to cry —cry—because I cannot believe I kissed him on the ride down.

Long fingers wipe the matted hair out of my eyes, and I want to climb into a hole and allow my hair to cover me up.

I cling to Beau's arms like I'll bury myself in quicksand. I'll wrench them from the sockets and beat myself to death.

Beau barks, "Where we goin'?"

Leo, blood dripping from his philtrum, cuts Beau an ice-cold look.

Beau's hands clasp my leg so tightly, I cry out.

Leo slams on the breaks. Slices a look of complete and utter loathing at Beau.

"Just get her to a hospital!" Beau cries.

Leo cranks the wheel to the right and guns the truck at the same time.

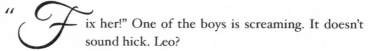

"Fix her!" One of the boys is screaming. It doesn't sound hick. Leo?

I've never felt so cold. Stars blink overhead, showing off a canopy of these weird knobby pines.

Loblolly pines. I read about them on the drive down.

Seagulls flutter across the sky, trying to find a perch. Someone chants something dark and foreign.

As I blink to force my eyes to stay open, all I can make out is the faint outline of Leo hovering over me like a vision.

Severe lines jut from his vessel's face from missing too many meals. His bloodshot eyes rove over me, and his hair hasn't been washed in months.

The man who's chanting reeks of incense and looks like he's never washed his hair in his life. His long beard quivers in the magical air, and a sound almost like music clangs from his metal necklaces.

I think vaguely of how Eva said she hates New Orleans. The filth and darkness of the streets, the dark magic. *Counterfeit*, she called it. But the magic surging through my sinews and muscles tells me that this power is very real. Not holy, but existent. Like sparks of electricity, it pops and sizzles up my back.

The vestige of the figure spelling me is missing half his teeth. He stretches out his aged, wrinkled hands. He showcases stiff, fingerless gloves. A crumpled hat and black vest remind me of Wolf and his ghost tour enactment. I'll never forget our artsy tour guide in San Antonio.

Another masculine figure paces in the background. The droopy cowboy hat planted in his hands tells me it's Beau. I can't think about him.

An empty red and blue playground hovers in my periphery, and as this witch doctor plies me with magic, I can't help wondering if it's possible to grab Eva and Raylan and never, ever leave home again.

Vinegar, hot and biting, surges through my system.

I think of Mr. Harris hovering over that trailer desk, and how he *promised* Leo would be born. But he didn't—he wasn't —and if I go to sleep, I might never wake.

What if I die before I ever get the chance to talk to Leo?

CHAPTER 23 - EVA

The universe didn't shatter, but it definitely shifted. Still waiting to see what exactly that entails. Beau texted and said Leo's friend was patching up Frost. Weird, and I can't even believe I'm not with her right now. But someone had to stay behind to help Raylan deal with the sadistic sister, and that sure wasn't gonna be Leo or Beau. What I'd pay to be a fly on that wall right now . . . I wonder if dueling pistols will be involved?

For now, Raylan and I sit on the back porch swing, swinging in silence to the sound of the Gulf's waves and the creak of the chains. I catch him staring at where we just uncuffed a homeless dude from the railing. As long as Tess isn't also secretly a cannibal, we should be able to navigate through this.

We used those handcuffs to chain Tess to her own toilet, until she wakes up and we figure out what to do. I convinced Raylan to give her a little something to help her sleep longer. It suits a double purpose, giving us more time, and giving that nasty knob on her head more time to chill out.

"What just happened?" Raylan suddenly barks. I slowly

shake my head. This is another minefield I have no idea how to cross. "She had him locked up here this whole time." He pounds his fist on his knee. "*Tortured* him." His voice trembles like he's a five-year-old who was just told Santa isn't real. I'd find it crazy adorable if it weren't so freakin' tragic.

"I'm sorry I didn't tell you earlier." I trace his thumb with mine, looking for reassurance. "I honestly didn't know what to do."

He gives an un-reassuring hum. I'd told him what happened as best as I could, tiptoeing around the fact that I'm pretty sure his sister is psychotic.

"Let's take a walk, babe." I push off the swing, pulling him with me. He doesn't fight, so I suppose that's a good sign.

Crossing the side of the dark green pool where he almost drowned, I squeeze his hand tighter. I kick off my shoes to walk in the sand, relishing the soft grains between my toes, but Raylan stays all tied up in his. A couple of steps in, though, I notice the sand is covered in small, dead, brown fish. As far as I can see, the line where the tide hits the sand is drawn with thousands of their little rotting bodies. Another effect of the Despairity? My breath quickens at the thought. I am so *sick* of them and all these terrible creatures turning everything ugly.

A second later, a salty back-alley dumpster smell reaches our noses. Not awesome, but I try to calm my breathing and pretend the fish aren't there. Raylan's hair is puffy from him running his hand through it too many times, and I'd do anything to take this burden off him. He stares at the fish like they're an insane algorithm in Calculus he's trying to figure out. I lightly tug on his arm to get him to walk with me.

"Well," I say a little too loudly. "Regardless, it's nice to see Leo again."

Raylan gives me the side-eye, and I gulp. I know he isn't trying to be mean. It's just his emotional range is kind of like from simmering anger to mega-volcano erupting rage right now. There's always some anger there, beneath the surface, but he usually smothers it before he acts on it. This may just be too much for him to handle.

So, back to quiet it is. We walk for what seems ages past the remnants of docks, just posts now that a storm carried the platform away, and the flocks of pelicans that like to perch on them. The sky is full of those little clouds that look like a quilt, all stitched together.

"She's always been kind of larger than life," he finally says to a landing pelican. "She always wants to be the *best*. The decisive leader. Getting people to pay the big bucks for her help. Always thought that was a little shallow, but this is just crazy."

I make a mental note to ask more about this pay-to-hunt plan later.

He runs his free hand through his hair again. "There has to be more to the story."

I nod and stay quiet, not really believing, but hoping.

"Leo, though." His voice cracks, and my heart breaks a little bit. "I'm sure he's gonna be okay. And Frost. Maybe it was an accident?"

A grand piano drops from the sky onto my chest. How to phrase this? "Babe, did you see Tess when she shot Frost?"

He stops walking. "What?"

My breath comes faster. "She didn't even switch her aim until the *very* last second. Like, she seriously wanted to kill Frost."

Raylan snatches his hand from mine. "Seriously, Eva?" Both his hands go to his head like he can block out the very idea. "She would never!"

"She would never lock up and torture Leo, either, right?" I shoot back, and instantly, I wish I had said something more kind. But, I did mean it, so I don't take it back.

"I just need to talk to her," he says, shaking his head furiously.

"Look, I care about you so much." I grab the bottom of his gray T-shirt, wanting nothing more than to kiss him until he's forgotten about this whole business. I try to gently pull him closer, but he doesn't budge. "I would *never* want to make things harder for you. But she's dangerous right now, Ray."

Finally, he looks at me, thinking, his jaw pulsing. His eyes are the exact color of the ocean behind him, where the water turns from brown to stormy blue. He puts his hand on mine, but it's not the sweet caress I love so much. It feels—transactional. I stagger a half-step back, and something jams into my bare foot. Yelping from the shooting pain, I pull my foot up to see if I stepped on a nail or something. A little slimy creature has lodged itself into my heel—one of the thousands of fish has come after me!

Blinking the shocked tears away, I look at Raylan's strong hand still holding mine. He always insists on taking care of me when I stab myself in the kitchen with a knife, or massages my hands when they're tired from target practice.

He looks at me with a coolness I haven't seen since that day back at the Alamo. When he could only focus on hunting so he wouldn't have to feel the pain of his awful upbringing.

I steel my nerves to free myself from this devilish fish creature. It's not biting me, it's got several spikes on its head, and one is jammed in my foot. Trying not to fall over or impale myself on several more fish, I hold my breath and prepare to pull.

Raylan's calloused hand squeezes mine, so I let go and look at him. The edges of his eyes drop with softness, and he kneels in the sand, placing my hand on his shoulder so I can keep my balance.

"I can get it," I mumble without conviction.

He holds my heel with one hand and yanks the fish with

the other. The darn thing snags, shooting pain up my calf. It's insane how much the little thing hurts. I stifle a whimper as he pulls harder, bits of skin tearing with it. Then it's out. He presses his thumb on the wound to ease the pain, but I can't help but think if this happened yesterday, he'd have kissed it while I giggled and protested about germs.

Trying not to be helpless, I ease my foot out of his grasp and help him up, taking the fish from him. I chuck it into the water, where it gives a sad little splash, like it was nothing more than a trampled flower. I ignore the blood pouring from my heel and let it mix into the germy sand. Let's add an infection to my list of problems.

I remind myself that Raylan's giant heart sometimes means it takes him a little while to process things. With a softer voice, he squeezes my hand. "If she's dangerous, she needs my help." He takes a step back, his boot crunching a dead fish, and suddenly, our hands are barely holding each other. I didn't even realize I was still holding onto him for support. "I need to focus on her. Focus on my family."

He hasn't said the words yet. I can stop this from happening. He's not a stranger. He's my Raylan. The guy who picks me up from school with a Diet Coke and a snack almost every day, and insists on texting "good night and sleep sweet" in our late-night conversations.

I act like he hasn't put up a wall. Like I don't know that his loyalty to his sister is the one thing that could trump his loyalty to me, Frost, and Maggie. I smother my desperation with nonchalance and say, "Of course, you can help her. I won't get in the way. I could help."

"Sorry." He gives a little sigh and lets go of my hand. "This one's not about you." He looks out to the water and tosses my heart out there with it.

"That's not what I meant!" I swallow, trying not to sound

hysterical, but suddenly, my throat feels like a rusted pipe. "Just that it doesn't have to be either-or."

He twists his body further away from me. "I'm going to check on her." He stalks back to the house, and I fall to the sand.

CHAPTER 24 - FROST

*W*hen I come to, my neck's so stiff, I half-believe I'm dead. Mostly dead? That phrase sounds vaguely familiar.

Beau cradles me like when we were in the truck—no. The fingers gently holding my arms are missing their nails, and there's dried blood on the backs of his hands and palms.

What am I supposed to say to Leo?

My fingers shoot to his, my cold fingertips pressing into his knuckles because I thought he would always be gone. Like I'm born to be a traitor, all I can think is, *Oh my gosh, I kissed Beau. Kissed him and hugged him while you were locked up.*

"You're awake." Leo's smile is so gentle and loving that it disembodies my heart and turns it into a wastebasket. A brown, thatched roof swims behind his head, reminding me we're at a park. Old, rusted-out swings creak in the background.

I try to make sense of what time it is, but the black, starry sky doesn't give the time up, and I wonder where his scary witch doctor friend went.

I end up cracking the lamest of jokes. "You aren't filling up diapers."

Leo's smile is so full of love that I fight the urge to wrap him up in my arms and kiss him until my arms and lips hurt.

But the smile disappears just as fast. "Got sidetracked." He doesn't look away, but he's not seeing me when he stares back.

He's thinking of the past weeks of torture. How Tess tortured him for weeks on end. I'll *kill* her. Throw her down in Eva's mining shaft.

My leg twinges like it's being devoured by . . . I don't know what. But it's a sharp pain, a reminder of how I didn't ever check to make sure Leo actually left. I trusted Maggie and Mr. Harris.

How very stupid I was.

I want to ask Leo if he thinks Mr. Harris is a co-conspirator with Tess—no way Maggie is—when another creeping sensation flutters over my leg, and the need to see what's going on with it is more overwhelming than the pain itself.

Leo's arm blocks my view.

"You cut your face." He runs his knuckles along my hairline, and a flutter of fantastical tingles surge across my cheeks and forehead.

To be in his arms. . . . I close my eyes, unable to grasp the truth of the moment. To actually believe I'm awake. I had somewhat forgotten the sound of his voice—the patience, the centuries of wisdom. The quiet confidence.

This tickling sensation above my knee, though, has me lifting my head fast, but again Leo blocks my view.

"It's better you don't see," he says.

"I just need to know what it is." I flex my abs, trying to lift my head high enough to peer all the way around his hand, only for him to press back on my shoulders.

"Frost, lie down."

Something cool squirms on my leg, and panic claws its way up my throat. "What is it?"

A hissing sound ripples up my leg, and all the air traps in my lungs. "No no no no no." I know that sound. *Snakes.* I grip the cool, thin lip of the park bench.

I whimper in fear, feeling the teeny tiny reptiles dig into my flesh, and Leo runs the unhurt parts of his calloused palms up and down the length of my biceps. He'll need to rub me faster, hold me tighter, because I absolutely will not allow snakes to make a playground of my skin.

Footsteps whack the pavement, and the leisurely gait tells me Beau's approaching now. Where else would he be? The boy *proposed* not a full day ago.

"She's awake?" He clutches his cowboy hat to the front of his plaid shirt, which is speckled with my blood. What few people know is he's embedded tiny blades into the brim that only extend when he throws it sideways, like a frisbee. I don't know why I'm thinking about that.

Leo's protective hands stiffen around my calf, and for whatever reason, this amplifies the tickling sensation from the snakes on my leg.

I whimper, not on purpose.

"You're hurting her!" Beau scrambles toward Leo and me, tripping on the raised crack in the cement.

Leo's arms go absolutely rigid—like he'd love nothing more than to go back to his old ways of distilling pain from the most susceptible human targets—but that is not who he is anymore. And it's not Beau's fault that I've allowed him to spend more time with me.

"I can take a shift," Beau drawls. "Like back at home."

There's this uncomfortable cloak of silence before Leo's hand hovers over the necklace around my throat.

The necklace Beau gave me.

The earthy taste of too-dry dirt tugs through my throat.

"What is this?" Leo asks, voice low.

"It's none of your business." Beau postures like he's a wild stallion. One hand rests on the sheath of his hunting knife, and the other casually rests on his wide, brass belt buckle that's successfully blocked a few shots. But if I were Leo looking at Beau for the very first time, all I'd see is a pompous, self-aggrandizing cowboy covered in camo.

"He's an acquired taste," I assure Leo, and I meant to say it quietly, but the sudden hurt in Beau's eyes tells me he's heard.

Beau spins around, dropping a wildflower he'd held next to his hat, and tears off for the playground.

Watching the wildflower flutter to the ground, Leo's grip tightens.

"He really is a good guy," I say, feeling hollow.

He doesn't say what I'm certain he's thinking. *I'm locked up for months, and you make friends with* him? Leo knows of my distaste for all hick-related things, but he wasn't there. He doesn't know how Beau helped me line each and every stump hole with rock salt.

"What did he mean?" Leo's voice tightens. "When he said he helped you with a 'shift' back home?"

Heat flares across my cheeks. "There's no contest."

Leo doesn't say a word, so I drive home the point best I can. "You were gone, and he was here and—" More tingling sensations shoot from my leg.

"What about UT?"

"I decided not to go."

Leo's bloodshot eyes widen in surprise, and it pains me to see his starry-eyed hopes for me dying.

I'm like that wildflower Beau plucked. Intriguing in a way. At first. But without any real aspiration to become more.

The tickling sensation washes through my leg. Like those creatures are licking all the way through to the bone.

I grip his arm. "Why are there snakes on my leg, Leo?"

"Dom put them there to facilitate the healing process."

I can handle seeing them. I can. So I shove Leo's arm to the side and stare at the miniature reptiles, wondering why I've been so stupid.

CHAPTER 25 - EVA

*N*o. This is unacceptable. Just an overreaction. I get it that Tess is all the family Raylan has left and after all he's been through, he's not thinking clearly. So, after a few minutes of ridiculously bawling my eyes out, I decide this is not how the universe shifted. It's just a challenge. And right now, he's alone in the house with that she-devil.

I tell myself these things, sitting on this beach by myself, far away from home, careful not to move and get myself stabbed by ornery little catfish that cut you in their death.

Except, I know Raylan. The change in his eyes? He's set. The image brings the tears again, but that's not going to do me any good. Standing up, I dust myself off and try to wipe my face, but my hands are too sandy. I decide to head back to the house, too. I'll just keep a low profile so he doesn't push me further away or say more uncharacteristically mean things.

I start to limp back, 'cause my foot hurts oh so bad. Also, must find something to clean it out so I don't die of flesh-eating bacteria if I somehow escape Tess alive. I make my way to the front porch, where there isn't a wall of windows for them to see me.

I'll tiptoe my way into my room until I can figure out another plan, which needs to include checking on my sister, who has been shot by my ex?-boyfriend's sister. Who was holding her ex?-boyfriend hostage until we rescued him with her new boyfriend. Yeesh. Yes, I will focus on the very weird drama that is my life and my throbbing foot instead of the fact that the *probable* love-of-my-life just dumped me. Yes.

I open the door, cross the foyer, try not to get blood or sand on the ridiculously expensive rugs, and dang it, the floor creaks so loudly. I freeze, but I hear muffled voices from the other side of the house. She-Devil must be awake, so I ninja-monkey-run to my room and close the door as quietly as I can.

I plaster my ear to the beige painted wall between us so I can hear better.

"I'm saving lives, Raylan." Tess sounds groggy, but I can feel the daggers of her words from here.

"By torturing my best friend?" He keeps his voice level.

"A Blurred One."

"A Blurred One who tried to make things right."

"You should have my back. I am your family. Not him, not them."

I want to just go ahead and shoot her through the wall right now, but I suppose I might hit Raylan. And then he'd definitely stay broken up with me.

They're quiet for a moment, and my ear is getting raw from being smashed on the wall, so I switch ears. She speaks up again, but more calmly. "I thought I could appeal to his supposed good nature to help me hunt. He's all I need to lure Blurred Ones into bodies so I can kill them. But all he wants to do is go be a baby."

I silently mock what she said with the idiotic expression

she should be wearing. I notice Raylan doesn't have much to say on the subject. She keeps blabbing.

"If you've got my back now," she says, "we can catch a different Blurred One. Maybe your more typical evil Blurred One would enjoy the killing."

Diabolical, but it could work.

"Of course I have your back," Raylan says. "You've just always said you wanted to hunt alone. And you didn't have to go and shoot Frost."

"You didn't have my back today," she snaps. I can't believe he puts up with this.

"Well, I have it now," he says, his voice rising again. I hear footsteps, so I jump away from the wall and onto my bed as quietly as I can. They don't come in the room, but their voices are loud as they walk right past me in the hallway outside my door. "Just leave them out of this, okay?"

"We'll see, little brother. We just need to stop for some snacks," she says cheerfully, like none of this morning happened. "Wait 'til you see my latest cage."

My head spins at how little he's fighting her. Like he's just shutting down. The front door slams, and they leave me like I'm yesterday's dishes.

CHAPTER 26 - FROST

*M*y leg's become silly putty by the time Beau
lays me in a hammock near a cabin downriver
from the park. It's a little hideaway Leo knows about from
that witch doctor who patched us up.

An old, rusted-out wire curls like a garden snake across
the goosegrass, and I'm so relieved the *real* snakes on my leg
finished the job.

The fringe of Beau's hair tickles my neck as he assesses
my leg. "Looks like it's healin'," he says, almost like he wishes
it wasn't. Not that he wants harm to come to me, but he'd
like to offer his own rescue if he can.

Even though Leo's a full ten paces away, I can feel his deri-
sion for Beau as he sips more of the herbal tea from his
friend. The herbs are supposed to help him heal from what
happened with Tess, but from the looks of things, I'd say
Leo's still a few hours from purging the rest of the rock salt
and holy water from his system. Yellow pus from the screws
still covers both the inside and outside of his palms.

Leo takes a measured step toward me, and Beau protectively blocks him with his arm. The movement is so sudden, so unexpected, that he accidentally knocks the cup out of Leo's hands.

"Beau!" I cry as the three of us watch the cup fly to a mound of trampled thistles.

Leo's shoulders stiffen as we all peer at the now-empty cup. Leo can still heal, but Dom was offering him a way to speed up the process with who knows what kind of herbs he used.

"I know what you are, *Beauregard*," Leo seethes. "You should leave. Now."

I try to sit up as razors shoot through my skull. More aftermath from the snakes chomping on my skin, I guess. But Leo has to see it was an accident.

"Beau was only trying to help."

Leo extends an injured hand, and the utter amusement on his face tells me he has a multitude of ideas for what to do with my friend. But Leo must read my mind, because he's suddenly dropping his Blurred One, I'll-suck-away-your-soul glare. He glances at me and says, "It won't be long until I'm back to normal."

The wind whispers through the reeds and thistles, reminding me that we're still very far from home. Tess just shot me in the leg, which means she's not only willing to hurt Leo, but anyone who stands in his path.

"Where's Eva?" I ask. Maybe she has ideas for how to patch things up.

It's as if my sister's reading my mind, because my phone suddenly chirrups with her playful ringtone. Leo pulls my cell from his dust-covered pocket, and he briefly locks eyes with me before glancing down at the screen. There's a picture of Eva lying on her belly, pretending to drink from a tipped-over bottle of the world's largest Diet Coke.

Leo smiles a little before passing over the phone.

I snatch it up, hungry to hear my sister's voice. I need to tell her I'm okay, that Dom patched me up, and ask if she has any ideas about what to do with Tess. But when I raise the cell to my face, the line's already dead.

Seeing the look on my face, Leo gently scoops up the phone and redials Eva's number before wordlessly placing it to his ear. But Eva's probably still around Tess, who possibly has the phone company in her pocket, too.

"Sure ain't the huntin' trip we imagined," Beau groans.

Leo shoots Beau a look like he'd like nothing more than to permanently prune Beau's ability to speak at all.

I'd *like* to explain that having Beau here is now a matter of conscience—he helped us take out that witch doctor and, because of him, I might still have a job. Something light as a feather, tickles my arm. Figuring it's a mosquito, I lightly brush the back of my arm before reaching up toward Leo for my phone. But he's scrolling through the contacts feed, no doubt looking for Raylan's number to see what's going on.

The tickling happens again, but it's something much bigger and cooler than a mosquito, and I look down to find a fist-wide, olive-colored snake slinking down the hammock rope. *Zombi.* The snake that can permanently take out Blurred Ones.

I haven't a clue how it got here or how long it's been around—if Leo has to currently have the screw in his face for its bite to prove lethal—but Leo still hasn't fully healed, and he's only about twelve inches away.

He doesn't see the snake, so I leap from the hammock.

It seems my body's still a little too elastic from Dom's magic. When I reach for the dagger in my boot, all I hit is a few of the tassels on the boot's edge.

I can't risk losing Leo the very moment I got him back, so

I do the unthinkable and reach for Zombi's nasty, scaly skin. Better to suffocate it to death than risk Leo getting bit.

Strong, freckled hands hold my shoulders back, so I do the thing they'd never think me to do. I break away and pull off my shirt. Because we need a blanket, and we haven't got a blanket. My shirt's just taut enough to cover Zombi's head and two-thirds of her scaly body.

Beau's mumbling something about "not exac'ly intendin' to get her naked," but I have only one aim.

Prevent Leo from getting bitten.

I dodge another set of arms and grapple for Zombi like she's a squirming toddler about to see her mom. Both of the boys are yelling at me, running to catch up as I limp along, but I must protect Leo at all costs.

Zombi wrestles like a live extension cord. No, much more lively than that, and if there are more snakes like this in Louisiana, there's no way I'm ever coming back.

Smelling faintly of cucumbers, she pumps angrily, trying to free herself from my shirt.

Woodpeckers smite the trees, echoing the *pound-pound-pounding* pulse in my head. I tear off for the brackish bayou right in front of the cabin.

Maybe, just maybe, if I release Zombi into that water, she'll forget she wanted Leo. We should kill the snake, but I don't trust my own aim at the present, and the boys aren't exactly in a cooperative mode for combat.

Bearded moss hangs in heavy tufts from the trees. The numbing sensation in my leg still makes it hard to stagger on, and as I lurch through the thin, papery moss, Zombi hisses.

But she's a newborn, just a newborn, about to take her bath.

Mud sucks onto my boots, and I'm just lowering Zombi's sleek frame into the room-temperature river when something *cold,* like a syringe full of fluids, strikes my thigh.

Right where I was shot.

Icicles shoot up and down my wound, and I gasp.

I can't move a muscle as I sink, headfirst, into Zombi's bath.

CHAPTER 27 - EVA

*A*fter hearing Frost's voicemail message for the thousandth time, I give up and call Maggie. Hopefully, she can stop hacking up wendigos and being mad at me long enough to talk. As usual, she's as dependable as Depends and picks up on the second ring.

"Hi, honey." A sweet, girlish voice greets me in place of Mags' usual boisterous tone.

"Mom?" I ask, racking my brain for the last time Mom and Mags hung out. They still like each other fine but don't have much in common past Frost and me.

"Yes, dear." Her kind voice batters my defenses, but I don't want her to worry. "I'm here with Maggie, she's—" Her voice becomes muffled as she's obviously pressing the phone into her shoulder. I could use a hug from her right now. "Eva, Maggie would like to speak to you now. I'm going to stretch my legs."

"OK," I squeak. "Thanks, Mom."

"OK, sweetie." She's always so formal on the phone. "Bye."

Mags' muttering filters through the phone, along with scratching and bumping, as Mom passes Mags the phone.

"EVA, YOU OK?" Maggie asks. She always talks about ten decibels too loud on the phone. It's almost enough to make me smile. I try to sound like I haven't been crying for an hour straight, and I don't have a snot-filled nose to prove it.

"Yes, Mags, but I've been better." I play with the little tufts of navy blue yarn on the quilt on Raylan's bed.

"What's wrong, darlin'?" The instant concern in her voice makes the waterworks start again.

"Everything. And Raylan dumped me." There's no hiding the crying from my voice now, with it all cracked and honky. I know there are more serious concerns at the moment, but this one is making it pretty hard to breathe. It gets worse when she doesn't answer immediately. I know it's not out of lack of love for me, but that she loves Raylan, too.

"WHAT ON EARTH HAPPENED?"

"His stupid sister! She freaking had Leo locked up in her basement." I'm yelling now and get up to pace the room. "She tortured him! She's crazy! She shot Frost!"

"WHAT??!!" she literally roars.

I quickly add, "She'll be fine. Leo and Beau are taking care of her. Tess got her in the leg. Leo's okay, too." I don't add that I'm not actually with Frost. I'll figure out how to get wherever she is next. "But everything is so messed up. Can you get down here? We need you."

I think she put the phone down, 'cause all I hear is a string of muffled curses. Then, more clearly, she speaks to me again, with a deliberate tone she only uses when she means serious business. "Eva, you know I would be there in a heartbeat, but I'm a little laid up right now, and I'm working on something big." She makes an exasperated grunt. "Listen to me. Stay away from Tess."

I choke on a laugh as I eye my surroundings. "I'd love to, buuuut."

"No 'buts,' Eva," she barks. "She's worse than you know." Her voice quiets a little bit. "She and I had a bit of a disagreement after you and I last spoke."

My eyes pop wide. "Did y'all fight?"

Maggie clears her throat, clearly uncomfortable. "A bit, yes." She sounds so quiet, almost defeated. I've never in my life heard her this way. "Argued 'bout her leaving a trail of bodies from here to Mississippi."

"She is a hunter. Doesn't that mean she's just doing her job?"

"Not all of them were supernatural creatures, Eva." She pauses, letting me decipher what she means, and I remember the homeless guy Tess had chained up. I stop pacing. She really did want to kill Frost. Mags would never condone killing an innocent person. She's always trying to take care of people and animals to compensate for all the violence in her life.

"Did you call her out on it?"

"Yeah. It didn't go too well."

I stop studying the set of gnarly throwing stars displayed on the wall like art. Do I hear a little shame in her voice?

"Just stay away from her. And you get on home, or I'll drag your carcass home as soon as I can get down there."

I'm almost speechless. "Mags, what happened?"

"Just promise me," she snaps.

My fingers twitch to yank a throwing star off the wall and carve something to pieces. She doesn't talk to me this way. What am I doing to make everyone hate me right now? But she adds more softly, "Promise me, Eva."

"I promise, Maggie." I use her full name instead of my usual sass, since she's putting up these walls.

"Good." Another woman's authoritative voice comes

through the phone that doesn't sound like Mom. "I best be going. Eva, take care of you and yours, and I'll call you as soon as I can."

"Okay," I say, resigned.

Maggie humphs under her breath. "Raylan will come around. Until then, you need some therapy. You good on Blue Bell?"

At this, I do smile. 'Cause Tess at least has enough sense to be fully stocked on the perfect ice cream. Well, she was, *wink-wink*. "Yes, ma'am. All right, well, you be careful, Mags."

"You, too. Love you, Eves."

I smooth Raylan's quilt back down so it's not so obvious I was in here. "Yes, ma'am. Like a seagull in a hyena shop."

CHAPTER 28 - FROST

I close my eyes against the cool, green, murky silence. Lungs scream for oxygen, arms and legs as heavy as titanium. I can't move a muscle, but venom courses and surges through my leg like a frenzied, trapped rodent.

Darkness.

I can only make out the sleek tail of Zombi as she slithers away—and dirty water's filling my open mouth. Can't. Shut it. I weigh six hundred pounds. Seaweed traps me beneath errant branches.

In my mind's eye, I can see myself screaming for Leo, but he needs to stay far away. Can't risk Zombi finding him.

Something lands on my legs, disturbing the river's depth. A vice-like grip grabs me around the biceps and heaves me up. I have no control of my neck and head, so, like I'm the newborn baby now, my head falls back. I look straight up at the sky.

Gray and colorless.

Which oddly reminds me of Maggie's coyote pelt back home by the front door. How funny it is that I've always had an aversion to a stretch of fur that never hurt anyone.

Those strong hands release my biceps and cradle my head and legs. Above me, seaweed sticks to the side of Beau's cheekbone and, a few paces off, Leo coughs up a long trickle of blood. Dom's herbs—Leo didn't drink enough to speed up the healing process. He's more fragile than I thought.

A female figure—Tess—curls a relaxed Zombi over her arms, proving my choice to release Zombi was a wasted effort. With the biggest smirk I've ever seen in my life, she plants her all-seeing eyes on the damaged boy I love.

"Looking good, Leo," she says. "Not as resilient as you thought?"

The breeze tickles my skin, and I shiver. My shirt's still floating somewhere behind me in the bog.

Beau wraps a thick woolen blanket around me that's as coarse as a cow's hide. I try to lift my head to face Tess straight on, but the venom from Zombi is coursing through my veins like gunpowder. Any second, I'll be dead.

Tess sees the fear in my eyes. "Calm down," she says. "Zombi's venom only kills you if you're possessed by a Blurred One."

My heart *thump-thumps* in gratitude, but Leo's still in danger with Zombi in her arms.

"I listened to Chevelle the entire drive over." She paces. Lovingly, she pets Zombi like the creature was a good girl just now. "It really is the best music for turning a hobby into a salary-paying job." Her eyes gleam with a self-satisfied confidence I don't think I've ever felt in my life.

What's more, I have a feeling this is Tess' favorite part. The anticipation, like she's a wolfhound on the hunt.

Another figure hovers just an inch behind Tess. Eva? No—Raylan. Taut shoulders display a ripped T-shirt, and all at once, I need to know where Eva has gone.

No doubt Raylan will help us out of this mess. He'll tell his sister to pack up her fashion accessory and head straight back to her gaudy beach house. He'll explain that we don't hunt for pay, because we're not mercenaries. The underprivileged, as well as the rich, need help.

I expect Raylan to say something like, *Back away, Tess,* but my sister's boyfriend doesn't budge an inch. He merely has this mask on his face like he's a brainwashed marine who's been given orders to listen.

Tess wrestles with Zombi in her arms, both of them locking eyes, and I think I'm going to vomit. "Did you know that it was Marie Laveau who infused Zombi with enough venom to permanently take a Blurred One down?"

"I musta missed that history." Beau clutches me tighter in his arms.

Sheer delight shines on Tess' heavily made-up lips. "That detail wouldn't be clear to the uneducated. Of course," she says, anger lighting her eyes, "if I'd known before today that Leo killed my parents, there's *no way* I would have let him live."

Using all my strength, I try to lift up my head. Wait . . . what is she talking about?

"Monsters need to die." Tess affectionately pets Zombi, the creature's scaled body slinking like an optical illusion. "What I don't understand," she says, "is how you could ever *fall in love* with one?"

The gunpowder coursing through my head is going to blow like a bomb.

Leo grounds himself near a maple, not losing me from his sight. I think maybe, with the flick of a wrist, he'll send Zombi flying and snap Tess' neck, but the puss on his hands is a reminder that he hasn't healed yet.

"I mean—" Tess glances at the stoic Raylan. "Do *you* think you could ever fall in love with a demon?"

Raylan cuts Leo a look, but it's hard to read what he's thinking because that mask of his doesn't slip. Raylan's shoulders are slumping, though, which tells me he's not exactly in a fighting mood.

"The thing is," Tess grumbles to the reeds on the muddy ground, "I *want* to be nice, but we have a duty. To kill monsters. All of them."

A surge of feeling trickles up my fragile neck tendons. It takes a bit of effort, but, slowly, I'm able to lift my head. As I do, I feel the strength coming back to my arms and legs, but not enough to slide from Beau's arms.

"You sure do have a high opinion of yourself," I tell Tess.

She laughs like she doesn't find me funny at all. It's as if she knows every single thing I'll do next. "That is because I'm passionately content with who I am."

"Or maybe you're just a narcissist," Beau mumbles under his breath.

Beau must feel the question in my gaze, because he adds, even quieter, "Takes one to know one."

I've enough feeling in my fingers to squeeze his arms.

"Hold down Leo," Tess tells Raylan, in full-blown battle-mode now.

Raylan, however, doesn't move an inch. Thoughts flicker through his eyes. "Let's move on. There are much bigger threats than Leo."

Tess pulls Zombi tight, and Zombi hisses so loudly that she's the sound of all three Despairity on the hunt.

Tess lowers her guard enough to laugh her most vicious laugh that's not really a laugh at all. "What, because he's a good little boy now? Need I remind you, he KILLED OUR PARENTS."

I don't know why she keeps saying that. But I *do* know this is the last time she'll be dragging Leo's name through the mud.

She needs to be seen, be worshipped. Beau was right; she *is* a narcissist. Why else would she need to have the nicest house on the beach? The highest quality boots, the nicest truck? Every other hunter I know understands the impracticality of standing out.

No wonder Raylan's been caught up in all her self-loving drama. She's the only family he has, and she is manipulative. But she has to see that Leo is not the enemy. He's proven himself time and time again.

Tess pulls Zombi so tightly, the olive scales shimmer like petrified rocks. Tess is taunting her. She *wants* Zombi to be pissed. And when Tess settles her calculating gaze on me, I think maybe, just maybe, she's going to launch the snake at me instead. But all at once, she launches the snake straight at Leo's head.

Panic surges through the muscles in my arms and legs.

I try to launch myself at Leo, but Beau's greedy hands are holding me back.

"Let me go!" I give Beau a hard hit to the ribs, and though he grunts a little, he doesn't budge.

Raylan, of all things, tears off toward the parking lot, and I can't tell whether he's being a coward, or if he's running for Eva, or what.

The snake slithers up and around one of Leo's shoulders, and an invisible butcher's knife splits apart my gut. With his unhealed wounds from the screws, he could die in half a second.

Tess pulls a screwdriver out of her pocket that's a little bigger than the ones Eva and I lug around. Hatred fills Raylan's sister's eyes, and she's speaking that foreign Creole language.

She lifts her arms as soft, melodic vowels fall from her lips, and Zombi curls behind Leo's neck. Reeds rustle like flutes and clarinets, and a trio of shadows lurking behind bald cypress trees tells me the Despairity have come back to witness this.

Leo stiffens.

The impassivity on Tess' face suggests this is something she's wanted to do for a very long time. I know Leo has done some terrible things, but he didn't kill her parents. Raylan wouldn't be his friend if he did.

The cypress trees and pockmarked ground swirl around me, and I *must* get air in my lungs.

Impossibly, I twist and wrench myself from Beau's grasp. I pull the dagger from my boot and fling it at Tess' freaking head. I would have made my mark, but she ducks and growls. She maneuvers around me and circles her hand in the air, urging the snake to get on with killing Leo.

Beau dive-bombs for my feet, and I scream for him to hold back. So, closing his eyes, as if purposefully deciding to do whatever I say, he dive-bomb's Tess' boots instead.

Finding my coordination, I snatch the other dagger from my boot and throw myself across weeds and roots to where Leo stands perfectly still.

Beau and Tess roll and wrestle on the ground, but I'm with Leo. I can save him now.

I think about how Leo played tea party with me when I was just a little girl, and he was maybe four thousand years old. I sink the blade into the meatiest part of Zombi's green-scaled flesh.

This hissing sound curls from Zombi's fanged mouth, and I'll have to do better than that.

I'm just raising my knife, rain-drops dripping from the sky, when Leo shouts, "Beau, stop!"

From the corner of my eye, Beau is also lifting his knife. But not at Zombi. At Tess.

Grunting from the effort, Leo raises his wounded hands and, despite Zombi wrapped around his neck, he telekinetically forces Beau to stagger a few paces back.

Beau snarls, "This ain't my first picnic," as Zombi constricts in three tight loops around Leo's neck.

"Don't. Kill. Her," Leo says between breaths.

Zombi flashes her fangs, revealing a creepy, pale mouth.

Leo tries not to move as he murmurs, "We are better than that."

Beau laughs like Leo's hilarious.

Footsteps echo through the woods. Raylan emerges through the trees with a .40 Smith & Wesson I don't think I've ever seen before.

"Tess?" Raylan calls, voice flat.

His sister barely registers his existence until he cocks the large handgun. "Stop."

As Tess' gaze settles on the pistol, her concentration gives way to bewilderment. Her eyes widen, and her jaw goes slack. "Where did you get that?"

Raylan steps around a toddler-sized boulder as he keeps his gun aimed at Tess.

Her surprise gives way to incredulity. "So you're going to shoot me now?"

Raylan's eyes flicker with danger. "Stop trying to murder my friend."

But the animosity shining in Tess' eyes proves she doesn't intend to stop any of this, so I raise my favorite dagger and, without thinking about the consequences, lunge straight at Zombi.

And graze a huge portion of Leo's neck.

CHAPTER 29 - EVA

I manage to steal Beau's overcompensating truck and track my sister down at this hideaway cabin in BFE, thanks to her overprotective friend locator app.

Tess' big ace truck is sitting right out front. This day. I let out a full ten-second sigh and pull up to a railroad tie curb.

Nice place. Romantic wispy trees and a bayou for Frost and her two boyfriends and me and my—Raylan. Minus Tess. How's he going to feel about her and Mags beating up on each other on top of everything else? I'm so not excited about being the messenger on this one.

I pause before getting out, gathering myself, and pull my hair up into a messy bun. All I can think is to show Raylan I'm strong and not work. Not an addition to the drama that obviously has him so messed up in the head, but helpful instead.

Hopping the ten feet down from Beau's truck, the crunch of gravel centers me a bit, and I take a deep breath of the musky forest air. Instead of chirping birds, though, I hear yelling from the other side of the house. Of course there's yelling. Tess is here.

I pull my gun from my belt holster and run as quietly as I can to the back. I stop to listen, channeling my breathing like Frost taught me, before turning the corner.

Raylan's unmistakable voice hollers. "You can't just go around killing whoever you want, Tess!" Killing? That word launches me around the corner, gun searching for Tess. Frost hovers over Leo, and Raylan and Beau look like they're both about to Hulk out, all twitchy-like. I relax a tad at not seeing any bodies, although there is plenty of blood. Tess gives me a quick once-over and turns back to Raylan.

"I didn't kill anyone," she says coldly, probably very disappointed.

Frost, bracing Leo's neck, shrieks. "Tortured, maimed, trapped, mutilated?" She's unsteady on her leg, and holy smokes, it looks terrible.

"Not everyone," Tess snaps, "finds traipsing around with boyfriends as important as keeping loved ones safe."

I'm pretty sure Frost's blood is about to boil right out of her body. She eyes something on the ground. Her favorite dagger, and right next to it, Zombi. The putrid snake chopped in half. Good freaking riddance, and go, Frost!

"Raylan," Tess says with sweet compassion that's absolutely opposite from her tone two seconds ago. "I will do whatever I need to protect my family. If people are going to choose the wrong side, that's on them."

OK, Lady Darth Vader. "You have *got* to realize," I say, "it's not always that simple." I purposely do not lower my gun. Which may have been dumb, 'cause now Tess pulls hers on me before I can blink. I gulp. I suppose now's not the time to bring up the fact I know she and Mags fought.

"Tess!" Raylan roars.

"Eva-lou's got a point," Beau decides to pipe in.

"You." Tess shakes her gun with anger at me now, pretenses of being cool and calm melting right off her fuming face. "I trusted you. Welcomed you into this family, and look what you did."

My hand's shaking. "I did what I thought was right."

"You did wrong," she spits, and I'm pretty sure I'm about to die.

Raylan lunges like a pent-up lion. He hits her on the wrist, making her drop her gun to the ground. She throws her elbow up, about to jab him in the throat, but he dodges it.

Twisting, Tess kicks the back of his knee, trying to get him to the ground. He drops to his knee, but like a super sexy special ops soldier, he uses the momentum to pull her down and into some crazy armbar thing.

"That is enough," Raylan growls. "Leave." Then, a little softer, "I'll come talk to you later and give you your gun back."

My heart tears a little bit at the hurt on both of their faces. Would I ever be able to do that to Frost?

Tess turns her head, which looks really painful against the hold he's got her in, so she can look him in the eye. "You're choosing them?"

"Don't you dare put this on him," I snarl, but Raylan keeps his cool.

"Just go," he says and releases her. "I'm trying to protect *all* of you."

Taking a final anguished look at Zombi, she throws a hand in the air and storms off. Like she's scared that if she stayed, she might start crying, and she'd hate to appear like she's actually human.

Leaving Raylan to process what just happened, I run to Frost, who looks like she's gonna collapse completely any second. I can't help myself, though, and I wrap her in a giant hug.

"Are you okay?" I ask.

"Are *you*?" She squeezes me tighter.

"Will be. Better now for sure." I let go and glance at her leg, which still looks terrible. I shoot Leo a look, but immediately fix my face, because he's got a big ole chunk missing from his neck.

Leo says, "I'm sorry," at the same time Beau says, "Seriously," and Beau is back by Frost's side like white on rice.

"I'll get ya back in the cabin," he whisper-booms to Frost.

I will follow her and take care of her in two seconds, but first . . .

I launch myself onto Leo in the tightest hug possible, minus the fact that I have to avoid his torn-up neck.

"*I* am so, so sorry." I sniffle into his chest as I try to erase the memory of twisting that screw in his face. I swear I'm going to get my tear ducts removed. "I didn't know what to do."

"You freed me, Eva," he says in his melodic voice. "Thank you." I squeeze him once as tight as I can and let go.

"Well." I finally let myself look at Raylan. He's about as decipherable as alien hieroglyphs right now, staring after where Tess took off. That's a puzzle for later. Right this second, it's Frost's leg and Leo's neck we need to focus on.

I slide my arm around Leo and start guiding him toward the cabin, where we can hopefully start mending all our wounds, inside and out.

CHAPTER 30 - FROST

I wish we could go back to when things were simpler. When Leo and I were kids, and we built forts out of pillows and blankets. His blond bangs hung in his eyes, and he was so happy, he laughed with his eyes closed shut.

But no, instead I'm lying on a stranger's bed, flat on my back, fever still high from Zombi's bite, worrying whether Tess is going to murder us in our sleep or not.

I killed her snake. I killed the one thing that could permanently kill a Blurred One. She sort of flipped a lid, aiming her gun straight at my face, then punching some poor, unsuspecting maple tree instead.

I'm glad I killed Zombi, but I'm also a little insane for doing that.

Water drips from the thinly planked ceiling as it continues to pour outside. Some type of rodent scurries beneath the floorboards, and I'd do anything for a little alone time with Eva so we could just talk.

How did she handle things with Raylan? Why is Tess so psycho? And how is it that I have two boyfriends?

I wish I'd been at the beach house to hold Eva's hair, to squeeze her hand when things blew up. Eva mentioned it when we came inside, avoiding Raylan when he tried to talk to her about it. At least I found another shirt to put on.

Hovering a few feet away from me, Beau tucks a bottle of Ibuprofen into his Wranglers' pocket.

"Thanks for the painkillers," I say, not really knowing what else to tell him, so I leave it at that.

He looks like he wants to broach an assortment of topics —how he really feels about me, the fact that he proposed before we came down. Leo's alive. Not sure what he'll do about that.

Beau does pause, though, looking at the black vial dangling from the chain on my neck, and I'd completely forgotten about that necklace. Good thing we don't have to add Lindy showing up to all this mess.

I give Beau a little smile, grasping the tiny vial between my pointer finger and thumb. He has to know I *am* grateful for it. I don't want him to get any big ideas about where we stand, though, so I close my eyes and turn my head like I need to sleep for a while.

Feeling like a complete and total jerk.

Luckily, Beau sighs softly, taking the hint. He gathers the cloth and whetstone he'd been using to clean and sharpen my knives and quietly treads out of the room.

Eventually, I think maybe the coast is clear, so I reopen my eyes. When I do, though, I must be delusional, because Leo's staring at me from the doorway with newly washed hair and a clean button-up shirt, and I've never seen a more handsome man in my life. Eva screams something about a spider being in the front room, and Beau's telling her he'll take care of it.

I know I'm not seeing delusions, though, because Leo's watching me with a wide bandage on his neck, and if I'd created him within the houses of my own mind, there's no way he'd be wearing that.

My cheeks warm as I remember all over again that I am the cause of that, but Leo just smiles at me like I gave him a paper cut.

The skin above his lip's nearly healed, and only faint scars remain of the wounds on his hands. Hands which played tea party, took me ice skating on the lake. *Frost,* he said when we were children, and he pointed out the beautiful, thin, white layer of frost on my window glass. *You are like that.*

Zombi's venom surges up and down my leg like uncorked baking soda and vinegar, but I merely press my leg down further into the scratchy comforter. Better for him not to worry that it still flares up.

He takes a tentative step closer, like if he moves too fast, I'll startle and fly off like a baby bird. "How is your leg?"

I can hear the care in his voice, and it is so good to hear him ask me that. I don't want to move, to speak, because part of me still believes he's not a real image.

He leans against the doorframe, and my mind's suddenly reeling back to when he leaned in the doorway of the storage room back at the house. I had joined him and put one of his metal-tipped cigarettes in my mouth.

My leg twinges and courses with heat, but I shoot him my most confident answer. "I'm an Abram. I can handle it."

His gaze flickers with pleasure before fading into something less light. "I never dreamed she would shoot you. And Zombi. . . . Tell me you are all right."

I smile despite the ninja peppers running through my quadriceps.

"I can't believe you chopped it in half." Leo grins on my behalf.

"Don't forget the part where I ripped off my shirt and saved your butt."

I don't realize that Leo's joined me on the bed until the springs squeal in protest. His knee brushes softly against my own, and he smells of soap. My heart rate sprints into overdrive. I want to cup my hands around his beautiful face, hold onto this moment.

Gently, he places the back of his fingers on my forehead, and it's like I know what he's thinking. *We should get you something for that fever.*

And it's like he knows Beau already brought me Ibuprofen, because the springs are suddenly shrieking again as he shoves off the side of the bed.

"It didn't take you long to allow Beau into your consortium." He paces over a matted green throw rug, his eyes saying something else.

There's nothing I can do but stare at my hands. "I— thought you left."

"I wanted you to be happy." He leans against an old, noisy pine chest. He avoids my gaze, looking to the ridiculous tassels on my boots strewn next to my bed. "I suppose it's penance."

I do my best to get up from the bed, my leg shrieking in protest. I yearn to say, *Don't say that.* I'll place my hand on his cheek. Tell him *he'll* always be my love, that I still can't even look at a map of Texas without tearing up. Instead, I say, "What did she do to you? When you were locked up."

Through the window, Leo stoically watches a fluffy-tailed gray squirrel gather nuts. It stops and stares at us, mewing like a cat.

"Were you caged the entire time?" I have to ask.

He shrugs like we're speaking of the time it takes to iron his best suit pants. "She grabbed me the moment the warlock sent me off."

I picture Tess grabbing Leo the minute she saw him and slamming him into a devil's trap. Faceless witch doctors holding up drills, chanting bits of Creole, and screwing his face—like we did to Knox.

I fold up my uninjured leg and tuck it underneath my chin. "How did she intercept the message you got from God?"

"There was no messenger."

"Wait, what?"

An ironic smile twists apart his once playful lips. "That was a fabrication."

I feel my lower lip tremble. No. This is not happening. "It was all a lie? By Tess?"

He nods like he's trying not to show me the pain he's feeling deep inside his chest. The terrible truth that he was never actually promised a human life. "I escaped once. Was assisted by Dom."

That's why he took me to that park to find Dominick after I was shot. So what's Tess' ultimate game? Her final motivations? I know she wants to be the big, bad hunter and put an end to all monsters, but is that really all of it?

"I need to show you something," Leo says, leaning away from the pine chest. "I should have shown you long ago, but I skirted it."

Cautiously, he strides over to me, stepping over that green mat, and settles himself next to me on the bed. His body heat is so balmy and inviting despite my fever, and I'd rather just wrap my arms around his shoulders. And kiss. But he's raising a self-assured hand to my cheek, and I know what this means. I'm not entirely sure I want to see another one of his visions.

So I turn to the side. He's going to show me another reason why he believes he's evil. But he's not evil. When will we agree on that?

My throat feels like it's double-lined with cayenne pepper and wasabi. Zombi's venom flickers and flares everywhere but mostly near my hamstring. I have to force myself not to shake it out.

"It's better that you know." Gently, Leo takes my hand, and somewhere in this little dilapidated hut, a clock ticks. I wish he would just *talk*. Say what he wants me to know instead of showing it, because it's always worse when he shows me the past.

"I wish you didn't have these powers," I murmur as I let him squeeze my hand. I knew it would happen—I'm half expecting it—but the moment he closes his eyes, a gust of wind picks me up and shoves me into a distant land.

The sharp scent of hair dye is the first thing I detect. Likewise, a trailer with a small stove and a window looking out to a neighbor's rusted-out refuse bin.

As I try to get my bearings, as I try to get my eyes to adjust, I realize I'm holed up, knees tucked beneath my chin. I'm below a folding table on filthy, scratched-up linoleum.

"YOU'RE A PIECE OF SH—" a man in a stained white shirt says.

He keeps saying that, and I want to cover my ears. I already want to go back when his worn boots crunch a beer bottle into the linoleum.

A hastily thrown together box of needles and syringes lay at the foot of a bed where a woman lies face-down on a comforter. Her red and green reindeer stockings are covered with a pale-colored powder, and the bruises marking nearly every inch of her skinny arms tells me she's addicted to drugs.

"YOU THINK WE CAN AFFORD THIS?" The man kicks aside a wadded-up blow dryer, which rattles like a fractured skeleton. He shakes a box of hair dye promising "premium quality, platinum color."

"I need my next score!" He wrenches the woman's now-platinum blonde hair so she will face him—and the similar nose and chin say she's an older, female version of Raylan.

Her eyes are closed like she won't be waking up anytime soon, and the man loudly curses again.

Leo shifts in a seat to my left. His dirty blond hair is gelled to the side, and he's in the same vessel of medium-tall height. Hunching low over a thick wad of Post-it notes, he mumbles, "Hit her."

The angry sound of bone hitting bone *cracks* across the single-wide trailer.

I expect the woman to cry out, but she's so far gone, she doesn't wake up, and Leo again murmurs, "Hit her."

Her red-stockinged feet will twitch. She'll curl into a ball. Defend herself. But she just lies there, immobile as the Smith and Wesson on the counter to the man's left.

This isn't the Leo I know. He's supposed to be telling the Despairity to hold back. He wouldn't come into a drug-afflicted home and rage carnage such as this.

But he merely sits there. Flicking at the powder with his bare hands.

"How could you?" I ask as Leo coolly brushes a pile of white powder into a slip of one of the Post-it notes.

In the memory, Leo avoids my eyes. "Now, the gun."

Springs squeak as we hurl back to the present, and I can almost taste the dank smell of the bayou cabin on my tongue. I jerk my hand away from Leo's. A sheen of sweat covers the length of our palms, and somewhere nearby, the ceiling drips.

"How could you?" I cry again.

He doesn't say a word.

"Leo." I flinch away from him. "They were his parents."

He looks down at his newly-healed hands. At the finger-nails that have nearly completely regrown.

"I told you I was far more vile than you'd ever expect."

A migraine slits through my skull. I'll close my eyes and drift off to another dreamland. But he's showing me this vision, and I need to know what I'm dealing with.

I take up Leo's wrist. Grit my teeth and nod for him to go on.

As I funnel to the past—slink and whirl to this psychedelic vision—an acrid smell washes over a trash-filled lot. Hinges shriek from a rusted-out screen on a window. A breeze teases my face, and I turn to see an unruly junk pile.

Broken boards, rusted out tools. Old tires with vines and dirt covering the rubber confirm they've been there for eons.

An unsympathetic Leo with dead eyes and an unusual amount of facial hair emerges from the single-wide trailer. His double murder twists apart my gut.

His shirt, unusually crisp, tucks neatly into his pants. His hair lies a little too much like Knox's, with too much gel in it. Leo's just placing one of his old Dunhills in his mouth when his eyes suddenly spark with life. He's caught sight of a skinny Rottweiler that is chained up so tightly, its fur's been pinched off.

Without a word, Leo releases the pet, which bows its head at his feet before collapsing on the ground.

Leo's just strolling past the broken boards and rusted-out tools and tires when a sixteen-year-old boy—Raylan!—comes into view. He's kicking and screaming in a lake, surrounded by three dark spirits.

The Despairity. I could blow them into a million pieces, the maggots.

Like a specter, Leo somberly watches the girls. Like he's forgotten how to feel. Like he's never laughed his entire life.

In unity, the Despairity reach and try to shove young Raylan beneath the surface, but he's a fighter. He screams and thrashes. One of the Despairity complains the boy's putting up too much of a fight, and Leo's looking like he wants to skip the ordeal altogether when his gaze registers on something else.

When I turn, I see what Leo sees. The boy's sweater says,

Frosty the Frickin' Snowman. Only the "y" in "Frosty" is missing, so all it says is "Frost."

Leo's eyes linger on the word. Like it gives him pain, but he does not look away from it. And it's like I can *see* the cycle of emotions.

She told me to leave. Raylan looks to be about sixteen, so I must have been about fifteen. Eight years since I last saw him.

She said she won't see me anymore.

But if our adventures climbing trees and ice skating on shallow ponds have taught him anything, it should be that children are just children.

It's as if he's reading my mind, because he turns away while holding up a hand.

"The boy is an innocent," he says.

The memory funnels back to a muted-hue prism when the real Leo in the cabin pulls back his hand.

He doesn't say a word, but it's clear he's ashamed of what he did. Because he only stares at the rough hardwood.

"Raylan forgave you?" I don't know how to stay silent.

Leo merely blinks. Like he's gone half-deaf.

Tess wasn't lying. About any of it. My voice cracks, because this is *far* more than just the two of us. "Does Eva know about this?"

A sharp wave of guilt flashes through Leo's eyes. He glances up briefly before looking down once more and shaking his head.

The ceiling drips. That noisy, gray squirrel is at the window again when Leo mutters, "I have long known that it is something I need to admit."

"I thought you said Raylan forgave you. So why would he tell Tess?"

"The bonds of family are hard to suppress."

"Don't tell Eva." I shudder, thinking of my sister's fragile state, of how she treasures Leo's friendship so much. "For her, loyalty means a lot."

CHAPTER 31 - EVA

*I*t's getting late, and the way the moon reflects off the river all wavy reflects the mood of us here in this Louisiana hideaway. Shaky, and still pretty dark.

With Frost passed out and Beau who knows where, Leo sat with Raylan and me in this too-small living room and told us all about his time with Tess. How she nabbed him straight from Mr. Harris' house, so his defenses were down. He thought he was going to heaven. She overpowered him with help from witch doctors, using spells as she screwed in the sigil, and locked him in chains carved with more sigils to keep him weak. And that was the pleasant part. Apparently, having your fingernails grow back quickly isn't always a good thing.

Then there's the thunderstorm cloud that's just chilling in between Raylan and me. Leo has the decency not to say anything, but after awhile, he excuses himself to "go sleep for the next three days." Frost has been in and out of consciousness all day. I need a hot minute to talk to that girl. But for now, it's just Raylan and me in this shabby but beautiful cabin by the bayou.

I grab the threadbare throw pillow next to me on the

couch that's embroidered with "Go Jump In A Lake" and hug it to my chest. I've got to break this silence before Raylan takes off.

"I'm sorry about your sister," I venture. I can't even say her name anymore. Like saying it out loud would give her more power somehow.

I listen to the cuckoo clock on the wall tick eleven times before he answers.

"It's not your fault," he says from his statue-still rocking chair, but we still can't look at each other. "I'm sorry for blowing up on you like that."

Well, that's something. "I totally understand." I scratch the pillow with my nail, thinking what to say. I want to ask him if she's always been like that, but I'm scared that's assuming he's ready to say anything against her. "I never wanted to come between you two," I say quietly.

Twenty more clicks of the clock tick by with no answer. Guess I better rip off the Band-Aid. "I talked to Mags."

Raylan finally glances at me but only for a second.

"Did you know she and Tess got into a fight?"

He grunts. "Yeah, they've been fighting since the second they met."

"No, like physically beating each other up."

His eyebrows shoot up, and he scratches his head.

"I think it was pretty bad." I watch his reaction, but his mask is firmly in place. His shadowed face looks exhausted.

"That's not good." He rubs his face with his hands, like he's trying to wipe away the dark circles under his eyes. Pausing, he puts his hands on his knees and puffs out a breath he's probably been holding all day. He looks at me, and the tilt of his head makes me think he's about to come join me on the couch so I can hold him. We can figure this out together, just like we did after my dad died.

Instead, he asks, "How about we go night swimming?"

"Um, ok?" Random? I've got no idea why this is a good idea right now, but I'm not about to argue. I know sometimes I just need a break before I can handle something. Maybe he's doing the same.

I mentally check what underwear I'm wearing, since there certainly wasn't time to go grab a swimsuit. Sports bra and some pretty decent black underwear? Should work, especially since it's dark. Maybe a break from all the crazy is smart.

Since I'm usually the one with the crazy ideas and he just dumped me, I let him take the lead. He doesn't disappoint.

"Well, let's go!" He takes off toward the back door, walking with forced lightness, like an RV with hundred-year-old shocks. I follow, completely intrigued and utterly confused.

We pick our way down the stone path to the dock, still barefoot from being in the house. Besides a few stray sharp objects, the stone feels warm and smooth underfoot, despite my bandaged foot. Thankfully, no demon catfish here.

The river is so still and quiet. I'm sort of terrified of getting eaten by an alligator, but I know Raylan wouldn't have us do this if it wasn't safe.

I busy myself with dipping a toe in the water so I can figure out Raylan's next move. Sure enough, he starts pulling off his un-ironically ripped T-shirt, and then he just plum takes off his pants so he's in his boxers. I'm so glad he's facing away from me so he can't see my jaw drop or my paranoid scans for people nearby.

"You gonna join me?" he asks, and I blink but try to stay cool. I suppose we're broken up, so I don't need to be too worried about "decency."

He prods me with his elbow, like we didn't just have one of the most stressful days ever. "Don't worry, I'm not gonna look." He promptly jumps in the water.

"Well, I certainly am glad I wore my big girl panties

today," I mumble to myself while he's under the water. I strip as quickly as I can and jump in before God, and my daddy's ghost, have too long to judge me.

Ah, the water is just slightly cooler than the warm outside air. Perfect Indian summer night. The second I resurface, he splashes me with a giant wave of water.

"What the heck is that for?" I gasp and almost choke on water and a laugh. I try to splash him back, but he dodges me.

"For you being too beautiful for words."

I have to tell myself to keep treading water. "Uh, thank you?"

He doesn't answer and just splashes me again. Now I'm all kinds of confused, so I settle for launching myself at him, tackling him with both arms and both legs like a monkey, and we both go underwater. He knows me well enough to know exactly where to push to make me squirm. He pokes right under my hip, and I let go and splutter to the surface.

The second I hit the air, he grabs me from behind, and we both go under again. We go back and forth, just having fun wrestling around, splashing, chucking mud at each other, and generally blowing off steam until we're heaving for air. When we quiet down, my arms, conveniently, are still wrapped around his shoulders. His legs are powerful enough to tread water for the both of us. And his arms aren't moving anywhere.

I play with his short, wet hair, every bit as nervous and conscious of every movement as when I first met him, instead of the second skin his has become in the last few months. It's like I'm feeling the angles of his shoulders or the dip of his collarbone for the very first time.

A sound catches my attention back by the house. I can barely make out Frost's lanky figure, followed by Beau. I guess she's feeling better. Wonder what Leo would think about those two on a midnight stroll.

Raylan's staring at me, the moonlight shining beautifully off his perfect cheekbones, and his eyes almost glow. He pulls me closer, and I'm all too aware of how little clothing stands between us, but he's playing with my hair now. Always a gentleman. Since I'm slightly higher than him, he raises his mouth to mine, and I don't hesitate one bit.

His usual taste, novel since thinking I'd never get to kiss him again, is mixed with the earthy flavor of the river water. A tiny, annoying voice in the back of my mind says he's not thinking clearly, but I've had a crappy day, too, and I'm not really thinking clearly, either, so I lose myself in him.

He pulls us closer to the dock so he can prop us up easier. Now no one could see us unless they were right here. Ugh, if there were ever a time to not be a good girl—but I just relax and continue to let him take the reins. His fingers get tangled up in my wet hair, then explore the uncovered parts of my body.

I'm able to forget about all the terrible things that have happened since coming down here. Focus on his broad chest instead of Leo being locked in a basement. His ears that still drip with water instead of my sister getting shot. His soft yet so strong lips instead of how Tess' gun pointed right at me. Letting it all go.

CHAPTER 32 - FROST

*B*eau gallantly takes my hand as we step over a fallen log. My leg burns, but I don't want to show him this weakness. I want to tell him he and I are over, but he deserves a conversation—a final conversation between the two of us.

It's like he's reading my mind, because he says, "Do you remember how we met?"

The moon shows just enough light for us to see where we're strolling in the woods. The trees almost look like people crowding round to see just how my breakup with Beau will go. The more aggressive ones lean closest, whispering that I'm heartless and shouldn't let such a good guy go. The lurkers at the back, though, are the worst. They're the ones who will spread the rumors that I'll never follow through with my commitments to provide for my family and protect my sister.

I shake my head to push away my psychosis.

"You don't remember?" Beau sounds hurt.

I spin to him, startled.

Do I not remember how I met Beau?

Of course, I remember.

Unbidden, my mind flitters back to the evening when Eva insisted that I go to a barn dance. I hadn't properly washed my hair or clothes for weeks. While I sat, playing the piano, Eva shoved a pair of brand-new Levis in my face and told me to "tweeze the unibrow."

So I ambled off for the shower, wishing more than anything that I was going to that barn dance to meet Leo. But he was gone, I was alone, and the only way I could move on was to forget Leo.

"Truth is—" I can't fight back a smile. "I didn't want to go."

Beau hooks his thumbs through his Wranglers belt loops. "But you're really glad you did." He waggles his eyebrows.

I look away to the trees—to my conspirators. They'll tell me I was way reckless to forget Leo, and I was equally as reckless to so quickly pick up Beau.

I try not to remember it—that night three months ago— but amidst the hay bales and beams that held up a rickety barn, Beau had presented himself pretty much the same way I see him now—in a plaid shirt, massive belt buckle, and Wranglers. I rolled my eyes, telling myself that *of course* I would find the cowboy that was so stereotypical, when suddenly he said with far too much kindness, "Care to dance?"

I don't know why it took me so much off guard. I guess I'd equated all kindness to Leo, and I knew it was silly. I knew it wasn't fair. With the smell of freshly baked apple pies wafting through the barn, I told him the one line he couldn't resist.

"You might want to ask someone else."

A dimple flashed in Beau's cheek. "You are irresistible."

There was no cleverness to Beau's speech. Nothing to catch me off guard. He simply asked me if I was having a nice time and if I wanted some pigs 'n' blankets.

Crickets chirrup around us in the bayou now, and it

reminds me that the trees aren't the only ones privy to the conversation between Beau and me. For all I know, Dad's spirit could be around, and Leo could have followed us outside and be listening to every word.

Spanish moss drips from gum and cypress trees like newly shaved pieces of fur. A pool of water dips below our weeded footpath, and, without permission, Beau takes my hand and lifts me over the pool.

"Hear that?" Beau suddenly lets go of my hand. He tilts his head to hear a croaking frog. "Bet he tastes *great* with Tabasco."

"You're emphasizing the fact that you're a hillbilly again."

An atypical sulking expression flits over his brow. "Hillbilly is what I am."

Listless, he suddenly kicks an already beaten down mushroom. He paces over spindly reeds and resilient ferns, and when he pauses in front of a tree that's been rotting in the water for a while, he turns to me and says, "Remember when you ordered the eggnog shake at the diner, and I reassured you it tasted like vomit?"

"You got me the mint instead."

"Remember how I trained you to be a waitress?"

"You're a terrible teacher."

If the dynamics hadn't changed, he'd be wrapping me in his arms, and we'd probably be kissing, just like we did on the way down. But now I feel soiled. Dirty. Because, without even knowing it, I was cheating on Leo.

Beau says in a charged voice, "I like you."

His declaration makes me pause in front of one of those spritely ferns. It's not something I haven't heard before. But he's being sincere. Honest. And it pains me that I can't give him what he wants to hear back.

"I like you," he repeats, unwilling to hear what's right in front of him, the truth, "because you are hardworking. An' compassionate. I like you 'cause every time Mama tried to spook you, you simply rolled up your sleeves an' counted the cash at the register. You *proved* that you are invaluable," he adds, and I crinkle my nose. "But that's not the only reason why I like you. I like you, Froster, because you are one mesmerizin' barrier."

My chest twinges a little. What does he mean?

He waves his hand as if that's not what he meant to say. "I like you for other reasons, too."

He can't just tell me that I'm some "mesmerizin' barrier," then pretend he never said that.

"Mama has an emotional connection." He tugs one of the pieces of Spanish moss. "An emotional connection to me, and you can help sever it."

My heart ratchets up to triple speed, and I don't know why. "Just leave her in a foreign country," I say, wringing my hands, "and run the diner yourself."

Beau lowers his voice, and for some reason, a chill runs up the back of my neck. "You know I can't do that."

I don't know why, but in that split moment, Beau is playful and uncomfortably adorable, true, but *something else.*

Perhaps it's the way he's standing. Maybe it's the way he's inching toward me with his knife in hand, but somehow I *know* he's a predator.

I gulp down the fear that's risen in my throat. I don't know what he is, but I know he isn't regular. "What are you?"

He lowers his voice to a whisper and starts circling me where I stand by that fern. "You," he says, "can help me defeat Mama."

I flinch at the word "defeat," because it sounds both so real and terribly wrong. She's a terrible boss at the diner, true, but I can feel the avalanche of truth getting ready to crash down.

Beau tried to kiss me for ages, but I didn't let him until *I* decided it was time. "Has a girl ever refused to kiss you, Beau?"

That dimple in his cheek flashes as he shakes his head. "Not until you."

It could be just because most girls in Bloodcreek smell like they've bathed in cigarette smoke. Or maybe it's because we share a knife-throwing obsession, but this look of frustration flits across Beau's eyes. "Of course, *he* had to ruin all my luck an' come runnin' back here."

A toad croaks over and over, and from three feet away, Beau looks upon me with a grim smile. "I didn't want to tell you so soon, but I suppose now's as good a time as any to spill."

A heavy feeling settles over my stomach. Please don't tell me he's actually not Beau but Wade, who's always been hiding in plain sight as a shapeshifter.

"Froster," he says with a slight tremor in his throat. "I'm a ghoul."

My lips are smiling, because ghouls eat dead people, so he's not, but then he's skulking toward me in such a practiced, premeditated way that I'm reminded all over again that he's an extremely adept hunter for how little he actually does it. And there's no way Maggie, Raylan, Eva, and I would have allowed him into our group if he hadn't proved his worth.

He toys with his hunting knife, and I expect him to say that he means to eat me now, when he apologetically says, "Well, I behave as a ghoul. I'm actually one of the seven heads of the creature of the Whore of Babylon. Though I prefer 'whore-ghoul.'"

I assume he misspoke—that he's devising an off-kilter plan just to get the drop on me before he slits my throat.

"See, I thought if I got you out here an' explained my point o' view, you might actually hear me through."

"What do you mean to do, Beau?"

He flashes another guilty smile. "Kill Leo."

My heart drops to my stomach like a stone.

"For the love of pearl! He *is* a Blurred One, after all. Plus, you kinda always said he has to be born!"

My hair sticks to the side of my face as I try to make sense of what he's telling me now. Water sloshes in my boots as I automatically back away, and mud sprays my arms.

I force myself to look straight back at him as my head flares. "You're hungry. You're not thinking right. That's why you think you need to kill Leo."

I grab my dagger from my boot, but a lot of good that'll do. Beau taught me everything I know.

I have to get back to the cabin. Protect Leo, and the idea tears a laugh through my throat. Like I'm worthy of protecting a Blurred One.

Warn him, then, because he's capable of protecting himself. Has been for years.

But Leo was recently injured, and he might not see Beau coming. Except he *did*. He said he "knew what Beau was." Why didn't Leo explain what he knew?

I suppose there wasn't time, what with Tess and Zombi showing up so soon.

And now, I can see it in Beau's eyes—the apologetic but ravenous desire to end Leo—and how in the heck did I end up with another supernatural boy in tow?

I take off in a run, humidity crawling through my lungs. A white-tailed doe tears off in the other direction, and Beau's boots clomp the earth as he follows.

About a meter or two behind me, he drawls, "I'll make it quick 'n' painless. I just can't let him get in the way of what I have to do!"

A sickening thud and crackling of bones echo behind me as he clambers over a collection of sinkholes. "Sorry!" His voice rings with embarrassment. "I'm just so hungry! Had to eat that toad."

My shirt catches on a scraggly Japanese Maple. I try tugging on the cotton, but it only bounces around. I give it a slice of my blade, and I'm free—leaving only three-quarters of my shirt.

Without meaning to, I glance behind me in time to find Beau guiltily sucking up the tail end of a still wriggling frog.

My heart flies to my teeth when Beau shoots me a mournful frown. "I *know* it ain't an appetizin' sight. I've just never gone so long without food before."

I fling my dagger right at his skull.

My aim is true. It actually stabs him between the eyes, but he grips the bony handle of the blade like he's made of Play-Doh. It makes a goopy, sucking sound when he tugs it from his skull.

"You have to lob off my head." He hands me my blade like I didn't just try to murder him. "But you wouldn't do that to me, would you, Froster?"

I grip the necklace clasped round my throat, about to rip it off, when he holds up his hands.

"I wouldn't do that!"

"Why?"

"Mama's still on the warpath! That spell's the only thing hidin' you."

I try to call his bluff, guessing being a barrier means I'm hard to read somehow. "If I'm this supposed 'barrier,' Lindy shouldn't be able to sense me anyhow."

"She's a hunter." He holds out his palms. "An' you haven't exactly been good at coverin' your tracks."

I don't know why, but I feel like I can believe him on that account. Maybe it's because he doesn't seem to relish his true nature. Maybe I could get him on some special diet restrictions. Maybe he could just eat toads.

His shoulders sag as he ambles over a pile of maple leaves in the thick sludge. "I wanted you to finish her off two days ago, but she has her own powers."

He runs his fingers through his now wild hair. "She got you to forget her chasin' and huntin' you. She doesn't like you, 'cause you threaten to take her boy from her. When you do that, she weakens in power."

In my mind, I see his mom gripping the back of Betsy and shaking her hard.

Tall, thin heels of her high boots match a whip—which she pulled out of her purse.

I close my eyes, trying to hold onto the thin, slippery strands of the memory she stole, but that's all I can find right now.

"She couldn't eat me." I suddenly remember.

"When you first started workin' at the diner, I took a shine to you, so Mama tried to suck out your soul. But—" he laughs a little nervously "—you side-stepped her, no problemo. I thought *maybe* you had some sort of mystical powers and were a witch or somethin' like that, but that's before I saw what a terrible waitress you are."

I lob a rock his way just to see if it'll do any damage.

He ducks without any real effort at all.

He cups his face in his hands in bewilderment. "No witch would show up to work, day after day, and be so terrible!"

"Hey!"

He smiles again, but his eyes shine like he's on the verge of bursting into tears.

But first, I need to know how he and all his siblings fit into this, because all of a sudden, this is making sense. "Your brothers and sisters are the other heads, er, creatures of the Whore of Babylon?"

A softness—a look of relief—washes across Beau's brow.

"To free yourself from your mom, you want to marry me, because I'm some sort of barrier."

"That's right." His voice is small.

"Your brothers and sisters are the other six heads of the creature. But if she dies, don't you die as well?"

An expression of earnestness flits across Beau's eyes and mouth. "I don't know how to explain it, but my gut says if she dies, we don't."

"That's quite the logical line of reasoning."

"She *beats* Awan and Grendel," he says, like those aren't unusual names. "She scares Awan so bad, she won't eat, Froster!"

I think of the pony-tailed twins that had hopped down from the slide. The boy who got away after scrambling out from under the table.

Still, Beau has to see that I'll never simply stand back and watch him do what he wants to do, so I grip my knife and consider lobbing off his head just to make this end for sure. "Killing Leo won't protect your brothers and sisters."

Beau's smile is so pained, I can feel his misery all the way to my toes. "And that right there is where you is wrong."

CHAPTER 33 - EVA

Raylan and I hightail it, soaking wet, toward the commotion in the cabin. Frost's unmistakable shriek has me running like my foot isn't bandaged, or that I'm in nothing but my knickers. Raylan is faster than me, curse him, so he makes it to the porch steps a full five seconds before I do. He grabs a grapefruit-sized rock nestled there on the ground, and I almost catch up by the time he leaps up the stairs and bursts through the door.

We quickly scan the room for trouble and find Frost's boys. Leo, using his powers, has got Beau pinned against a wall across from the couch where Leo was sleeping. Beau is either surprisingly strong, or Leo is still weak, because Beau manages to grab a crawfish figurine and chucks it at Leo.

"Can everyone just stop trying to kill everyone else for a second?" Frost yells, but I reckon these boys aren't hearing anything past their testosterone.

I flinch as a snow globe gets thrown, then redirected by Leo. Raylan makes to lunge at Beau, but trying to heed my sister's plea, I grab his arm to hold him back.

"What the heck is happening?" I holler as Beau tries to grab the iron fire poker nearby. "Calm your butts down!"

Beau heaves his torso free from Leo's invisible hold just long enough to snatch the poker before Leo slams him back against the wall. Beau's man bun's come undone, so his hair falls in his face, making him look fierce instead of his usual cocky swagger.

Frost looks equal parts pissed and terrified. "Beau's some kind of whore-ghoul, and he's hungry, and he's kind of gone mad and is really focused on Leo!"

"Whaaa—" Raylan and I say at the same time. Uh, gross? I guess that explains why Leo's having trouble keeping Beau pinned.

"You know," Leo says, hand outstretched, trying to keep Beau pinned to the wall, "I've been attacked enough lately." The fire poker sails back at Beau and embeds in the wall right between Beau's head and the Longhorn steer head mounted there.

Raylan and our guns are on the other side of the room, so we can't reach them without risking getting impaled. I look around the old Southern Living magazines and yellowed doilies on the sofa table for another weapon. Raylan's eyeing the curtains like he'll yank them down to choke Beau.

Beau manages to get a knife out of his pocket and throws it at Leo's head, but Leo dodges the blade enough that it slices right through the now-pink skin on his neck where Frost accidentally got him earlier. He shouts in pain, and Beau's body slumps to the floor when Leo releases him.

Beau wrenches the fire poker out of the wall and struts over to Leo, but Frost throws herself in front of Leo as a shield. In three seconds, Raylan races across the room, snags his gun, and has it against Beau's head.

"I don't know if this'll kill whatever you are." Raylan's

voice is equal parts terrifying and sexy. "But it sure as hell will hurt."

Leo gently pulls Frost to his side, so she's no longer in Beau's path, and puts a tired hand on Raylan's shoulder. "No more killing."

Raylan's shoulders fall a smidge, but his eyes blaze. He's had a long day, too.

Leo gives a small sigh and traces the faint scar on his philtrum lightly. "We need to find a way to coexist," he says, like it pains him to admit. "I have a feeling things are about to get bad, and we could use him on our side."

"We can't trust him," Raylan barks, gun still steady, and right then is when I realize we're standing in front of everybody in our underwear. I suck in my stomach and fold my arms over my chest. Uh, no judging, Frost. "He'll try again." Raylan still argues.

"We need him," Leo says firmly.

"We did just fine without him," Raylan says.

"Babe." I try to make him see reason. "We don't know what Tess is up to. We might need all the help we can get."

"Tess is the best hunter in the country," Raylan seethes. He holds his gun steady, pushing the tip of the barrel into Beau's temple.

How can he be so bullheaded? "I think Leo and Maggie would beg to differ."

Raylan shoots fireballs out of his eyes at me, and I fight conflicting urges to roll my eyes and flip him off. I manage to just match his glare. With a growl, he lowers his gun and stalks over to his duffle bag, rummaging through it for some clothes.

Beau's tense muscles relax a little. "Thanks for the positivity, y'all." Being stopped from fulfilling his revenge or whatever, I'd think he'd be more angry, but his eyes flash with guilt before he tries to shoot us his easy smile. Like he's pretending everything's gonna be a-okay, but it most certainly is not. Frost keeps looking between the three men, unconvinced this won't be blowing up again.

Leo, ever respectful, releases Frost's arm and distances himself from her just a smidge.

"I'd wondered when your hunger would manifest," Leo says, his blue eyes open and earnest. "Ghoul hunger urges are some of the hardest to suppress. That said," he reluctantly adds, "I do owe you a token of gratitude. Thank you for watching out for Frost."

"It was my pleasure," Beau answers, not exactly looking Leo in the eye. "Sorry I tried to kill you." He still avoids eye contact as he holds his hand out for a handshake, but is he already over this, for real?

I reach behind myself for the epically awesome wolf blanket on the couch. As I wrap myself up in it, Leo gives Beau his hand, and they shake. "I'm sure we could find you an alligator in no time," Leo says, all forgiveness and awesomeness.

Beau eyes Frost like she's literally made up of sunshine and unicorns, but his eyes are wide with dashed hopes. A frown rolls over his face before his features harden like clay in a kiln.

He hurls himself at Leo, teeth going straight for Leo's wounded neck. Frost, Raylan, and I lunge to try to help, but before we move more than an inch, Leo raises his hand. He freezes Beau, then sends him flying back to the wall where he started—skewering him on the giant point of the mounted Longhorn.

CHAPTER 34 - FROST

*T*wo beats don't pass before Raylan grabs up his pistol again and presses the barrel into Beau's head even harder. "Is your aim off?" he asks Leo, "or are you *still* letting him live?"

A little abject, Leo ducks his head, hair hanging in his eyes. "He hasn't done anything I can't forgive him for."

"He tried to kill you. Even after you shook hands!"

Leo glances at me before looking away. "The important thing is Frost is protected."

Raylan throws his one free hand up in an uncharacteristically dramatic fashion. "This has nothing to do with her."

"IT HAS EVERYTHING TO DO WITH HER!"

The entire cabin draws silent. Eva clings to her gray wolf blanket, and Raylan looks like he's about to spit daggers.

In all our time together, though, I've never heard Leo shout. He got angry at Knox, true, but always with a cool measure of collectiveness. Raylan's hit a nerve I didn't even know Leo had. With bloodshot eyes and a tremor in his hand, Raylan's time with Tess has definitely taken its toll.

Coughing up a string of blood, Beau tries shimmying off

the antlers, but the fact that he just tried to kill Leo means he gets to hang there for a while. He actually makes it halfway up the sharp slope of one of the antler's nubs when Raylan shoves him into the wooden wall.

"Come on!" Beau squawks like a vulture. He looks like he actually means it when he says, "Leo's standin' in the way of my 'happily ever after.'"

I have to fight the urge to lob off one of his ears here and now, but Beau traps me in his puppy-dog gaze. "Are you really goin' to let him do that to me, Puppy Chow?"

Eva pulls her Glock from the side table. "If you *really* wanna live, not another word, Beau."

"But I wouldn't be a true gentleman if I didn't tell you what I was intendin' to do all along!"

Raylan sidles up to Eva like they've never been closer, but the decision to kill Beau isn't so crystal clear. Beau may have just tried to woo me with his own twisted saga of the supernatural—and he may have attacked Leo—but the truth of the matter is, he told me it's because he wants to *protect* his siblings from his mother. Plus, he really does like me, and I'd be lying if I didn't admit that attraction.

I sidestep Eva and Raylan to get a little closer to Beau. "You can't blame your jealousy on your hunger pangs, Beau. You may be hungry, but we've been hanging out for months." I grab a tiny dagger from my sleeve. "So deal!"

Raylan smiles at me like I've never said anything that made more sense, when I add, "Despite that," I lower my voice. "You okay?" I reach out to touch Beau's well-formed shoulder.

"And I thought— " Raylan stops mid-sentence. "You are unbelievable!"

I feel my own eyes widen at Raylan's hard line in the sand. "He doesn't stand a chance against Leo."

Eva glances up from her phone, which she's apparently

swapped for her gun. She's texting like a madwoman. "Mags confirms it. No whore-ghoul stands a chance against a Blurred One."

Raylan glares at me, and for the first time, I can see the cool and detached resemblance to his sister. How they both know when it's time to turn off the compassion and just hunt. But that isn't me. Call me weak, or divided, but I don't know if I have a switch at all.

Eva scampers around the couch, the little blanket wrapped skiwampus around her. And I still can't believe the two of them were in their underwear.

"Raylan," she says. "It's all right."

A muscle feathers along his jaw. "So you're going to order me around."

Hurt, sharp and raw, flicks across Eva's gaze. "Who are you right now?"

Raylan throws his hands in the air. "I'M NOT THE BAD GUY HERE!"

A random cuckoo clock goes off. Leo spins away and leans his head against the wall. Even Beau has the decency to stop squirming on those antlers.

Eva's voice has never sounded so detached. "I never said you were."

For the first time in a great, long while, everyone Eva and I care deeply about is squeezed into this tiny hut. Except Maggie and Mom. The ideal scenario would be that we would all get along. We'd be discussing how to convince Tess to let Leo alone, and we'd go back to Bloodcreek. Roast s'mores at Maggie's and burn hobo dinners.

What Raylan needs to see is that things aren't nearly as "black and white" as Tess is making him believe. Beau's a whore-ghoul, but that doesn't mean he doesn't have any semblance of good in him. Leo's a Blurred One, but he's one of the most incredible beings we know.

"Do you really believe Beau deserves to die?" I turn to face Raylan.

But the muscle still pulses along his jaw, and I'm reminded all over again of why he listens to Slipknot and other metal. He has so much pent-up anger.

When he doesn't even hint at an answer, I say, voice even smaller, "What about Leo? Would you really kill him, too?"

Raylan's face becomes stone. "All I'm saying is, maybe Tess has a point. What's the Whore of Babylon, anyway? Because besides Leo, all the creatures I've seen will turn on you eventually. A snake is a snake. It *will* strike."

His gaze falters from Eva's terrified eyes over to Leo. A look of indecision falls over Raylan—like he's remembering what Leo showed me. How he was the Blurred One who took out his folks.

CHAPTER 35 - EVA

I suppose we've got ourselves a temporary ceasefire, but it's about as friendly as the Cold War in here. There could be nukes any second. I ordered us all some pizza to at least keep us from getting hangry and negotiated dinner time by tying up Beau in the back bedroom.

I want to live in the moment and savor this deliciously stringy cheese, but the way Raylan is glowering at everybody is a real appetite killer. I'm pretty sure if he keeps up his anger, he's gonna form a black hole right here and now, right under the table we're eating at. Goodbye, little crocheted doilies!

So we're at an impasse. Raylan cracks his knuckles, Leo looks like he just ran over the neighbor's cat, and Frost, like she ran over ten. Time to break the silence and get some truth bombs out of the way.

"So you kissed your hillbilly boyfriend," I say to Frost, wadding up my napkin and chucking it at the trash can. I miss. "Leo wasn't coming back. You had to move on." Raylan's laser gaze slides to me like this is a jab at him somehow. *Ugh, so sensitive.*

I glance at Frost to commiserate, but her face is as red as the pepperoni I just ate. Leo's hand freezes midway to his mouth before setting his pizza back on his napkin.

Oh, my goodness, she didn't tell them? Can I make anyone else's day horrible? Kill me, Frost. Do it now.

"What is a Whore of Babylon?" Raylan deadpans, and I'm so grateful for the change of subject, he is immediately forgiven for all rude behavior.

Frost throws her hands up in a "beats me" gesture, but she won't make eye contact with any of us. Girl's a terrible liar. I pop an eyebrow at her. That's all it takes before she's spilling.

"He didn't have time to tell me much."

But her jaw's clenched almost as much as Raylan's.

"Time before what?" I prod.

She doesn't answer, just closes off. "Maybe we should talk outside?" I glance at Leo and Raylan to see how offended they'd be if we talked in private for a bit, but Raylan leans back in his chair with such attitude, I've got half a mind to tell him to fix his face, like Mom would say.

He's deadly quiet when he says, "There wasn't time because he was in a hurry to kill Leo."

Frost gives a tiny sigh of resignation. "And eat."

"Seriously?" I yelp, and Raylan is half out of his chair already.

"No!" Frost cries. "He didn't really want to, it's just been a crazy few days and—"

"And so he thought he'd take a load off by eating someone?" Raylan pounds the table with his fist. The pizza jumps an inch. Frost looks like she's about to lose it. She is the nicest person since Emily Post, but back her into a corner and prepare for the ax to fall.

"And what, Frost?" I ask.

She sets her barely-nibbled pizza next to the crumpled-up napkins she's used to soak up the extra cheese grease.

"And, he's not the threat," she says, looking straight up at Raylan.

Raylan glares back. "I'm dealing with Tess," he says, tapping his thumb on the table. "She'll come around. Beau tried to kill Leo. How long till he gets hungry and turns to one of us for a snack?"

Frost straightens into that perfect posture she gets when she's feeling extra stubborn. "He wouldn't have been able to kill Leo. No one can, now that Zombi's dead."

"Raylan," Leo's smooth voice cuts the tension in the room to a more bearable amount. "Tess tried to kill Frost."

"SHE DID NOT!" Raylan shouts. He balls up his fists, clenching, trying to calm down. I'm equal parts furious he is acting like this and devastated for him. I want nothing more than to hold him like he held me back at home when we were shooting, but I know he won't have any of it right now.

"Okay, Raylan," Leo soothes. "We'll figure out what to do about Tess later."

I'm terrified, but I raise my hand a little. "Since we're laying it all out on the table, y'all should know that Tess and Maggie got into a huge fight." I can't even look at Raylan, but I can feel his eyes burning me to a crisp.

"What, when?" Frost cries, grabbing her phone like she'll call Maggie right this moment.

"Not totally sure. You know Mags." With a sigh, I put down my pizza. "I called her earlier, and she played it off, but I have a feeling it was pretty bad. Mom was with her."

Frost's thumbs fly across her phone. Probably texting Mags. "So that's why she hasn't been answering my texts."

The worry that's been brewing in my gut just solidified. "Maybe, yeah," I whisper and dare a glimpse at Raylan.

He shakes his head incredulously. "I'm sure it wasn't that bad." He pushes out of his chair so abruptly, it falls over. "I'm going to call Mags and talk to Tess."

I know how big-hearted he is beneath that soldier exterior. How he brought Maggie flowers to show he cared while she was taking care of a sick kitten, and mowed our lawn all summer since he knew how many memories it holds for us.

But I also know he doesn't want to hear anything from me right now. I've been the bearer of too much bad news. So, I look to Leo, his oldest friend. I eye-point to Raylan, silently screaming, "Help him!"

Muffled yelling comes from the back bedroom. Leo stands, his old wooden chair squawking with the movement. "I won't let any of you get hurt."

Raylan huffs quietly, then coolly gathers his things and leaves.

CHAPTER 36 - FROST

Raylan's gone, but Eva, Leo, and I form a semi-circle around Beau. He's still tied up in a chair in the back room, next to a matted rug and cedar chest, packed with a few gallons of salt and holy water.

It's a wonder that he traipsed around my property for so long without me detecting him. I suppose holy water and salt don't affect whore-ghouls?

My leg twinges from the venom. I guess I'd stupidly hoped it would leave my system by now. My head spins, my mouth is perpetually dry, and I could have a hundred and thirteen-degree fever. I wipe my sweaty palms on my pants, praying I can continue to handle myself.

I'm sure Beau would be yapping if it weren't for the fact that he's gagged by a blue dish towel. His arms are tied back by the same rope Knox used once upon a time to tie up Eva. One look at my sister, and I know she remembers.

The chair Beau's sitting on doesn't look all that stable, and I'll bet he could break it if he really wanted to, which makes me think we have a shot at him being reasonable.

"Has Maggie said anything else?" I murmur to Eva.

She doesn't move her eyes from Beau. "Just that whore-ghouls can't take out Leo."

She sighs over-dramatically while folding her arms. "I sure liked things a lot better when we were all on the same team." Her eyes trail to the window where Raylan's truck had been parked only moments before.

"You deserve to eat a beignet," Leo says, catching us all a little off-guard.

Eva's eyes brighten temporarily at the thought as Leo smiles, and I love how the two of them get along so well. Yet another reminder not to mention that Leo took out Raylan's folks.

Beau watches me with that hungry look in his eyes again —no, not hunger. He's looking at me the same way as when Lindy told him he was worthless with a broom.

"Beauregard." Leo takes a medium-sized step forward, creating a loud creak in the floor. "Are you ready to be released to eat the dead alligator?"

Eva makes a gagging noise, and I reach up to hold the vial hanging from the chain round my neck to calm my nerves.

"We want to trust you, Beau," I say, remembering how he used to always help me refill the ketchup bottles in the diner.

"We can't babysit him," Eva says, "if we gotta worry about what Tess has planned."

Beau's beaten-down eyes stare up at us, making him look just about as threatening as a pinecone. "You don' like me," he says around the towel, "'cause Mama stunted my growth."

Eva looks to me, and I don't know why, but I look to Leo. But I won't know anything until I look to Beau.

Taking a teeny-tiny step, I find the same creak in the floor that Leo found. "How?"

Beau speaks pretty adeptly through the towel. "Anytime Mama don't like how we act, she boxes us up." Saliva darkens the dish towel.

Leo, Eva, and I stare down at him—at the cowboy hat that's laced with miniature daggers and the pointy angle of his shoulders, trying to figure out what to do. Did Lindy spell me when I invited this creature-boy into our circle?

But Lindy wants me to stay away from Beau.

Sighing, Leo reaches down and removes the dish towel from Beau's stretched-out mouth.

"You're awfully forgiving, Leo." Eva eyes the way Leo calmly unknots the rope.

"He doesn't pose a threat," Leo says, like he knows.

Beau dramatically stretches out his mouth. "I know, before, I was talkin' with my tongue outta my shoe." He closes his fingers into a resolute fist. "But this time, I promise to keep my laces pulled."

Eva's fingers twitch like she's tempted to re-tie him with that rope. "Please tell me I don't sound this idiotic when I play with my words."

Leo shakes his head in camaraderie with Eva, and I lean into Beau. "I'm sorry your mother is awful, but I need to know I can trust you to not go after Leo."

Beau raises his newly-freed hand to cross his heart.

"One misstep," Eva almost snarls, "and back to the chopping board."

Taking in her surroundings, including the cedar chest with unused holy water and rock salt, my sister suddenly huffs. "What the H is our next move? What if Raylan goes all Brutus because Tess cons him with all her manipulation-hoodoo?"

Beau cracks his neck from side to side in an obnoxious display of being freed from the ropes.

Eva throws her hands into the air. "FROST, CAN I TALK TO YOU?"

While I'm not too keen on leaving Leo and Beau alone,

the panic in my sister's voice has me placing a calming hand on her shoulder and steering her from the room. "Sure."

We're well past time for girl talk, anyhow.

I expect Eva to pull me into the kitchen, but she tugs on my sleeve—all the way past the kitchenette dining table and around the old musty couch and through the front door.

She makes sure the door is firmly closed before she spins to me, her hair flying out as her eyes stretch wide in fear. "What if he never comes back?" She's speaking of Raylan, so I don't say a word. "What if he joins Adolph Tess-ler and her supremacist plans to rule the world?"

As Beau and Leo's voices rumble from the inside of the hut, I ignore the urge to listen to what they're saying through the door. "They're family, Eva." I try to find the right words. "Families always have to deal with issues."

I think of how I stabbed our own dad in the back, and then how I've failed to come clean about Raylan's folks. But then I know I've already said too much, because Eva's eyes are stretching as wide as her holster.

She lowers her voice, sounding an awful lot like Maggie's. "What do you know?"

I glance at the door. It sounds like Leo—or Beau—is raising his voice, and please, don't let them kill each other.

Eva twists the fattest of her three rings on her fingers. "What do you know?"

I run my tongue along the front of my teeth to ground whatever I'm going to say to a thin sliver of truth. This is *not* the conversation I need to be having with her. I absolutely do not want to tell her that Leo's responsible for the death of Raylan's folks. Her fingers don't stop moving. Now she's gone on to tying about thirty knots in her hair.

Reaching out, I grasp her hands to house them inside my own. "He'll *see* Tess' true colors."

Eva's troubled eyes slightly soften at my words, but then

they narrow, because she's always been able to detect my lies —or a veiled truth.

Forcing myself not to panic, I keep my heartbeat as steady and slow as I know how. Because Eva *can't* know this about Leo. If she thought she might be losing Raylan *and* Leo, she would be absolutely devastated, and we need to be on high alert.

I squeeze her hands, which have stopped twitching. "Can we go back inside now?"

Guilt for not coming clean churns through my heart. Even if it's Leo's story, Eva would want to know. It involves her boyfriend, but she already looks down on me for having a soft-spot for Beau.

Slowly, her eyes soften, and she lowers my hands with a nod. "By the way, I am *so* sorry about spilling the beans about you kissing Beau."

Despite my mortification at that truth bomb, my lips stretch into an earnest smile. "It's okay."

Eva heaves a sigh of relief, and I pray she doesn't remember her unanswered questions and try to drill me later.

CHAPTER 37 - EVA

*F*loating along in an old fishing boat, I shake my head and swat a fist-sized dragonfly away from my face. "There has *got* to be an easier way," I say, totally annoyed, but smile a bit at Frost to lessen my tone. Apparently, one four-foot alligator isn't enough to satiate Mr. Man Bun's hunger, so we have to feed him again instead of winning my boyfriend back from his evil sister. "It's like we have a pet zombie."

Here we are, way deeper in the bayou than where I kissed my amazing, maybe ex, maybe not-ex-boyfriend last night. It's way more swampy back here, like where we met Tess. Plants *everywhere*, surely hiding all kinds of terrifying creatures. I hold back a shudder.

Frost seems right at home, though, steering the boat like she's a regal Cajun queen. "Just relax," she says. That's a fine thing coming from her. "Maggie's grabbing Mr. Harris and coming down. They'll help us figure out this mess."

Leo acts like this is the most interesting sentence in the world, with the way he's staring at her, and Beau sniffs the air like a bloodhound.

"And Beau just needs to eat a little more so he'll be totally under control," Frost says, way too naturally.

I gag, only half-pretending. "And you kissed that mouth," I whisper to her. Frost gives me a "hmph," and Leo's eyes droop, because darn these boys and their supernatural hearing. "So," I continue, unable to help myself. "Will the new saying be, 'look what the Beau brought in'?"

Beau stops sniffing just long enough to playfully narrow his eyes at me. "You know I could kill you before you even scream, right?"

"Mmhmm, and you really want Raylan to cut you into itty bitty pieces after you do?" I look at him lazily, like he doesn't scare me in the slightest, but that look could be a little bit lying.

"We should almost be there," Frost hollers over the motor. Distract instead of contend—one of Frost's many peacemaking skills. "Anything yet, Beau?"

He sniffs the air again. "I think there's a gator o'er yonder." He points to a thicket of cattails about fifty feet away. "Don't taste good, but it's alive, and I could use a good wrestle." He winks at Frost, who promptly turns redder than a red delicious apple. She turns the motor down, and we slow, drifting closer to the thicket of trees. Beau motions for her to cut the engine.

The bayou is silent now, except for birds rustling nearby. Beau pulls off his cowboy boots and T-shirt and daaang, all right, he's got abs, but I roll my eyes at Leo for moral support.

Beau slips into the water quietly and wades, almost chest-deep, over to the trees. When he gets about ten feet from the nearest one, he stops and grabs a floating branch. He chucks it at a log near him, only, oh man, that ain't no log, that is a huge alligator. Seven, eight feet long? It lunges at him so fast, I wonder if it's been planning on eating Beau this whole time.

The alligator opens its huge jaws and snaps onto Beau's torso, then plunges under the water, Beau in his grasp. Frost yelps behind me, but I can't look away. After the initial splash, there's not much movement, and I wonder if the gator already killed Beau. Poor Frosty. She grips her dagger, ready to help at any moment. Thankfully, she's smart enough to not jump in.

Leo reaches out a hand and raises it, telekinetically pulling both bodies out of the water. Beau and the gator are both still very much alive, thrashing, tearing, the gator with its teeth and claws, Beau with his teeth and apparently very strong fingers. They hover there until Leo uses enough force to make them freeze.

He speaks like a hostage negotiator. "I will let go in five seconds. Make your move then." Frost maneuvers closer, but there's still not a clear shot. "Five, four, three, two, one."

Leo releases them, and within the next two seconds, Beau snaps the gator's neck with a loud crack. He sinks his teeth into the soft hide underneath, then they hit the water again, making a giant splash that soaks us all. Lovely.

Moments later, Beau stands up, kill in hand. With a wicked grin, teeth covered in sick, brownish blood, he says, "Y'all want some?"

---

*I*t's the kind of dark that makes you see things that aren't there. I close my eyes and open them again, testing the darkness. There's next to no difference. I throw my arm over my head, then turn to my side, careful not to hit Frost's wounds. We're crammed in one of the cabin's full beds, boys out on the couches. Although Raylan's not back yet. That bugs for sure.

Frost is as silent as a rotting jack-o-lantern. I can never tell if she's sleeping or not. I'm not quite ready to shut my mind up enough to zonk out. I'll be surprised if Frost sleeps at all, knowing her two boy toys are in the next room.

"Frost?" I whisper so quietly, I'm not even sure I said it out loud.

"Mm."

There are about a million and a half things I want to ask her, so it takes me a second to decide on a question.

"What are you gonna do about Beau and Leo?"

She's silent, but I know she's just thinking. I try to see my hand in the dark while waiting. No luck. Just kind of a presence only the sixth sense could pick up. No street lamps exist around here. There's no nightlights, no moon. Not even a digital clock to create a glow.

"Leo still needs to be born," she finally says. "If there really is a way." Her tone is clipped but level. We're not getting anymore into that right now.

"And Beau?" Another long pause. So long, I think she may have fallen asleep on me. "Frost." I prod her leg with my toe, 'cause now that the question's out, I've got to get an answer. Besides, who knows when we'll get a chance to actually talk next? Especially with three boys, an evil sister, witch doctors, Blurred Ones, *Whores of Babylon?*

She flips on her side to face me. "He asked me to marry him."

"Shut. The. Front-freaking-door. Are you kidding me right now?" I'm dizzy all of a sudden, and I'm still lying down.

She sighs like she's just lost about fifty pounds of tension. This must be what she was holding back earlier. "I know he really likes me. Maybe even loves me. But there's more to it than that."

"How romantic. Like what? And holy smokes." My mind is suddenly begging for a visual. "How and when did he propose?"

She actually giggles a little bit.

"Wait a second, you're actually thinking about it?" I bolt straight up and grab my phone to illuminate us a little bit.

"No, not at all," she says, like I'm being ridiculous. "It has more to do with getting away from his mom. She sort of loathes me on account of me being some sort of supernatural barrier."

"Say what now?"

"I don't really know why, but when his mom tried to eat me—"

"EAT YOU? Who is not a homicidal cannibal these days?"

"Well, she tried to eat my soul." She flops over so she's facing me in the little bed. "She wiped my brain, but after a little jogging and Beau's help, it's coming back. I don't know how to explain it, Eva, but I think I've always known I could do this."

I want to laugh at her, at the ridiculousness of the suggestion. This entire situation. But there's no humor in her voice. Silent is the most respectful I can be.

"When the Despairity came after me," she says, "I don't know why, but I've always been able to block them out somewhat. Or I was learning to. I can't explain it."

"Dude . . ." I think of that day of being snared with Knox in the devil's trap, the Despairity trying to feed on Frost for so long. She should have been toast.

My phone flashes for a second, and my heart skips, hoping it's a text from Raylan, or at least Maggie. Nope, just a spam email. Frost's foot brushes against my leg, so I try to scoot over as much as possible. My phone lights up the floor for a half-second. I glimpse several long, thin, sliding shadows on the wood before the phone dims again.

My blood changes from a nice lazy river to freaking polar plunge arctic cold, my finger lingering on the home button.

I'm totally just seeing things, but my skin crawls like the shadows. My heart has no need to freak out, make me want to scream and run for the hills. To prove it, I press the button and aim the screen toward the wooden floor.

Nope. Not seeing things.

CHAPTER 38 - FROST

*I*t's like someone's set a fully-heated iron on my leg. Zombi's venom seems to rejoice in the pain—likes the intrusion—but I can feel my own body and blood fighting it.

I press my hands to my head, because something like mythological sirens are shrieking in my ears. Eva and I knock elbows, so she must be doing the same.

Something long and skinny drops like a bowl of spaghetti from the ceiling with an audible *thump* as it hits my thighs.

I think maybe it won't be bad—that I can shove off whatever dropped—when the all-too-recognizable feeling of an arm-sized snake slithers up my stomach.

Cool, rigid scales creep along my belly. A tongue flicks into my belly button. As I push down my shirt, I half-wonder if Zombi's been resurrected and come back to life.

But this snake—it's sleeker and smaller, and I whimper as Eva laughs that freaked-out laugh she only does when she knows we're screwed.

Another snake slithers from the direction of her head and

up the side of my forehead. Its tongue flicks in and out of my ears like used dental floss.

My mouth, my lips are frozen solid.

Scales and coldness slip over the thin T-shirt covering my chest. On either side of me, two snakes snatch at my wrists. They constrict and squeeze, as if by wrapping around my wrists, they'll strangle me to death.

One of them digs for my watch. It tugs and pulls, chafing my skin. It needles its skinny body between my flesh and the metal clasp.

When the watch doesn't budge fast enough, slippery scales glide against my mouth. A wet-tongued tip knocks against my lips. It begs to crawl inside, smelling vaguely of seaweed.

I don't know what to do, how to get them off. For some strange reason, Dom's low chanting ricochets inside my head. Maybe this isn't real? But I thought Dom was a friend.

More snakes wrap and tug around my arms. They pull—yank—me further into the lumpy comforter.

And the screaming sirens aren't just in my head. Wails are coming from the snakes themselves, as if they're fighting to tie me to a gurney now.

But I have to know Eva's okay.

More *tap-tap-taps* pry open my lips.

I want to scream to Eva that they're not actually real, but what if they are? What if I'm mistaken?

I squeeze my lips firmly shut, wondering about the fact that Beau said I was a barrier of sorts. Maybe I can *think* them away? Use my mind to force them off?

Eva's frantic fingers grapple for my own, feeling fierce and brittle. We lock hands, and I squeeze her fingers together so hard, she'll *know* we won't be defeated by this.

We won't die by snakes. I hope she gets the gist.

I'll raise my Glock, you raise your dagger. I swear, it's like I can hear her say this.

I think of my boot—down at the side of the bed—and Eva's gun on the nearby end table, knowing it's our only shot. I squeeze my eyes closed tighter, because the snakes begin to glow an alabaster white in the darkness.

"One," I speak through a millimeter of my parted mouth. "Two..."

A blinding flash of yellow light splashes me in the eyes.

Fresh humidity washes over my face, and my stomach's suddenly empty where the snakes used to be.

A gingham blanket's wadded up by our bare feet, and Eva and I are still holding hands like we're a pair of wounded mermaids drowning in the Lake of the Ozarks.

The muscles in my neck strain and my eyes blink to adjust to the light. An imposing figure lurks in the doorway. My mind automatically attributes it to a Blurred One that's been beckoned to join Dom's side when the disheveled hair and military-like aura reminds me of Raylan.

Raylan surveys Eva's and my hands, which are still wrenched together—and he glances around the room, all too aware that something's gone awry.

Eva's eyes shine with *panic—fear—joy*.

She must be thrilled to see him but doesn't know what to do with his sudden arrival in the middle of the night.

On top of that, Raylan's as unreadable as ever with that blank mask over his face, and I want Eva to tell him that Dom was somehow cursing us. But she settles her arms over her chest and rolls over like all Raylan did was find us sleeping, passed out.

An awkward beat passes before Raylan mumbles, "Sorry." He scratches the back of his head with one hand and lowers a pistol I hadn't noticed with the other. "Just got back and . . . thought I heard something."

I glance once more at my sister, wishing she would say

something, when she turns her head to look full-on at Raylan, seemingly trying to read his mind.

He doesn't say a word, though, and it's like she's waiting for him declare that he never should have left in the first place. When he doesn't, she grabs her pillow and hurls herself over to the other side of the bed.

Raylan looks so devastated that I reach for my boots on the bed's side so we can chat.

---

*R*aylan hunches against the side of his truck like the lost little boy I saw in Leo's vision. I want to tell him that I know—that I saw what happened—but how do I bring up the fact that the person I love actually killed his parents?

I watch a hand-sized tortoise wander off toward the woods, highlighted by a halfway fallen over light. "Dom used some sort of witch doctor hoodoo to haunt Eva and me."

Raylan grunts, probably thinking what I'm thinking.

If Dom can go after us without even being in the same room, we really need to get to the bottom of what's going on. Are Dom and Tess working together? But I know I need to tread lightly with Raylan. "Things didn't go well with Tess?"

Tears prick his almost-marble eyes, and I've never seen Raylan Wilks emotional, so I glance to the hut. For Eva. If she saw him like this, there's no way she'd be icing him out. Of course, he iced her out first, though.

His spine bows as he runs his hand over his face and says, "She doesn't get it."

I could ask him what made her get into the "let's be the most prestigious hunters" mindset, but I'm not entirely sure I want to know. Even though it's years later, Tess is probably still bouncing back from losing her parents. She left home when she was young. Hunting became the way to fend for herself.

"I went over there," he says, "to give her our parents' gun. Tell her I'm sick and tired of thinking of my friends as monsters. She blew up." His voice cracks. "She said, 'the only way to be the best hunter is to take them all down.'"

He pounds the side of the wheel with his fist. "I don't care about being the best hunter. Since when did getting that vanity trophy matter?"

I think of the calculated look in Tess' eyes right after she pulled the trigger and shot me in the leg. How she obviously wanted me gone, but she checked herself. Checked herself because of Raylan.

I feel my lips twitch into a smile. "She's quite the peaceable one."

Raylan shoves away from his truck so hard that gravel shoots toward where that tortoise took off. "What I don't get is *how* she can be so narcissistic. How can she make this about her when people are dying because of the bad Blurred Ones? It's like she doesn't actually care about helping people. Just about killing things and making money while doing it."

We're on thin ice, so I tread as delicately as I can. "I'm glad you don't hate Leo."

A lifetime of memories flashes in his eyes, and he looks so tired, so worn. "Never did." A muscle feathers along his jaw. Can he really just be a little older than me? Sometimes it feels like he's a decade older because of his time on the road and experience.

"Leo told me what happened. With your paren—"

Raylan holds up a firm hand. "That's in the past. What you have to understand is that loyalty runs deep with my sister. Leo was the cause of their deaths, but the truth is, we turned out a whole lot better than we would have otherwise because of him."

I imagine Raylan following in his father's footsteps, beating his wife. Or, when life got tough, turning to drugs like his mom. "But Tess might have turned out better if she didn't feel like she needed to provide for you and herself."

"She would have provided for us either way. What matters now is the fact that she feels justified in killing my friend."

A fissure of guilt twists through my stomach regarding my latest string of secrets. "Do you think we should tell Eva what he did?"

Raylan shakes his head. "Her friendship with Leo is one of the few good things she has."

"At least Maggie's on her way."

Raylan's relief is as palpable as a breath of fresh air when his shoulders relax.

As I watch a blue dragonfly zoom past, I think it's funny how I'm the one in love with Leo, and yet my sister has to be the one protected from what he did. Raylan says Tess has a thing with loyalty, but Eva's the same way. The two are more similar than I'd originally imagined. And yet, Tess shows us how loyalty can be twisted into something rotten, evil, and wrong.

Across the bayou, Leo and Beau saunter out of the front door of the hut. Leo tosses a football toward Beau, and I think I may need to get my eyes checked.

"Those two are getting along," Raylan says.

Maybe neither one of them needs much sleep, and this is Leo's solution for not up and murdering my summertime fling that wasn't ever supposed to happen. He doesn't feel justified in killing Beau, so "keep your enemies closer"?

I think Raylan may want to take a shot at our newfound whore-ghoul, but he surprises me by not so much as glancing at his gun. "You're in quite the predicament." He folds his muscly arms.

Leo lobs the football so hard, Beau flies back several feet

when he catches it. Beau gripes something about Leo being lower than a snake's belly in a wagon rut before launching the football like a missile back at him.

I shift my gaze away from the boys, because I can't deal with what has to happen next. "Leo's going to be born." And I remind myself of Beau's brothers and sisters, desperately needing freedom from their mom. "Soon Leo will be *poof!* Gone." I don't say what that implies—that I see myself in a relationship with Beau, because I absolutely do not. But how can I send Leo away when I'm all he has?

"I can't believe you dated the spawn of the Whore of Babylon."

I shove Raylan's muscular arm. "Not everyone can fall in love with a human."

I don't realize Raylan's smiling until it's gone. He angles his body away from me and pulls open the tailgate of his truck. "I need to get my sister to simmer down." He climbs into the truck bed and shoves open the lockbox.

"Eva really wanted to get along."

Raylan laughs a little. "No way that's going to happen." He rifles through the layers of ammo. "Not when Tess realizes Eva threatens to steal her 'Queen Bee' status.'"

"What?"

"I never told you?" Raylan smiles his darkest, most ironic smile. "Eva's a far better shot than Tess."

I have no idea how Eva would react if she realized she was a threat to Miss I'm-the-Best-Hunter-In-All-the-Land. Throw a party? Or temporarily be a worse shot, all to smooth things over with Tess?

"The two of you make quite the team." I have to show that I still approve of their relationship.

Raylan grabs a pistol, Leo's revolver, and some screws before shoving them into his front pocket. "We better get ready. My sister's on the warpath."

CHAPTER 39 - EVA

"Oh-my-gof-I-needed-thish," I moan, mouth stuffed to capacity with beignet. Leo licks some residual powdered sugar off his fingers with a smile. I'm relieved to see his fingers seem to have recovered from his time with Tess.

"It certainly helps lighten a situation," he says, expertly steering Raylan's truck without getting sugar or slobber on the steering wheel. I had him drive so I could eat faster, since it'll only take a few minutes to get back to the cabin from the little bakery. I don't really want to stress-eat in front of Raylan right now. I didn't sleep too well after being mauled by imaginary snakes, so I stole Leo away from his masculinity match with Beau for some friendship catch-up and to grab the breakfast of champions for everybody.

"I mean, seriously," I say after I finally swallow. "Who knew hunting would involve so much drama?" Leo's face falls a little but smiles again when I hand him another delicious beignet. "Shiz has definitely gotten weird. I mean, why's your buddy Dom taken to terrorizing us at night?" I catch the laughter shake Leo's shoulders, and it's a reminder of how much I adore him. How much we've all missed his good-natured badassery. "And you are so much better than Beau."

He doesn't say anything back and gracefully takes a bite.

"Leo, I didn't even know it was possible to be sophisticated while eating these fluffs of sugar."

He chuckles softly, and it's such a pleasant sound, I wish we could just drive around a little longer. The swampy landscape fascinates me, like the water is constantly trying to fight back against the land and take it over. It's everywhere. Makes Missouri seem so tame.

"Mags texted," I say as we drive over yet another bridge. "She and Mr. Harris should be here late tonight. Good ol' Mr. Harris. Who knew he was a stone-cold warlock? They'll both be happy to see you."

Leo shifts in his seat. "They'll help keep you safe." His phone rings over the truck's sound system. The lit screen says "Dominick" is calling. He meets my eyes grimly before answering.

"Dominick," Leo says, all pleasantry gone from his face.

"Da girl ok now," Dominick says. It sounds more like a statement than a question. His voice over the speaker is so gravelly, I imagine his throat wrapped in barbed wire. Like the man needs a handful of throat drops.

"Yes, Frost's wound is getting much better, thanks to you, my friend," Leo replies, his tone measured, "though none of us are fans of the snake spell you cast last night."

"I did that to furtha clean da wound," Dominick rasps.

Leo's lips twitch. "Mmm hmm."

"You bring her to me," Dom says, "and I finish my work."

I shoot Leo a *heck no* look.

Leo's brow furrows just a tiny bit. "I believe she has recovered—"

"You bring her, or pain will return. Worse," he adds. We're pulling up to the cabin again, my body instantly becoming alert at the sight of it, knowing Raylan is inside. I honestly have no idea where we stand right now, and my sugar buzz has now left the building.

"OK, we'll come as soon as we can," Leo says as he parks next to Beau's truck.

"You come tonight." Dominick's voice lowers and becomes impossibly raspier. "I'll need da moon."

I pull down the vanity mirror to make sure I get all the powdered sugar off my face and shirt. And pants.

"Very well," Leo says as he smiles faintly at my futile brushing. "Thank you again for all your assistance." He presses the screen to end the call, and his hand hovers there for several seconds.

"Why'd you agree to go? He's totally evil."

"I'm not sure about taking Frost, but I want to see why he's turned against us." He opens his door, so I grab the goods and follow him out of the truck.

"He says like it's a walk in a park," I tease.

"Hoodoo can be dark and unpredictable, but perhaps he can be reasoned with. Or maybe he knows how to reason with Tess."

I cock an eyebrow.

"I'm trying a new, more proactive approach. But yes, we should be careful. Let's talk inside with the others." We've reached the door, and his face reflects the same mixture of emotions I feel. He pauses, one foot on the porch step. "Keep doing what you believe is right, Eva. You and Frost will both do incredible things."

I jab him in the side with my elbow. "I've missed your pep talks. And such a positive outlook for a guy who was just tortured. For a dude so supposedly evil, you're amazingly awesome."

"You, Frost, and Raylan have cleaner souls than I could achieve in a thousand lifetimes."

His reference to Raylan and my goodness makes my heart sink in forty different ways. "He is amazing." I can't even voice the other words. *Too good for me.*

Leo twists so he's fully facing me and puts his hands on my arms, which are full of food. "When will you believe me?" he asks softly. I feel so much love radiating from him, I wonder if this is what it's like to have an awesome big brother. "Have patience. You and Raylan are like two melodies that are still finding their rhythm, and when you do, you will be harmonious."

I can hardly stand to hope, and I'm pretty disturbed at how Raylan has managed to turn me so stupidly infatuated since the moment I met him. But if Leo's right, I'm not doing anyone any favors by being a whiny wuss about it.

CHAPTER 40 - FROST

Feeling the weight of the throwing knife in my hand, I lightly grip the back of the handle with two fingers, just the way Beau taught me to.

Like I'm holding a hammer, I'm about to strike the wall. Only the wall's about fifteen paces off. And, since he cursed us with snakes, it's meant for Dom.

I cock my arm and release the metal handle, causing the blade to whistle through the woods.

Tip embeds.

My aim's a little to the left of the heart of the cypress. It's not my best throw, but I've been throwing a little over an hour, so my arm's obviously tired.

"That'd scare a buzzard off a gut pile," Beau says as he rests casually in the hammock. "Course, you moved your wrist a little to the left."

I glance down at my wrist. *Did I?* Zombi's venom feels a little like ghost peppers surging through my system. Though I'm pretty sure I threw the knife exactly the way Beau taught.

Like I'm coming down from a caffeine high, I shakily grab another dagger from my boot. "I always keep it straight," I say, centering myself by staring at a mushroom. I *won't* swoon a little to the right.

Beau's newly put-on spurs jangle as he saunters over a purple-fringed plant. *Sometimes*, he says about the spurs, *they put me in the hunter mindset*.

"How long have you been a cowboy anyway?" I ask as he plants himself so close that I can smell the aftershave wafting off him.

"Been a real long while," he drawls.

"But nothing like 'I was born in the eighteen hundreds' kind of old." I'm fishing for an answer.

"Why would I dash one of the only remaining sex appeals I got?"

I must be making a funny face, because he all-out laughs. His teeth are maddeningly straight, and his saunter after filling up on alligator meat is alarmingly nice.

Maybe he detects my latest disdain, because he says, "I think I'll keep bein' mysterious for a while."

Curling his hand over mine, he shows me for the twentieth time how to throw the knife. Straight on, no movement at all to the left or right. It's an action he's shown me a thousand times. An action, too, that I wouldn't have to be practicing if Tess hadn't waltzed into our lives.

Sensing my souring mood, Beau drawls, "It's almost like you're apologin' for throwin' it."

What he doesn't know is, maybe I am. Maybe all this throwing and planning is too stark a reminder of what I did to Dad.

But that was months ago, and we have new enemies at hand.

The truth of the matter is, Dom or Tess *could* get Eva. Even now. They could get Leo. And Lindy . . . Too many variables for me to sleep at night.

The image of the foreclosure flashes through my mind,

and my fingers tighten around the back end of the metal handle of the knife, eager to send it off.

But Beau lightly nudges his thumb on mine. "Keep your thumb pointed forward at all times."

I nudge away his arm just as Eva's dark hair and Leo's sophisticated gait appear in tandem around the hammock.

My eyes flit to Leo's, but his face is an unreadable mask. Like he's angry. Is he really concerned about these advances from Beau? He has to know that, next to him, Beau's like a second-hand eighties dress.

"Hunter meeting!" Eva calls.

Raylan emerges from the woods, where he's been doing target practice himself. He holsters his .45 as he and Eva pretend seeing each other doesn't affect either one of them at all.

Eva plants a sassy hand on her hip. "Dom thinks he can just demand to see Frost."

Leo silently stares at the vial on the necklace sitting at the base of my neck.

"After haunting you in the middle of the night?" Raylan's brow crinkles.

Eva's voice brightens. "Right?"

Leo's voice, though, cuts a little too eerily through the cypress tree-filled wood. "Shouldn't we be worried about *another* foe descending upon us?" He's still glaring at the chain clasped around my neck. Beau must have told him it's to keep Lindy away. So does Leo not believe him now?

Beau turns his back, purposely biding his time as he saunters off to retrieve my knife. "I know how to keep Froster safe."

Leo's jaw flexes. "When you're not hunting crocodilian to keep your hunger at bay, adolescent."

Eva's eyes widen at Leo's tone, and Beau giggles as he pulls my dagger from the trunk. "Froster'll be just fine. Just as long as she keeps on that necklace."

Recovering herself, Eva waves her hands like she's waving down a speeding car. "Uh, hello? Are you ready to hear my plan, or what?"

Leo's demeanor visibly melts as he digests what my sister's trying to tell us. Settling his ageless eyes on her, he asks with a cheerful glint in his eye, "Like the time you claimed 'breakfast' was Diet Coke poured over Beaver Nuggets?" He actually winks, and I full-on laugh.

Raylan cough-coughs, covering his mouth.

Rolling her eyes, Eva says, "More like the time I tied up Knox with that chain and choked him to death."

"*Nearly* choked him to death," I have to say, slipping my knife inside my bootstrap.

"Not helping!" Eva lifts her hands with a cry.

Seeing the laughter in my sister's eyes, though, gives me what I need to settle everyone down. We can do this. We can work together to keep back whatever Tess is planning. And Dom.

"Maggie's on her way," I say, "but that doesn't mean we have to wait for her to set things up."

Raylan nods. Sheer appreciation shines in my sister's eyes, and Beau slaps the wicked bowie knife on his leg.

"I been *waitin'* for you to say it's time to tan some hides!"

I don't know what's worse—that Leo hasn't said a word the entire drive over, or that I'm actually glad we haven't talked. Because, where Leo's concerned, I don't know how to act.

I've loved him for so long, almost building him up to be a god in my head. But both of us know he's far from that.

Waves lap at the shore as we speed away from the cabin. Seagulls flap their wings, and with Leo's longish hair flapping in the breeze, to any stranger, we might look like an ordinary couple going out. I'm grateful to Raylan for letting us borrow his truck. I doubt Tess would let anyone touch any of her things as easy as that.

I watch through my open window, wishing we were going out for nothing but frozen yogurt. We'd go to the movies, and we'd talk about what class we'll be taking next.

"You think I should have gone to college," I say as we roll past an abandoned flea market. Angel statues remind me of the above-ground cemetery where Dom insisted on meeting us.

Leo's gentle hands loosen around the steering wheel as he pauses in thought. "I—" his jawline flickers as he tries to find the best response "—think you should become the person I know you are."

"Maybe I'm happy." The inner regions of my chest cavity, though, feel as empty and languishing as an ancient crypt.

Leo clicks the turn signal, preparing to turn left. An abandoned gas station waits for us at this intersection, and my heart beats in time with the turning signal.

Why won't he talk?

I take in the vanished cuts along his newly shaved jaw. The humble confidence he naturally exudes without even knowing it. I hate that he was locked up for so long and tortured by Tess. She took his innocent hope to be a better person, and she twisted it into a tool for her devices.

It makes me wonder how many Blurred Ones she'd planned on luring with his help.

We drive past a throng of egrets lurking like upside-down umbrellas in the wetlands of the marsh. Some of them flap their wings, and I think how freeing it must be, to go wherever they want.

Leo's voice is low. "I thought we had a deal."

"Well, now I have a mortgage."

Pain flickers in his eyes, and I know it's not pain he's feeling for himself, but the pain he's feeling on my behalf. He sees how, all too prematurely, I've been stripped of my childhood.

Leo looks to the farthest left corner of the windshield, like he doesn't dare look me in the eye. He murmurs, "You are supposed to better yourself."

I know he's trying to be a pushing, positive influence, but that's never going to work, because he's always going to leave, and I need to live my life.

"You're not supposed to *be* here," I whisper.

Swallowing, he reaches over to take my hand, fresh tears pooling in his eyes.

CHAPTER 41 - EVA

*B*eau yanks the wheel of his old beat-up Chevy so hard, I fall onto Raylan as he slams into the door. I grit my teeth against throwing an insult at Beau's crazy driving as I try to straighten up. Not all of us have super-human reflexes to keep us balanced, and we wouldn't have to rush to be Leo and Frost's backup for their meeting with Dom if Beau didn't have the bladder of a pregnant lady. Raylan must be deep in thought again, because he doesn't grumble, even though his head hit the window probably hard enough for it to shatter.

"Think Leo'll be takin' off after this hootenanny?" Beau asks, weaving between a dump truck and an old minivan. "Ya know, continue his quest for the betterment of his soul?"

"I don't know," Raylan and I mumble in unison.

"I'd treat her good, ya know."

I fake-stifle a laugh. "Yeah, until she actually falls for you, then you'd be back to chasing the next girl who didn't immediately fall for your pretty smile."

Beau exaggerates a gasp and covers his mouth. "You think I have a pretty smile, Eva-lou?"

He's so outrageous I have to chuckle despite the tension. "You're such a player. And now that I think about it, probably a really old one." I brace myself on the seat as we fly around another pot-holed curve, then check my phone's GPS. Still another eight miles.

"Leo's old," Beau retorts.

"But Leo's awesome." I wink. Then I add more seriously, "But yes, both choices are less than ideal."

Beau purses his lips but nods. I feel a twinge of empathy for him, sitting next to Señor Statue over here.

"Well, all right. You'ns think Dom and Tess are in cahoots?" Beau asks, and I'm relieved, since I've wanted to ask the exact same thing. I was right to hold back—Raylan's face could fry Beau's clean off, but a breath later, he softens a little.

"Maybe," he admits, barely audible over the truck's roar.

Two points to Beau, as he just nods curtly.

"I'm sure it'll be fine," I try to soothe. "We're just coming in behind as a precaution. Throw Dom a little more off his rocker if he tries something fancy."

I put one tentative hand on Raylan's arm, ready to pull back at the slightest flinch, like I'm attempting to pet one of Beau's gators. But he doesn't pull back. He freezes still as an ice sculpture, and my heart sinks a little more. Right. Not wussing or whining, just refocusing on a battle strategy.

"You got any tranq bullets handy?" I ask the air in the truck. *"Just in case,"* I drawl.

I feel Raylan's eyes flit to mine. "Yes." A verbal warning shot.

Beau slams on his brakes at a stoplight that's too red to ignore. "I gotta machete in the back, and a killer bite," he adds.

I think I manage to hide my grimace.

"You two just focus on Dominick," Raylan orders. He's

our natural leader when it comes to hunting, so we don't argue. "I'll talk to Tess. *If* she's there."

I don't think talking's gonna cut it, but I ain't gonna step on his hopes. Four miles to go. I check the clip in my 9mm one more time and twitch my foot to feel the dagger in my boot is still secure.

"It's going to be okay," I tell all of us and shoot a desperate prayer upstairs to help make it true.

CHAPTER 42 - FROST

*L*eo turns off the ignition as we pull up to the cemetery. An overpass brings cars shooting past us from the sky, and neither Leo nor I say a word, because neither one of us is ready to get out.

An old semi rumbles past, and I think how simple it would be to wave down the driver and ask him to pick us up and drive us somewhere out of Tess' network of hunters. Somewhere out of the country.

Despite this, I know I'm safe with Leo, even if we have to stay in New Orleans, but that doesn't mean I'm ready to go out into the big bad world. I want to hit pause and stay here in Raylan's truck, munching on the sweet corn puff Beaver Nuggets abandoned on the back seat.

As the wind whips through the Spanish moss on a nearby oak tree, massive cement tombs warn us this is not your typical place. Thousands of dead corpses loom inside walls, not planted below our feet. It makes me wonder if there will be ghosts when we go in, how much rock salt I should pack.

The distance between us on Raylan's bench seat shrinks as Leo soundlessly scoots closer.

Venom courses through the weakening flesh of my hamstring, and when Leo presses his thigh into mine, I think my very skin will ignite.

He is here, and I am here, and I cannot kiss him.

I'll kiss him. He's my very air; my other half.

My heart twitters and swirls. A dizzy canary in a birdcage. My palms ring with sweat, and I can feel my head pounding with every heartbeat. What if I'm deluded? What if he no longer likes me like that?

What if, for whatever reason, after seeing me with Beau, he changed his mind?

Leo's age-old, depthless eyes scan my face like he's memorizing every single freckle and scar. The simple and ordinary shape of my nose and chin.

His breath hitches so quietly, I almost don't detect that it's happening. "You are so beautiful," he says. Like it causes him pain.

Outside my window, the wind rustles the oak's hundreds of miniature leaves. I spot a crow taking perch near the top, which should warn me that something terrible's about to happen, but I'm not ready to miss or skip past our time together.

The simple truth of the matter is, I could live a century as a hideous hag, locked in a corner, if it meant I could once again hear that phrase.

"You are so beautiful," he says, reading my mind.

I squeeze my eyes shut, memorizing the earnest yet sturdy sound of his voice.

I open my eyes. He's not sure of what he's about to say. Smiling uncertainly, he says, "Kiss me, Frost."

He reaches up to cup the side of my face. And when I lean into his vessel's smooth fingers, the wrist that has moved many times to protect me, I love him so much that my chest swells with panic.

"I love you," I say. I don't throw around those words care-lessly. I am a girl, and he is a Blurred One. From clichés, we are exempt.

Anxiety and love swirl like a time-bomb in his eyes. They say time is slipping by much too fast. We're here to meet Dom, but he leans in anyway.

I have known him so long, I have memorized this face, so when his lips close over mine, and my eyes flutter shut, I can feel the earnestness spelled across his cheeks.

He is my moment.

I reach out to slip my hand between his back and the seat and grip the back of his suspenders, because it won't be long until Zombi's venom has me floating out of my mind.

He finds a hole in the knee of my pants and slips a hungry finger inside. His skin isn't even his, and he's turning me into a barren wasteland of sweat.

"I love you." He breathes into my ear, sending railroads of pleasure tracking down the side of my face.

"I love you." I kiss the smooth whiskers sprouting from his jaw.

We should stop; we shouldn't keep on kissing, but, for all I know, this could be our last moment together, so I lift the lever to recline his seat.

We rock back, and Leo clicks off his seatbelt. My head flips sideways at the sound of the belt retracting into the plastic device, so I curl closer into his chest, remembering how, when we were kids, he let me win checkers every single time.

"Leo," I breathe. The angle of the seat makes me feel suspended in time. I nudge his lips with my lips. "We'll *find* a way for you to stay."

He presses his lips to mine harder, because there isn't time. He wraps his hands around my hips, his fingers as warm as the oven mitts he used when we baked when I was young.

His voice comes out short and far too strangled. "You are my life."

I wish he didn't say it, because it helps me see his pain. How is it that he made the decision to be born at all if it hurts him this way?

"We'll find a better solution." I pull down one side of his suspenders. I have to fight the urge to peel off more.

Something loudly buzzes behind me.

When I turn, I find his phone, loudly rattling between the console and a plastic orange and red CD case.

When I catch Leo's eye, the look on his face is so forlorn that I can't help laughing.

I brush my hand along his arm, which flares with heat. "It's okay."

Leo shoots me a look that says he'd rather do anything than answer the phone, but he slowly reaches down and accepts the call. *Raylan* flashes on the screen.

Our hunter-friend's no-nonsense voice carries easily from the miniature speaker. "We're about fifteen minutes away."

The Metairie Cemetery sign groans on the iron fence like things are about to go awry, but I am with Leo. We should be all right.

"Wait," Raylan says, "until we arrive."

Leo kisses my hand so hard, my bones give way. He kisses my earlobe, which sends happy little particles dancing along the lower half of my face.

Zombi's venom crackles—shoots from each and every one of my veins—but I don't want to think about Zombi, so I settle my gaze upon Leo's face.

He's pale. No, he's deathly white. His lips are blue, and he looks like he just might faint.

I raise my hand to touch my mouth, recalling in vivid detail how our lips covered each other's—several times—and my love and saliva mixed with his.

No, no, no. No. He can't be regressing to when Tess tortured him. *NO.* I didn't just infect him with Zombi venom.

But he doesn't have the screw in his philtrum. He should be okay.

"I knew the risk," he says, "but it was worth it to kiss you one final time."

As what he said sinks in, I can feel my own blood drain away from my face. "How could you let me kiss you?" I clutch his hands, which have grown clammy.

"I am strong enough," he says. "Dom says to meet him inside."

I put my hand on the door handle, but he presses a heavy hand on mine. "The only reason I let you come along is because—" his voice cracks "—I had to say goodbye."

I try pulling the metal of the handle, but he wraps my fingers in his hand as if they could be charred.

"Frost, you're not coming inside."

My heart threatens to flicker into flames. He can't make me sit here while he goes inside.

He raises his other hand like he's going to use some Vulcan mind meld and make me lose consciousness. A loud *THUMP* cracks across the cab. I turn my head, because it originated from behind us.

The harrowing sound of fingernails scratching the metal roof has me reaching for the daggers in my boot, despite the seat, steering wheel, and gearshift in the way. But Leo's fingers are still firmly holding my other hand; he's white as a bedsheet.

A tornado of wind tears open the door, pulling it off its hinges.

The unmistakable feeling of magic sweeps through gray-white hair and a knotted beard. Dominick.

Leo must sense my need to grab my daggers, because he

releases my hand. But Dom shouts something in Creole, causing Zombi's venom inside of me to solidify.

I harden. Like cooling metal.

Leo, stiff as I am, most definitely has Zombi's venom running through his veins, and I can't tell whether we're silver or something more fragile. Crystalline.

Leo and I clutch each other like frozen statues as the spirits of the dead lurk in Dominick's face.

Settling his vacant, soulless eyes on us both, Dominick laughs, long and low. "Time to atone for killing my Avi."

CHAPTER 43 - EVA

*B*eau careens his truck into the cemetery drive. Guess we're not going for stealth. Massive oak trees with Spanish moss loom over thousands of crypts, all shapes and sizes. Rows of them stretch as far as I can see, and since the sun just set, it's silent and still.

Raylan must see my jaw drop. "They do crypts or mausoleums because of being under sea level." His eyes crinkle with as he half smiles, and I can almost see my Raylan in there. "Otherwise, the caskets push above ground with even a little flooding."

"They're actually beautiful, aren't they?" I muse, taking in the forlorn angel atop an extra big one while we drive by. It looks like they reflect all sort of things about their occupants. I spot a cat statue, a sphinx, and gargoyles. If I still painted, this would be my inspiration for years.

What I don't see are Frost and Leo.

Beau pulls up to a fork in the path. "Which way, boss?"

Raylan sets his phone down with a grunt. "Leo's not answering."

Beau creeps the truck forward, and the beauty of the

moment disappears while we pass a spike with a skull planted on top. The skull appears to still have pieces of flesh attached, like it hasn't been missing from its body too long.

Raylan's voice is clipped. "Something's wrong."

Beau slams on the brakes, and I fly forward until my seatbelt catches me. "Beauregard!" I groan, but he ignores me.

"You'ns ready for a hunt?" He looks to Raylan for confirmation, who nods.

I could point out that Leo may just be distracted by my sister's hotness, but my gut's churning. A shadow darts behind a crying angel, and the warm scent of burnt sage seeps into the truck. I hesitate to breathe, like the air is cursed. Maybe shoulda waited for Mags and Mr. Harris. But no, we've trained. It's just Dominick and possibly Tess. I hope.

Beau parks the truck in front of a super-creepy mausoleum with more moss than granite, threatening to welcome us forever. The cross on top points to the sky, like it wants to skewer me right through my chest. Beau turns off the truck, and the silence pounds my ears.

Raylan runs his hand quickly through his hair, then cracks his neck. "We'll each take a row, but *stay in shouting distance* and stop when you spot them." Glancing at me to make sure I'm armed and ready, he grabs the handle with his free hand, his XD in the other. "Ready?" He's out the door before I finish saying yes.

Within minutes, I'm cursing myself for the millionth time for not being naturally faster. Even with adrenaline pumping through me, I'm no match for Raylan's long, muscley legs, or Beau's paranormal speed. Cheater. My only saving grace is I'm a little smaller, so I can hide more easily in the shadows.

We pass like twenty graves, seeing nothing but more rows of stone and the sinister outline of an old funeral home nestled among them. Finally, Raylan motions for us to gather together. I grab a stone obelisk for support and heave for air.

The tiny, spindly legs of a cockroach scuttle over my hand, and I jolt back. Two points for me for not screaming. It's grown dark enough that I can barely see Raylan's face, even though he's just a foot or two away from me.

"We're going too slow," Raylan says, voice so low I have to strain to hear over my heavy breathing.

"Can't you use your hound dog nose?" I hiss to Beau.

"I certainly am tryin', ma'am," he says earnestly. "All I smell is death."

"That could be good." Raylan's voice floats across the humid air. "Point us toward the freshest death."

Beau perks up at possibly being useful and inhales heavily once, chest rising. "I need a better spot." He turns and faces a particularly huge mausoleum, almost two stories tall.

"This'll do," Beau whispers and scrambles up the slick granite like he's just climbing onto a barstool. I've gotta admit, that's a neat trick. He perches up there like an oversized gargoyle and gives a quick whistle. I can barely see, but his arm is motioning for us to join him.

Oh, goodness gracious, I am going to break my neck before I even get to the fight.

Raylan puts his hand on the small of my sweaty back for a second and looks me in the eye. It's the first time he's really looked at me since the other night in the lake. He must sense my insecurity. I smile as bravely as I can muster.

"Let's use the tree," he says, voice of steel.

A giant tree Frost would know the name of looms next to the tomb. It's much more doable than climbing cut granite, but for my curvy self, it's still gonna be a struggle. Raylan laces his hands together to give me a boost.

"For Frost," I mumble to myself. I go for a running start and throw my foot into Raylan's hands, hoping some momentum will help launch me to the big branch above. By golly, it somewhat works. I get my torso solidly lodged on the branch, but my feet still dangle. I kick wildly, trying for traction against the trunk, simultaneously praying no more cockroaches try to be my friend. I'm just getting some purchase when big ol' hands are on my rump, and I know they ain't Wade's from the Alamo.

I stifle an exasperated squeal, but it's Raylan, giving me enough support to easily swing my legs up over the branch. "I could have done it," I call back down to him.

"I'm sure you could have," he says, and I can't tell if he's being sarcastic. I'm starting to get real annoyed by his attitude.

"Hurry up," Beau calls quietly. Right. Priorities. I haul myself up to the next branch and am pleased to see Beau's not too many feet above me. Six, maybe. Raylan's made it firmly on the first branch. Determined to not need his help, I hustle up the next couple branches till I'm high enough. The branches spread ten, sometimes twenty feet wide

With no help, I climb onto the tomb's roof and up to Beau. Raylan is right behind me, but I'm determined to ignore him as much as possible.

"What's going on?" I badger Beau. Better be good for getting us all the way up here instead of combing the cemetery for my sister.

"I can smell 'em," Beau says, motioning to his left. A disturbed massive murder of crows screeches and escapes an obscured threat not fifty feet away. "But, as y'all can see, I don't need to."

CHAPTER 44 - FROST

*W*e've gone to the land of the dead. Where limestone is carved into towering angels, sphinxes, and crosses. Crypts are tall as houses. Stone-chiseled spires scrape a bruised, coal-black sky.

Cement paths wind past mausoleums like we're in a labyrinth, and I *feel* their sinister pull—leading, beckoning. They'll never let us go.

I don't know how it happened. Somehow I ended up getting tied to an old, live oak missing half its foliage. I must have lost consciousness. The oak's not even bearded with moss; the crypts spooked away all of it.

In the gusty breeze, Dom's matted hair flitters like ruined feathers. His wrinkles split apart a leathery face. As he lights candle after candle, he folds his gangly legs together in front of him, uncannily limber for his old age. I can't believe he's Avi's dad. Avi—the love-spell-jinxing witch doctor we killed the first time we came to New Orleans.

He spreads his lips to sing a dissonant, minor-keyed tune, and it's the soundtrack of the dead. His ancestors have, no doubt, taught him it's for causing sorrow, for inflicting the greatest amount of pain.

Clutching a beaded necklace interspersed with bones and coins, Dom sways back and forth, causing the coins to loudly clank. He's communing with spirits, and I wish our resident warlock, Mr. Harris, would hurry up and get here with Maggie.

Incense wafts through the muggy air, giving off the scent of charcoal burning. Dom reverently runs a partially gloved hand along a statue, seemingly praying to a Roman-clothed man holding a cross in his arms.

Tess impatiently paces in front of a cathedral-carved mausoleum. She catches me staring. "That would be Saint Expedite. The Catholic and Creole saint. He stands between life and death. Dominick means to link you all so we can kill you more quickly."

I stare up at Raylan's sister, wondering how Raylan could turn out to be such a nice guy while she's such a "B."

Dom's milky-white eyes flicker to Tess' heavily made-up face, and while she looks like she'd take great pleasure in skinning my cat, it's impossible to tell what exactly is going through Dom's mind.

He continues to chant, his voice both eerily low and high. *"Prepare bagay ki te. Prepare bagay ki te. Prepare bagay ki te!"* Creole. Has to be.

I look again where Leo's chained to a rotunda's pillars. Like she doesn't want us to see each other, Tess chained him so that all I see is his back, suspenders and shoulder blades splayed. When he wakes, he'll do everything in his power to break us free. But he was going to face them alone and leave me in the car. Did he really plan on beating Dom and Tess alone, or was he offering himself up as a sacrificial lamb?

When my gaze settles on a tall, spherical urn at the center of the rotunda, Tess' dark eyes shine with delight. "That's where his ashes will go." Gravel crackles as she stalks toward Leo.

He must still have too much Zombi venom in his system to wake. When he regains consciousness, maybe I can convince him to stop Dom's séance. Knock out Tess so we can head back to our fortress in Missouri.

Feeling the severity of our predicament, I flex against the twine digging into the crook of my arms. If only Leo could smoke out before she confines him with a screw. But he can't do that if he's not awake.

Tess' full, glossy lips perk into a smile that doesn't reach her eyes. "We waited to be sure you gave him Zombi's venom." She laughs at our time together in Raylan's truck. "How does it feel to be the reason why Leo is neutralized?"

She shakes her head, smiling with no actual joy. "The thing about you, Frost, is you don't know where to draw the line."

If I could reach the dagger in my boot, I'd show her where I'd draw the line.

Dom sprinkles a sizeable amount of powder on a cat's skull, his voice ebbing and flowing like he's in another sphere, chasing Saint Expedite.

"*Prepare bagay ki te. Prepare bagay ki te!*" His tone reminds me of how he haunted Eva and me with those snakes. He made those nasty illusions drop from the ceiling. My body was convinced they were real, and I can't help wondering if their venom was as potent as Zombi's.

Dom nods toward Tess, like it's time for her to do something. Put a bullet in my head? Stick a screw in Leo's face?

Tess cheerfully locks her eyes on me as she approaches, passing a sphynx with an elaborate headdress and a bird carved above its face. Smelling of cosmetics, she leans over me and not-so-delicately wrenches my hand so she can pull off my watch with ease. I strain against the twine, trying to prevent her from taking it, since Eva and Maggie gave that to me. But she jerks the metal clasp against the back of my hand, purposefully drawing blood so that it marks the timepiece.

Tess stares down at her newly acquired watch, not bothering to explain why. "Leo here is a Blurred One." She struts off. "Therefore, he needs to die."

Stalking back toward Dominick, she passes an angel that's clasping its hands together to pray. She holds up the watch to the moonlight before smashing it against the concrete, and she hands it over to Dom, who accepts it without missing a beat.

As Dom sprinkles more powder on the skulls, Tess spins on her heel to saunter over to Leo, and I try to reach the inside of my boot with my pinky. So many tassels. And buckles. If I could just reach my dagger, I could cut the twine.

Plucking up a drill from the nearby pedestal urn, Tess pulls a screw from her jeans.

Leo! Wake up!

"I promised Dom here," Tess says far too breathily, like she works for star-sixty-nine, "that I'd deliver *everyone* responsible for killing his Avi."

The bitter scent of incense tugs through my nose as I try to just focus and breathe. Tess doesn't really mean to kill everyone. Raylan was there. She wouldn't want to kill her own brother. Would she?

"In exchange," she holds Leo's chin, coolly assessing his unconscious face, "he's agreed that Leo is mine. The witch doctor has no use for Blurred Ones. Besides, Leo was with me when you all murdered Avi."

From the inside of my boot, I curl my ankle closer. Bend it unnaturally far, because things like ligaments and bones shouldn't stand in my way.

Sensing my movement, Tess jerks her gaze toward me.

Not finding anything but me leaning unnaturally forward in an attempt to escape, she releases Leo's face. "He *murdered* my parents. Except you don't care. We're not your family."

A blinding-white image of Leo sitting at the card table in Raylan's childhood trailer flashes, unbidden, into my mind.

The bitter scent of the hair dye.

Raylan's mom, still passed out on the bed.

His Dad looming over her, fists clenched.

And Leo's harrowing voice: "The gun is by the sink."

Startled, I grab a fistful of dirt, which feels far too much like ash and death. Like we're running out of time. But that memory didn't come from me.

An impassive Leo with too much facial hair and hair grease nods, prompting Theodore Raylan Wilks to pick up that 9mm.

He tells Theodore Raylan Wilks to pull the trigger.

I squeeze my eyes shut, trying to push out the memories. "*Leo! What are you doing?*"

In the humid air of the cemetery, I look up to Leo's stretched-out back, wishing I could see his face. Maybe he's pretending to be unconscious so that he might attack Tess when she least expects it?

Still, when Leo wanted to show me something that happened in the past, he always did so while touching me. He can get into my head from several paces away?

Another splash of color crashes over my mind.

Orange and yellow French marigolds.

Purple and blue Iceland poppies.

Fragrant, but not in a good way. Smelling of body odor, fighting for attention at the cusp of spring.

"*I am the trained horticulturist.*" Leo mournfully seeps into my mind. "*I trimmed and pruned the most noxious of influences. I culled the weeds.*"

Oblivious to our exchange, Tess circles Leo like a tigress closing in on her prey. "Of course, Leonardo here was supposed to prove his use by helping me lure more Blurred Ones. I'd trap them and kill them before even more harm came to my family." Gruffly, she grabs the back of Leo's fair hair and wrenches it back so she can peer into his closed eyes.

"I *know* you're awake," she says between gritted teeth. "Time for you to pay."

Beneath her boots, twigs pop and creak. She raises her power drill to his face.

"Don't let her do this to you!" I scream into my mind, but Leo doesn't say a word. It's like he's given up. Once, he believed he could be born, but that was Tess' lie. How many hours has he had to ponder what he did in the past while she tortured him, and I was in Bloodcreek?

Sharp, metallic pruning shears float into my mind. They squeeze the pretty stem of two orange poppies. *"I did it, Frost,"* Leo says. *"I killed them because I thought they were weak."*

The drill whirs loudly. "You have to have seen this coming," Tess says to Leo.

Hot tears trail down my face. Leo's sheers keep flitting into my mind. I thought he learned that he's good enough to save. I thought he understood that he's not that person anymore, and it's time to move past the fear and shame.

"He's sorry for what he did!" I say.

A darker, heavier vision flits over my mind.

An impassive Leo watches the Despairity drown a young teenage boy. In his Christmas sweater, a scrawnier Raylan sputters as they hold his head under the water.

His arms flail. I can barely hear his muffled cries.

"We all make mistakes!" I shout while Tess tightens the screw in his face.

So Leo sends me visions I never wanted to see.

A bitter, old widower hunches in a recliner, waiting for his chil-dren to call on Father's Day. But he beat his daughters and son when they were children. Leo convinces him to strangle himself with the phone cord, because no one's going to call anyway.

A boy not much younger than me chokes his sister, so Leo tells him to get in the car in the garage. Crank up the carbon monoxide.

"Stop it!" I flex against the twine.

Leo's clear voice slams into my head. *"Use your knives to cut the twine."*

"I'm not leaving you!"

"You see I am not worthy of saving."

"We already discussed this! You're not like that anymore. You have changed."

The too-quiet air smothers me like a blanket as Tess lowers her drill to survey her masterpiece. Zombi's venom thrumming in my ears has the corrosive power of hydrogen peroxide.

If Dominick's spell works, everyone I love *will* die.

We'll never get to throw that epic birthday party for Maggie that Eva's always talked about. The six of us won't stop for crawfish on the way home. I'll never figure out what the heck to do with Beau now that he's a stunted whore-ghoul with plans to protect his brothers and sisters from his mom. Their enemy.

Biting through the fear, I fasten my left hand around my right bicep and, using the twine as leverage, I *yank*, pulling my shoulder out of place. A loud *pop* sounds as a thousand needles dig into my bones and nerve-endings. I'll grab the dagger, but first I have to fight back the scream. It threatens to pry my mouth apart, but I won't give our one fighting chance away.

My right arm and hand are limp like silly putty, but it doesn't matter. Doesn't matter. Leo's giving up, and he *has* to believe he's worthy of saving. I don't care that he was evil for longer than I thought. I know who he is inside.

Panting through the pain shuddering through the right

side of my body, I grit my teeth and flop my right hand forward. I connect with a mass of tassels, and I slip my thumb and pointer finger into the cove of my boot, wanting to scream like my arm's been chopped off. I manage to grab the handle of the knife, which is just as thin as the blade.

I flick it up, fix the cool metal in my hand, and fling it like a wet fish to my left hand. It fits like a glove.

I cut the twine.

With every ounce of my now-freed body, I take a step back and wrench my hand behind me. I fling the knife, wishing I'd practiced as much with my left hand as with my right.

My heart shoots to my throat as the knife flies wide. It uselessly hits the bird on the headdress of the sphinx. So I reach for the dagger in my left boot, but Dom seems to sense my movements, so he shouts a curse and sends me flying to my butt. My back cracks as I slam into the tree. And the twine wraps like snakes around my arms, even more tightly than before.

With the combination of Zombi's venom and my new self-inflicted injury, my shoulder screams with pain. I try not to cry as I attempt to settle my breathing.

Crows scatter and flap. Even they know it's not safe in this cemetery. Dom shouts other Creole words I don't recognize. His hair twirls with dark magic as fire bursts into the sconces attached to graves.

"Drop the drill, Tess."

Raylan's voice suddenly comes out like a warning shot. I could hug him, it's so nice to hear his voice. He emerges from behind a high mound of dirt with a stone soldier atop a horse, pointing a saber toward the sky.

Gripping his .45, Raylan maintains a confidence I could only hope to exude someday.

Like she's bored, Tess rolls her eyes. "You got here just in time to watch me burn the animal alive."

Raylan skulks past a stone Doberman that looks like it could rip out my throat if it wanted to do so. Raylan continues to hold his gun, not taking aim.

Tess slips the drill into the urn with a clatter. "Dominick knows not to hurt you, but your 'friends' need to learn to realign their priorities."

Raylan clamps his jaw as the sconces on nearby crypts alight his face. "Your plan has already unraveled." He nods toward dark figures lurking with feathered hats and painted faces.

Tess looks around, eyes wide. "You got witch doctors to work for you?"

Raylan shakes his head. "Nope."

Twelve or so men and women dressed like Dom emerge from behind stone coffins and statues of children paying their respects to the deceased. Some wear open vests. Others clutch skull-capped canes. Tess takes an unsure step backward before catching herself and reaching for the cigarette lighter poking out from the back pocket of her jeans.

Seeing that his sister really does mean to burn Leo, Raylan slowly levels his pistol at her face.

Tess' eyes widen further as unbridled shock tears across her face. "I am your family!"

When an irregular shadow leaps toward Leo, Tess suddenly whirls to grab the figure. I'm sure it's a witch doctor, but Tess wrenches the figure's arm so we can all see.

It's *Eva*! Eva—with dirt on her face and leaves in her hair. My sister plasters on a smile like she was hoping to be found. But I know that's an act, because I can see the fear in the way she bunches her shoulders together minutely.

Eva shakes her arms out of Tess' grasp like all she really cares about is the fact that she's making her jacket filthy.

"Yeesh!" Eva complains. "Not exactly the welcome I was hoping for."

Coyly, Eva attempts to slip a pair of pins into the front pockets of her jeans, but Tess grabs her wrist so fast, I'm reminded all over again that she's deadly.

"And I thought I found someone who shared my vision," Tess says. "I guess I was naive." She plucks up the lockpicks and throws them to the cement path as more witch doctors appear from around graves.

Glancing down at something in her other pocket, Tess says, almost like she hates to admit it, "I brought spelled blood." She glances at Raylan and even Eva briefly. "You can be protected if you link yourselves to me."

Eva guffaws as she attempts to dive for the lockpicks, but Tess snatches up her hair, and my sister yelps in surprise.

"Anyone who stands between Leo and me," Tess says, "dies tonight."

If I weren't tied to this stupid tree, I'd rip off Tess' head and give it to Beau the next time he needs to feed.

Angrily, Tess shoves Eva toward Leo like she means to burn them both alive, but Eva shoves back so hard, Tess staggers several feet.

Eva dives for the lockpicks as Tess cocks her gun. She points it straight at Eva. Right between the eyes.

Fear clutches my heart like vinegar and baking soda about to blow wide, so I grapple for my left arm. Because there's no way I'll reach my other dagger in my boot with my right. Adrenaline must be pumping through my system because, with a quick jerk, I'm able to use the twine to help me rip my other arm out of the socket before I can think twice.

Fingers shake. I didn't know I could be riddled with so much pain, but I'm in control.

Have to be.

I fumble over tassels and buckles and, blood pounding in my ears, I seize the skinny metal knife.

Twine groans as I slice.

It hurts—hurts worse than when Tess shot me in the leg. Hurts more than when I threw the knife at Tess the first time, but I swing my first dislocated arm, my right, like it's not attached to my body. I fling the blade through the air before I might pass out from the pain.

Tess is standing closer than before, and despite all odds, my aim strikes my enemy. The tip embeds in Tess' wrist, even better than the chest, where I aimed. But a gunshot explodes across the crypts.

On Raylan's shoulder, a red ring of blood grows.

Dropping her pistol like it just scalded her, Tess grunts and yanks out the blade. I simultaneously remember that she meant to shoot Eva. *Eva.* My ears ring with heat.

Before I know what's happening, Tess tackles her brawny brother by the waist. Like they're bear cubs, she feels like she needs to bring him to her side.

"I didn't mean to." Tess' voice pitches. "Raylan—" She presses her hand to his wound, which is already pooling with so much blood that if I killed Raylan by throwing that dagger at Tess, there wouldn't be any forgiveness for me.

The red wound isn't anywhere near any organs, though. It's on the shoulder, and wounds in the shoulder usually heal okay.

"Raylan!" Eva springs for the love of her life.

Pure, unadulterated rage tears across Tess' face. "You touch him, you die."

Eva flinches before turning two frightened eyes on me.

As the chanting of the witch doctors grows louder —"*Prepare bagay ki te! Prepare bagay ki te!*"—I know Dom and the others are using their magic to do something even worse than we had foreseen. He wanted my watch, and he prayed to

Saint Expedite. He still wants our speedy deaths. And, I guess, for all of us to be linked.

Burning incense coats the air so thickly, I cough to breathe. That only jars my newly displaced shoulders, which send a fresh wave of pain.

The fact that Tess didn't know the other witch doctors were coming means this is far more serious than a few of us dying. They have a grander plan. Something we didn't see coming.

A whirling rope comes out of nowhere and grabs Eva, suddenly jerking her away. A witch doctor with skulls on the brim of his hat had been about to grab her, and I am *so glad* Beau's here, lassoing like he was born with a rope at his side.

But, in terms of witch doctors, there's now about thirty, and even more are climbing over mausoleums like they're not even hindered by gravity.

Skull-brimmed hats jangle as clubs and pipes fill their hands. They chant, waiting for I don't know what, but they seem ready.

A man's skeleton-painted face contorts as bugs squirm beneath the skin. A few actually crawl from his nose to his ears in a neat trail of beads.

The witch doctor's possessed by a Blurred One.

Phantomed figures smile, gap-toothed. Wide.

More beetles scurry above and below their brows and cheeks.

This can't be happening. Can't be happening. I scream, "BEAU, TAKE EVA AND LEAVE!"

I can figure out how to free Leo. Surely, Tess will grab Raylan and escape. I can't feel my arms, but I'm free from the rope, so I can still break us free. But Eva fights against Beau's lasso like she means to save Raylan before they leave.

Tess rips off part of her shirt and ties it above the wound on his shoulder to cut off the blood supply.

I'm about to scream again for Eva and Beau to just go—find Maggie—when something *cold* presses into my neck. Like ice skates.

A long, gray-white beard whooshes with magic as the foul, mushroom-like breath tells me it's Dominick. He squeezes my aching arm as he closes off my air supply with a machete against my throat.

"You *all* be vessels," he hisses. "One large witch doctor, Blurred One family."

CHAPTER 45 - EVA

"We can't just leave them!" I growl at Beau. He still hasn't removed his lasso from me. "And since when do you run around with a freaking lasso?"

He tugs it, forcing me to stumble and almost trip on some smaller headstones. He's taking me with him, away from my loved ones. Raylan. So much blood. And Frost, whose skin stretched with a pain I don't even know the source of.

"Ya can't help if yer dead," he says.

"If *they're* dead," I seethe.

He stops pulling long enough to give a little slack in the rope. I seize the opportunity, swiping the tiny blade Frost made me stash in my gun holster. I aim up and slice the rope. I'm free, but to do what? I know I need to be smart about this. We're obviously so outmatched, I can't just run in there with a wink and a gun, or I'll get us all killed.

Beau's shoving me into the entryway of a tomb. "All right, all right, Evalou. What do you wanna do?"

Pleased he's not just treating me like a helpless damsel in distress, I meet his eye, determined to come up with a plan. "We need backup and medical help. Supplies." I scour my brain for possibilities. The trucks are far, police would just arrest us all, and if Mags could help, she'd be here already. An overzealous cherub grins at us above the coffin inside the tomb.

"Not much useful 'round here, I'm 'fraid," Beau says, putting a hand on a lean hip. "But they got lotsa bodies to munch on."

My head jerks up as an idea forms. "Gross, but not much to be scared of, either. Come on."

---

*B*eau punches the small glass pane at the bottom of the funeral home's window, and it gives with a crash. Surely, there's a stealthier way to do this, but there's no time. I don't say anything as I see blood ooze from his knuckles, and to his credit, he doesn't, either. After a small shake of his fist, he reaches inside the window and unlocks the latch. I'm pulling the window up just as his arm clears the glass.

"Lemme go first, Eva," Beau whispers, and I'm about to say "heck no," but a glimpse at his face makes me realize he's not being chauvinistic, just realistic. I nod quickly, and he's pushed himself through the window in seconds with the stealth of a jaguar. I'm right behind him, not with the stealth of a jaguar. There's a desk by the window, though, so thankfully, I don't fall straight to the floor.

Once inside, it takes a second for my eyes to adjust from the dark outside to the almost absolute dark in here. Guess funeral homes aren't big on natural light. I pull my phone out and switch on the flashlight.

"Keys," I whisper to Beau. "Find the keys to the hearse."

"Yes, ma'am." Beau complies. Thank goodness there doesn't seem to be an alarm. We certainly don't need the cops complicating this situation. I think of Frost, Raylan, and Leo with those crazies out there doing who knows what and feel like all the blood pools to my feet, leaving none to my brain. I'm a little woozy.

"Focus," I whisper to myself so quietly that hopefully even Beau's supernatural ears can't hear. I can't even tell where he is, but from the dim light of my phone, it looks like I'm in the office, and he's already found his way elsewhere.

I slide off the desk and open the top middle drawer, trying to keep my movements from getting frantic. No stupid mistakes right now. Nothing in the drawer. I move to the heavy side drawers with equal luck. A small blue box with a red cross on it is squeezed into the bottom drawer, though. Certainly could use a first aid kit.

But shoot, where would they keep the keys? Why don't I know how to hotwire a car? Why doesn't Beau?

"Eva," Beau calls softly behind me, but I still jump. I turn to him and blind him with my flashlight, but he grins, keeping his eyes shut, and jingles the keys in front of him.

"Good." I exhale and start to run out of the office. Maybe we can save the day with the hearse as protection. I grab onto the tiny ray of hope like it's a tether in outer space.

Trusting he can see way better than me right now, I grab the back of his thin cowboy shirt and let him be my guide, while I try not to step on him or trip. Plus, turning off my light will keep our visibility down.

We move quietly down the hall on the squishy carpet. "Garage is down here," Beau murmurs over his shoulder.

Funeral home garage. The image of a decaying, zombie-like body driving a car into the garage pops into my mind. Not helpful, Eva.

"You drive," I murmur to Beau. "Look for a hat or something to blend in even more. I'll hide in the back."

"Yes, ma'am," Beau drawls, like he's doing nothing but driving Miss Daisy. I envy his calm, although he's walking so fast, I have to run, so I'm sure he's worried about Frost. Just inside the garage, he finds a chauffeur's cap and pulls it over his man bun. "How do I look?" He gives a tiny bow before bolting to the driver's side door.

Right. My turn. Best not contemplate too long what else might be back there. I swing the back door open and peer in with my flashlight. Sure enough, there's a coffin. And not much room for anything else. I open the door enough to crawl in and shut it behind me. I climb aboard the coffin and knock on the window between the driver's seat and the back.

He slides the window open. "Why's there a window? So the driver can talk to dead people?"

I grunt a laugh. "I suppose they've learned to count the dead as company."

Beau clicks a button on the sun visor, and a ghostly moonlight barely illuminates the interior as the garage door slides open.

"All right, let's hustle." The hearse starts moving, and I slide a bit on the coffin. Remembering the ride over, I hiss to Beau, "But remember to drive like a funeral driver so we can get close!"

"Then run over Tess when we get there, right?" he says as he backs out of the garage. I giggle and can't really argue. My chest feels both buoyant and tight with hope and anxiousness. Just hold on, my loves, hold on.

Beau turns the vehicle around, and we're ready to descend upon the battle. He punches the gas.

CHAPTER 46 - FROST

*I*t seems fitting that Dom should be holding me hostage with a blade. I unnecessarily used one to kill a family member. Dad. In our yard. After Eva and I chopped stumps.

No.

Leo and I can't keep dredging up the past if we hope to escape.

Cloudy wisps of fog float across the cemetery—ruined pieces of silk that float toward Leo, probably the Despairity.

Are you okay? I try once again to connect with Leo in my mind. But all I can see is his back, his shoulder-blades pulled too taut as he deals with Zombi's pain. If I could just get him released from being chained to those pillars. His human vessel must be exhausted with Zombi's venom licking at his Blurred One spirit, priming his flesh for the moment Tess lights the flame.

Raylan moans from where he lies in Tess' arms a few meters back, and I have to hope that Tess will forget about her vendetta against Leo in order to help Raylan escape.

Dom's mushroom breath sprays across my face. "We fill you now," he says.

A man with red eyes and a black-painted face lingers close to me as more beetles scurry out of his ears and back into his eyes.

Dom *can't* do that to me. I have to save Leo—be in my right mind. Eva and I got permanent triquetras on the back of our wrists to prevent possession, so I should be okay.

With the jagged handle of his machete, he jabs the back of my knees. As he does so, the necklace Beau gave me catches on the hilt. The vial flies through the air and lands on the cement, shattering.

No.

Dom grunts with disinterest as I try not to worry about Lindy. Not one more enemy. The backs of my legs sting, and sweat drips into my eyes.

"You can try to possess me." I try to clutch my elbows, but my arms don't work. "Though my friends *will* hunt you down and make you pay."

Dom laughs such an evil laugh, I can feel the darkness seep into my chest cavity. Raising a gloved hand, he beckons for the other witch doctors to close in.

Shadows lurk in somber faces, and I've never seen so many child-sized heads on canes. One figure clutches a wooden reed with matching feathered darts. He discreetly passes the reed to Dominick.

Raylan moans from where Tess forces the vial of her own blood between his teeth. He sputters and coughs.

"Dat girl know nothing 'bout what we want." Dom drags me like a ragdoll toward his shrine. "She would kill *everyone* she gets her hands on but family."

Leo grunts as he tries to reach for the drill to pull the screw from his face. Blue, shimmery shadows circle him. The Despairity. Are they feeding off him or helping him?

The tallest one wraps her long, skinny arms around him and presses the crown of her head into the middle of his back, seemingly sharing some of her own strength. But the other two are hanging back. Like they're not entirely convinced they should help him today.

Fight the venom, Leo. I try again to reach him through my mind, but the screw must be blocking me.

Dom grips my chin and raises my face so that he can assess me in the moonlight. "A pretty vessel for a pretty deed," he says.

The tall Despairity helping Leo seems to overhear Dominick and pauses just long enough to look at me. A wintry chill speeds down my spine. It's like she can see into my soul with those black, fathomless eyes.

Dom's leathery fingers squeeze my nose and clamp over my mouth as the witch doctor with red eyes shoves the vial of whatever Dom created between my teeth.

I try to spit it out, but Dom squeezes my nose and mouth so hard, my entire head shakes.

Despite my best efforts to spit it out, the liquid goes down my throat. Tastes like horse feces. And my body convulses—an electrical charge placed between my teeth. I try to keep my eyes open, but all I can see is a prism of tar and yellow and green.

Greedy, oily tentacles flit inside my mind—a demonic octopus about to overcome my brain. And I can see them— Eva, Beau, Leo—about to be connected by the cephalopod's suction cups and attached to my mind. If I become possessed, they become possessed. Vacant, open orifices for any Blurred One who happens to fly by.

The octopus' tentacles snake down my arms, twisting like I stepped on it. Writhes.

In my ears, it shrieks. And just as I'm trying to cover my ears to soften the scream, that bright orange butterfly Leo showed me before in San Antonio overshadows the octopus. Like it has the power to do so. The octopus squirms and falls away.

Grateful for the butterfly's help, I lean into its paper-thin body. Tar drips from its wings, but it seems to be okay.

The moment we connect, though, I see Leo, the more facial-haired Leo, perched on a side staircase, outside the hospital when my parents first sent me away. I recognize the place from the vines shrouding the orange brick turret on the right side. The hospital isn't supposed to be in function anymore, but I'm not the only teen from a lower-middle income family who can't afford proper medical care. Plus, the doctors are most discreet.

And then I'm sucked into a memory that's not my own.

Leo, my Leo, watches through a dirty window as a trio of boys keeps nudging my tray. A roll and mashed potatoes slop to my lap as blood pools in my cheeks. I ask the boys to leave me alone, but they take that as encouragement and pull out my hair-tie to snap each other's legs.

Later, Leo tries waving me down as I trudge down the bleached, tiled hallway. But I'm so doped up on drugs, I don't know who he is, let alone have the confidence to look him in the eye.

He hands me my hair-tie, which I snatch up with greedy fingers and gather my hair into a bundle, because I hadn't been given a brush in weeks.

When the doctor sits me down for an assessment, Leo's spiritual form breezes through the window and shoves the doctor's head against the wall, so he loses consciousness completely.

"I'm getting you out of here." In his translucent spirit, Leo's form shines. He looks like the boy in the hall, but not. His form keeps changing.

He tugs on my shoulder, but all I can do is look up at him with drool dribbling down my chin.

"Frost." He tries to get me to see sense. "We must hurry!"

I stare at him like he's just another orderly, and his eyes ring with fear. "Why won't you listen to me?"

With a tender hand on my face, he searches the pupils in my eyes. He can see I'm not quite right. So, with his other hand, he smooths back the wisps that escaped the hair-tie and scoops me up in his arms. I punch him in the throat for handling me that way.

I don't recall this. This has not been in my memory, but it's like the octopus has shaken out the truth Leo hid from me. Or I hid from myself. The fact is, Leo tried to save me a myriad of times.

As I play tic-tac-toe with another inmate.

When I go for a walk to pluck the buttercups in the front of the building.

When I eat my applesauce, which the boys have mixed with the peas.

Each and every time I refuse Leo, he doesn't have the heart to take me out of there. He won't force me to accept him unless I agree to leave.

Like I've been shoved and forced to skydive from a plane, I suddenly shift to see seven-year-old me.

The matted hair, the freckles on my nose and upper cheeks.

I'm laughing with friends. The boys who'd bothered me earlier have stopped pulling out my hair-tie.

It's as palpable as when I lost my father. I can *feel* Leo's pain. His fruitless desire to still be friends.

I block him from my life.

He attempts to write me letters.

I burn them in the stove, not bothering to look inside.

Seeing there's nothing else to do, he sorrowfully looks down at the mud-caked staircase. Where would he go? Would he ever find a friend like me?

Against all odds, this late in the year, he sets his sights on the most beautiful of butterflies. It's orange with a black rim and spots on the sides. Just like my freckles. He thinks it looks like me.

Knowing it's impossible—that it's completely absurd—he has an idea of what he must do: He will give that butterfly to me. Not as an ordinary present, but imbued with something different. Something to help me.

Leaning down, he plucks it up tenderly, trapping it between his palms. He sneaks it his essence, like whispers of fog that would protect him from his enemies.

He tells it to guard me like the angel who accompanied me to my mother's womb when I was a baby. And he sends it floundering through the open window—to where I sit in front of a keyboard with chipped keys.

Fascinated, the little girl who is me holds out a finger. My hospital gown also has butterflies. But the moment I do it, this fantastical wave of warmth barrels over me. I'm being kissed by the sun, but also something dark. Something with thorns, but I don't find it scary.

One of the boys, seeing this unusual exchange between a girl and a butterfly, openly gapes. By the time he has the presence of mind to raise a finger and point it at me, the orderlies say it's time for our pills, and none of us would be trusted with outlandish stories anyway.

I know what Leo did. He gave me his power. Not all of it —just a fragment—but the most important piece. The piece that protected his core from the enemy. And all my life, it's been my fantastical barrier. No one could completely hurt me.

Dad would never successfully raise a finger against me specifically.

Apart from the few nasty thoughts from the Despairity, I would never truly be compromised.

Blinking back into reality—to the smoke and unusual shadows of the witch doctors filling the cemetery—I speak the truth to Leo so he can hear me.

I know it was you, I say.

CHAPTER 47 - EVA

I'm about to scream for Beau to slow down when I hear a *clunk* outside the hearse. "Did you hit something?" I holler at Beau. Before he can answer, the back door swings open. Grabbing my Glock, I twist and cock it, aiming to let loose on whoever's on us.

A voice I know as well as my own mother's rumbles through my cave. "I'd suppose that's you in there, Eva?"

"Mags!" I cry. Holstering my gun, I try to scramble toward her, but she stops me with a hand on my boot.

"Just sit tight. I'll squeeze in." Neither Mags nor I are tiny women, and there is no extra room. And the way Raylan was bleeding, definitely no extra time.

The front door opens, and the hearse shifts a bit as a bulky figure joins us. "Mr. Harris," Beau bellows.

"Beauregard," Mr. Harris says.

"Figured with witch doctors, we could use a warlock," Mags explains, trying to figure out where to fit.

"Oh heck, I know where there'll be room." I groan and roll to the side. Searching along the side of the coffin, I find a latch. Holding my breath against possible zombie or ebola viruses, I pry open the top and without looking, roll in. I feel something slick. I refuse to think of the corpse and determine not to look.

Mags slides as best as she can on the other side of the coffin. "All right, Beau, drive!"

He pulls away and finally, we're just a minute away from getting back to Frost, Raylan, and Leo. Having Mags and even Mr. Harris here gives us a real fighting chance, despite still being outnumbered. But the image of us piling out of this hearse flashes in my head, and I start giggling.

"What on earth are you finding funny in there, child?"

I have to hold my breath a second to stop giggling long enough to answer. "We're a Trojan Hearse!"

Mags answers with a groan. Then a giggle. It's enough to make me believe maybe we'll all come out of this alive.

"All right, I think I see something. Time to focus," Mags says.

I shift, trying to ready myself, but being in a coffin with some dead dude is more than a little off-putting. I wonder who this person is and hope their ghost doesn't haunt me forever for disturbing their "slumber." A curious itch tickles my mind, so, bracing myself for a truly horrifying outcome, I turn on my flashlight. Just a peek before we ride into battle.

The light sears my eyes, so I cover the bottom of my phone with my hand. I barely open my fingers a crack, but it's enough to illuminate the coffin. I choke, my eyes burning at the sight. A young woman. She's maybe in her twenties, but it's hard to tell because her body is bloated and ruined. I recognize the look from an episode of *Blue Bloods* with Mags. She'd been drowned. The slick thing I felt earlier was her decaying skin.

This could have been Raylan, back at Tess' beach house, if I hadn't somehow managed to scare off the Despairity. Raylan, who's out there bleeding right now because of yet another mess I've somehow gotten him involved in. I don't care if he hates me. If we get out of this alive, I'm going to go kiss him and hang on him like I'm a freaking barnacle.

"Here we go," Beau says, banging on the divider. "Mags?" I suppose she's our new default leader.

"Rupert, you're on crowd control," she commands, a natural-born general. "Beau, get Frost. Eva, you help Leo with whatever he needs." Her voice drops to a deadly rumble. "I've got Tess."

CHAPTER 48 - FROST

"So, your precious concoction didn't work," a high, authoritative voice says as Dom scrambles for more ingredients. The new arrival's quizzical eyebrows and tall, stiletto boots have me taking a step back from Dom's shrine.

Lindy.

"The child is a barrier," she tells a mystified Dom. "She blocked my advances easily enough when I tried to get inside her mind."

Dom glances at the other witch doctors, plan gone awry. Dirty, painted faces stoically watch Tess dab at Raylan's wound, and the Despairity fly in a cloud of charged smoke around Leo, hopefully decreasing his pain.

Dom looks like he doesn't know whether to kill me here and now or feed me that nasty potion that sent that tarred octopus into my mind. He pauses, watching the Despairity as if waiting for instructions from them. But they can't be on the same side.

Flicking her studded whip, Lindy parades past a pyramid crypt and a lion with a ring clenched between its teeth. Extending a dainty hand toward Tess, she says, "Ms. Wilks said she could use a little help cleaning up her enemies. When I saw all the lovely townspeople convening, I knew I'd found the proper place."

She coolly glances around at the now-quiet witch doctors. More of their faces writhe and contort with Blurred Ones' worms crawling into their bloodstream. One actually coughs up a fistful of cockroaches, which Lindy finds mildly amusing.

The air and dominance with which Beau's mom surveys the group, though, enrages me. She believes she's so high and mighty, when Beau and his siblings barely get enough to eat. I don't know exactly what she's done to them, but I would guess that she keeps them under lock and key.

Part of me thinks Lindy's going to insist that I turn around and get back to work. Maybe she learned of our foreclosure notice and has returned just to goad me. Is she going to join forces with Tess and Dom and the other witch doctors? I'm not skilled enough to take out everybody.

Lindy suddenly furrows her brow. "Where is my son?" She turns her head from left to right, taking in the bare chests and long fingernails in company. "I didn't expect him to abandon his little girlfriend so easily."

Raylan lifts his head from Tess' lap and hucks the dagger I used on his sister through the air. It implants in Lindy's neck —a rusted-out knife stuck almost prettily.

Lindy laughs her most girlish laugh, as if Raylan's merely complimented her cooking, when this choking sound suddenly shoots from her lips, and blood sprays over her teeth. Lindy's eyes stretch wide. She and I both stare at the long, immobile blade.

I imagine she'll be pulling it out soon—just like Beau did when I threw it between his eyes. But the gurgling loudens. A geyser about to release.

Lindy staggers, her corded whip dropping to the cement in a heap. Lifting her hand to delicately remove the knife, she wraps her skinny fingers around the handle, the bubbles in her mouth still dribbling.

There's this awful sucking sound like she's breathing through a broken straw, and she's just about pulled the knife halfway out when she violently shudders. Her elbows raise up involuntarily.

You have to lob off my head, Beau had said. Raylan must have nearly severed her spinal cord. Her nerves are going crazy.

Lindy staggers another couple of feet, her high-heeled boots clattering on the cement as she totters toward the sphinx. When she casually tilts her head a fraction to the right, the knife's handle accidentally grazes the bottom corner of the sphinx's headdress, and her head severs from her spine.

Raylan smiles as her head rolls away like a basketball. Leaning back into Tess' arms, he murmurs, "Now I know why Beau turned out so annoying."

Tess, though, just lost her single ally. She looks like she might implode any second, there's so much hurt and frustration in her eyes. She puts so much effort into appearing "logical" when she's probably even more sensitive than me.

She slips Raylan to the ground like she's done protecting him, and glances at a pair of witch doctors clutching canes. Planing her undeviating sights on me, she pulls the lighter out of her pocket and tears off for Leo, cement pounding below her feet.

I don't know where the Despairity went, but Leo doesn't even look alive.

I spin to free myself from Dom's clutches, but he grabs the back of my hair just as quickly. His greedy fingers pull my hair from my scalp, and his filthy fingers mirror the oily octopus that took over my mind.

I jerk my head to get out of his grasp. Hair tugs in pain. I try to elbow him in the groin, but my arms won't work, and I was *really* stupid when I did that to myself in the middle of a fight.

Dom's black, gummy smile stretches wide. He takes a fast drink of some murky potion before spitting it straight at my face.

The witch doctors' chants resume, a twisted, macabre orchestra sweeping the graveyard in a tidal wave.

Taking heart at my fear, Dom chuckles darkly. "We know who gave dat watch to you, child. Da sister with the even *prettier* face."

CHAPTER 49 - EVA

The hearse lurches, speeding up, then rocks violently as Beau slams on the brakes. We fly into action. Beau and Mr. Harris are out in the forray before we can even get the back door open. Even through the thick hearse walls, I can hear a chorus of chanting.

Mr. Harris' voice soon rises to meet them, sounding like a whole other person's. Still breathy, but so powerful as he recites spells. Chanting witch doctor voices respond to him, but he raises to a shout like he's commanding the Grand Canyon to up and close.

Mags shimmies out, and I whisper, "Safe travels," to the dead woman beside me while Mags yanks me out of the coffin. The second her feet hit the ground, she takes off like a pissed off bull at Tess. I know she'll take care of her, and then actually take care of Raylan, so I focus on my job. Try to be the hunter.

Glock ready to fire, head on a swivel, I focus on my mission: helping Leo. But there's so much chaos. Mr. Harris holds a small leather book in one hand, his other hand outstretched, faint orange light trailing his finger where he draws symbols in the air.

A small object zaps just inches from my face, hitting an unseen barrier, and falls to the ground. Shocked, I look at the feathered razor that just tried to embed itself in my face. Thanks for the magical wall, Mr. H.

The shadows writhe as I search for Leo. So many bodies lurching in rhythm but restricted now by spells. One moves more freely, a gray-white beard flashing in the moonlight, and next to him, I see the blonde glow of my sister's hair. *Frost.* My body flinches, trying to run to her, but that's not my job. Beau's lanky figure is already stalking Dom.

Thousands of roaches and beetles scurry across the soft grass, weaving in and out of view until they climb onto their masters, slithering down eyes and throats like a time-lapsed decay. I have to force myself not to brush off phantom insects and instead rush forward.

Leo's hunched by a giant scorched planter, not looking in much better shape than when he was locked up in Tess' torture chamber. Not ten feet away, Mags and Tess are going at it, and it's like a grizzly bear versus a jaguar. Different, but both so deadly. Raylan must not be far away.

Mags blocks a knife swipe from Tess as I sprint to Leo. Silver lining—he appears rather unguarded, but my blood *boils* at the sight of something round and shiny on his upper lip.

"Mama?" I hear Beau ask from behind me, where he was supposed to be freeing Frost. A quick glance shows me a headless body in leather that does look a lot like his mom. To his credit, though, he doesn't stop and instead looms between Dominick and Frost like an Old Western cowboy.

In the darkness, I kick something small and metallic. The drill. Snagging it, I set straight to helping free Leo. I'm going to start making him wear a metal mask so no one can ever do this to him again.

"Hey, buddy," I say, sliding down in front of him. "Let's get you up and running."

A sudden coldness envelopes me, like we're in an over-sized freezer. My favorite ugly friends must be here. I know nothing can fight the Despairity like Leo can, though, so I just need to free him.

A cockroach the size of my fist flies at my head, and I shriek, dodging it as Mr. Harris' spell, belatedly, turns it to smoke.

Looking where the Frankenstein bug used to be, I finally catch a glimpse of Raylan and his ruffled hair, laying by a giant tree. Not moving. Shouted curses pound my ears, echoing off the tombs. Beau and Dom are a clashing blur of blows. My body is getting colder by the second, and it's kind of hard to breathe.

"Eva," Leo says, his voice strained.

Right. One at a time.

"Sorry, man." I grimace. "Once again, this is gonna hurt."

Tess spies me fixing to undo her handiwork on Leo. "My brother's shot, and your brilliant idea is to help *him*?" She dodges a punch to the gut from Mags. "You're either ignorant or just really stupid."

The cold makes it hard to grip the drill. Leo grasps my hands to try to steady them. His eyes look desperate and frowning instead of hopeful.

"Come on, Leo," I say. "You're supposed to have all the faith in me."

"You want the faith of a murderer, Eva?" Tess hooks a punch straight into Mags' chest. I can hear the air expelled from Mags' lungs as she doubles over. Tess' next words are as cold and calculated as a giant anaconda. "*Your* friend *killed our parents.*"

There's no way. I search for Raylan to reject this prepos-terous idea, but his face is barely more than a shadow. Mags, recovered, throws herself at Tess, but Tess twists away before Mags can make contact. "Really, Eva," Tess calls. "Ask him."

I look back to Leo, angry enough that I land the drill right away. I grit my teeth and pull the trigger. Leo's eyes flutter as his blood drips onto his shirt, the screw tearing already-healing bone as it pulls out with a crunch. He's free.

"Ladies," Mr. Harris wheezes, still drawing runes in the air. "We must speed this up."

The witch doctors' movements are getting stronger. Bigger. A man with a terrifying mask of giant red teeth and snake eyes aims a blow dart at Beau through the spell. Thankfully, Beau ducks in time, but he's really slowing down. He's got Frost on her feet, and he punches while Frost kicks at Dom. Frost's arms hang strangely around her, and I wonder if she's been hexed or something.

Leo places his hand gently on mine, his eyes looking no happier now that he's free. The Despairity start circling us, almost like they're protecting us, but that can't be right or good.

"Eva!" Tess screams, chucking a granite orb at Mags now, of all things. "You could've been great! I welcomed you into our family, and you chose that *thing*. You deserve to die right along with him." She throws a kick straight into Mags' knee with a loud crack. Mag roars and reaches for her gun, but then she swings her hand back around to pull Tess' feet out from under her.

Tess, for the first time, looks ragged, sprawled on the ground with her eyeliner smudged on her face. Her sweat-soaked hair sticks to her forehead. She pulls out a large silver handgun, the one Raylan said belonged to their parents, and starts to sit up, aiming at Maggie.

My Mags. The most consistent, stable force in my life. The one person who has never once made me feel dumb or fat and has been there for me, not out of family obligation, but by choice. Before I can decide, before I can think, or breathe, I draw my pistol and shoot Tess straight between her shoulder blades. Because what else could I do? Gunsmoke tingles in my nose, and my chest shutters inward.

Tess falls back, face to the stars, and I can't believe I just shot her. Air leaves my lungs and won't come back in. Frantic, I look back at Raylan, but his eyes are closed, his skin almost as white as the stone around us. He—could he understand?

Something pricks the back of my neck, like maybe one of the darts got me. But, Raylan is dying. And I think I just killed his sister. "Mr. Harris!" I cry at the warlock who's keeping this from turning into a slaughter. "Can you help Raylan?" I get a breath in, but it's not enough.

The librarian stops his hold on the crowd long enough to see Raylan passed out on the cement ground. My baby's running out of time. Mr. Harris shuffles quickly to Raylan's side and moves his hands over the wound, but the witch doctor chanting grows louder, now unchecked. What are they trying to do?

Tess lays as still as Beau's mom, and I'm growing colder from the inside now.

Mags is alive, though. She hauls herself to sitting and unleashes her shotgun, shell by shell, on the witch doctors.

They don't even try to run while she unloads on them. And then I realize, they don't fall.

"They're possessed," I yell at Mags. "Time to get 'em wet."

She nods and grabs ammo from her other belt. Blue shells for holy water. Pressing the release, I let my clip fall to the ground and slide my holy water clip into place. I unload five shots on the snake-eyed masked man. He shrieks, and black smoke flies from his mouth behind the mask.

I turn to a woman with a feathered crown and shoot her. Between the eyes. She hisses at me, staring me down with a hole in her forehead. I fire four more rounds into her head until there's not much left of it. Black smoke shoots from her stump of a neck.

A raspy laugh booms from where Frost and Beau had been fighting Dominick. Beau's got Dom pinned to the ground with a machete to his throat, which, apparently, Dom finds hilarious.

Frost hurls a dagger into a giant guy's bare chest, her arms working at least a little. She leaps to me, dodging another feathered dart that tries to catch her muscular arm.

"Eves." Frost throws her arm around me like it's made of rubber. "Are you okay?"

I nod emphatically, not sure why she's asking, and turn to finish my clip on the giant guy. She shoots a worried glance at Leo, who holds an overly exhausted hand up at the Despairity, like he's trying to form some sort of peace treaty with them. They inch closer, and I smell their rot. I stifle a gag, but quite unexpectedly, I puke all my beignets over the ground. Sad.

Leo murmurs, distracted. "Eva, I was still right about you."

"What the hell is going on?" I whimper. "Did you really kill them?"

When he doesn't answer, I turn to Frost to tell her there's no way that he did that, but her eyes droop with guilt. Leo's hand slaps the ground. The Despairity fall on us like a mountain of water from a broken dam. Frost twists towards them and throws a hand out, a lot like Leo did. They freeze and . . . is this for real right now?

"Frooooost?" Since when has my sister been telekinetic, and why on earth has she been holding out on me? But I don't hear her answer, 'cause something small moves under my skin, and my legs are so wobbly, I have to steady myself on a marble pillar.

"Where is Eva?" Raylan suddenly demands, pushing himself up despite Mr. Harris' muttering.

I'm so relieved he's still alive that my head forgets to control the rest of me, and I fall to the ground. Despite having my face smashed in the dirt, I promise myself to shelve books for Mr. Harris for as long as I live.

Raylan staggers over and hunches beside me, gathering me into his arms.

"I've got you," Raylan's voice is both soft and rougher than I've ever heard.

"You're okay?" I manage to croak, searching his furrowed brow and pale skin. Then I feel the slick blood on his arm. Just a patch then?

He kisses my forehead and, grimacing in pain, grabs his gun. But his gaze lands on one of the many bodies on the ground, and he freezes. His face grows as hard and cold as the marble we're leaning on.

"I'm so sorry," I say, fighting back a sob. His brows narrow, and he shakes his head just a bit.

Something shifts inside me. *Moves.* And it's bigger now. Like the cockroach from before has wormed inside my body, and it's wreaking havoc on my intestines. A loud, wet cough escapes me before I know what's happening. Dark liquid covers Raylan's chest, and it smells *bad*. His eyes shoot wide.

"Mags?" Raylan roars, veins bulging like they'll explode. "DO SOMETHING."

A second prick hits me, this time in the soft tissue of my stomach. Raylan's head snaps in the direction of the assailant. Dominick holds Beau down now with his foot and lowers a giant reed blowgun from his mouth.

"Poison?" Frost's voice wavers, tearing her focus off the Despairity for a second.

"Ounja," Beau grunts from under Dom's foot. "To break down 'er protection. Ya need holy water and a silver chain."

Dom pushes harder, and Beau's voice becomes even more choked. "Keep 'em from gettin' in."

I'm trying not to be too self-centered, but I really don't feel good, and I'm pretty sure those cockroaches are playing gladiator inside me now.

"Raylan, try Maggie's trunk for the silver chain!" Frost's panicked voice cuts through my mind-fog. "Her knee's shattered, and I have to help Leo."

"But, Raylan," I groan. "I love you."

His eyes flash, soften, then harden again.

"I'm not leaving her." His voice has that stubborn, flat tone, but I sense indecision in the way his arms shift around me. The cockroaches win, and I have a coughing fit, spewing chunks of I'm afraid to know what.

"I don't have one." Mags' voice is cold. "We gotta get her outta here."

CHAPTER 50 - FROST

*E*va. She's not okay.

Her body twitches and convulses; something's trapped inside. She doesn't have the gift from Leo—can't stop it from taking over her body and mind.

Her permanent tattoo fades from her arm. The ounja's working its magic. What's happening to my sister's body?

I kick aside an angry witch doctor with feathers all over his head and spin for Leo. He's our best shot for freeing Eva. Maybe he can jump in her vessel and chase out whatever's crawled inside.

When I get to the rotunda, the Despairity leap from the shadows and jump on me like leeches. I grapple with their thin, slippery hands, and I'm still surprised they're somewhat corporeal. They don't have to contend with a slower, damaged body. What's more, the tall one keeps trying to slip past me. I swipe at her, but it's like she's trying to reach Eva.

To kill or possess her. I'll die before I let that happen.

Behind me, though, Eva clutches her stomach where the second dart struck her, and I want to gather her up in my arms, crank up the Depeche Mode, and put on another family movie. Maggie will show up with Beaver Nuggets. But that can't happen, because if I'm not fast enough, every single person I love could die.

Leo, are you there? I try to reach for him from within my mind.

Help Eva, he pleads.

An inky cloud floats toward my sister, an oily mark of grease streaking past the sphinx.

Beau's freed himself from Dom, but he's screaming about his ropin' skills being "mighty lesser," and Maggie drags herself toward the hearse. Maybe she thinks she'll ready the getaway. Raylan ducks to avoid a studded cane. He tries to grab Eva, but the witch doctor succeeds in hitting his back with a cane.

Mr. Harris and Beau make a nice wall between the rest of the witch doctors and us, but sconces are brimming with even more fire. Shadows leap across gargoyles. Angels flicker with a demented light. Graves rumble, and I don't know where the witch doctors' power ends. Can they raise each and every body?

I crash into a long-haired, skinny-as-a-rail witch doctor who slipped between Beau's and Mr. Harris' ranks. She pulls Beau off of Dom as I tug my final tiny dagger from my sleeve and, flexing against the pain, jab it into her eye.

The newly freed Dom grabs Eva by the hair and drags her over gravel and cement toward his candles, skulls, and other supplies. He can't get her possessed. I won't let him.

He lifts my smashed watch to read it in the moonlight. "It be okay, child," he tells Eva. "Sleep, don't fret."

He chants his repeated refrain, "*Prepare bagay ki te. Prepare bagay ki te.*" The other witch doctors join in with delight.

I can't even help her, because my barrier status means we can't be linked.

My baby sister's back arches. She's a feral cat struck by

lightning. Her head lifts to the sky, and her lips open as the blue murky cloud of the tallest Despairity slips between her teeth.

Eva's body contorts as the tallest Despairity inside her stretches apart her spine. The triquetra on the back of her wrist is gone. Like Beau said, the ounja must have caused it to disappear.

Her fingernails claw the air. Black smoke and beetles scuttle across her once beautiful face.

Beau and I sprint for my sister, his lasso in one hand, my arms hanging uselessly beside me. Beau shoots me an apologetic smile.

"I guess I lost my huntin' skills when Mama died."

"You're human?"

His mouth twitches a little too happily.

Eva screams, and I step away from Beau, my hip grazing the sphinx.

Eva flies right toward me. Her shoulders and chest slam into mine, and the ground cracks open as fire escapes sconces. Licks surrounding graves.

The witch doctor's magic must be done. My ears suddenly pound as the silence proves there's no more chanting. I must have bit my tongue, because my mouth tastes like batteries.

I lean down to my unconscious sister, pushing her hair out of her face.

"Eva?" I wipe at the dirt covering her eyes. I trace my finger down the tear-tracks running down her cheeks.

Mr. Harris runs up, panting and red-faced, as more fire consumes the grass around the graves. "We must hurry." He heavily breathes.

An engine roars as Maggie barrels through a throng of witch doctors in a hearse that looks like it has bat wings. Maggie rolls down her window and screams, "FROST!

HURRY!" She leans back and wrenches open the back door, but I can't go yet. Eva needs me.

Mr. Harris grabs my arm, which flares with pain, and Beau grabs my other. But I have to help Eva escape.

From the ground, my sister's charcoal hair gracefully falls across her face as she unfurls from a fetal position.

Leo, blood all over his face, closes in on our ranks.

"You need to go," he says.

I'm not leaving Eva! I shout into his mind.

"Eva isn't..." The fact that he doesn't finish the sentence means he's given up on the fight.

As my sister rises, her hair sparks with teal static electricity. Her lips twist into a sneer that opens up a fresh river of fear in the center of my mind.

In a primal move, she lurches to her feet. An evil soul marks me with her gaze. If I had been afraid of Dom or Tess or Lindy, that is nothing.

It's like she's the devil. Devil incarnate.

"Forget about your sister," the being says far too breathily. "She's mine."

Raylan crawls toward the hearse, eyes absorbing what my sister seems to be. He tenses like he's going to grab her, but she laughs like she hasn't a care in the world before telekinetically picking him up and smashing him into the side of the hearse.

Maggie throws open the door and helps Raylan to his feet before shoving him inside.

More orange flames wrap around the cemetery, and the two remaining Despairity swirl above Eva in a nebulous cloud, pulsing and crackling. I think, maybe, I'll just let one of them house me when Leo must read my mind.

He fiercely shakes his head. *You are uninhabitable.*

We must do something!

My shoulders splinter and sear with pain. Leo picks me up

in his arms and carries me to the hearse as that being inside my sister laughs in an alien kind of way.

Put me down! I try to push his arms, so he'll let me go, but they feel like they're made of rubber.

I leave you here, and you will die, he tells me.

Tears, hot and fast, build in my eyes.

More clouds of smoke puff toward us—more Blurred Ones coming—and beetles and roaches cover the earth as Mr. Harris draws an enormous rune to clear a path for us to escape.

I think we won't make it. So many roaches. They're towering. Beau's mouth involuntarily stretches wide open—he's about to swallow a big, fat roach—when Leo throws me in the hearse.

No! I smack my head against the window.

Leo grabs Beau by the collar of his shirt and shoves him beside me. Leo jumps in, so that we're all piled on top of each other.

Eva! I try to fight my way through the arms and hands, but they just leave her. How can they just leave her—to beetles and fire and Blurred Ones?

Through the window, Eva's face is a horrible, smudged smile as we peel away.

CHAPTER 51 - EVA

Eva's not home right now.

CHAPTER 52 - FROST

I don't even have the power to slouch as Beau drives. Mr. Harris reset my arms and gave me a few concoctions to make me heal faster, but all I can think is how we just left Eva behind.

We could have put her in a devil's trap. Like Knox. Kept her in a cage.

No one will even begin to entertain the idea. I hate to admit it, but I do believe Leo was right—if we'd stayed, we never would have survived. Too many Blurred Ones and witch doctors had power.

Clouds of smoke have been filling vessels the entire drive through Louisiana. We almost couldn't get out of New Orleans, so many abandoned cars blocked the way. I knew Blurred Ones were hungry for power, but I didn't know they were so organized in their plan. It seems like they're all gathering in New Orleans. I doubt any humans are wearing the triquetra tattoo, and few have the inner discipline to keep the Blurred Ones out.

Leo says nothing.

I sit impossibly stiff between Leo and Beau while Beau

drives. Air conditioning shoots at our faces, and I shiver from the sweat still covering our clothes and bodies.

"Leo," I try to speak to him. *"Why won't you talk to me?"* But he just stares out the window at hundreds of smoke-stack Blurred Ones taking over vessels en-mass throughout the city. News reports will surely share this. Or will the news crews be taken over and silenced, too?

Oblivious, Beau chatters on about his new human-status. "Imma gonna serve milkshakes with *every* meal. Milkshakes an' steaks! At Lindy's." He shakes his head, chuckling. "Actually, it's Beau's. Because it ain't Lindy's!"

Are you mad I couldn't help you? I try to keep my inner voice from cracking.

It takes a little while, but Leo's head gives an almost imperceptible shake.

Are you mad about Beau?

An even longer pause before he shakes his head again. That's not altogether convincing.

Leo's spent the last hundred or so years wishing to be human, and Beau gets human-status the minute Raylan ends Lindy. Does he feel like he's cursed? Damned? That he'll never be able to change sides?

Maggie told us Dom and the other witch doctors are using some sort of cloaking spell to prevent us from finding Eva in the city. We all believe Eva's still there, but New Orleans is the type of place that has entire civilizations hidden behind closed doors, nooks, and crannies. For whatever reason, both boys claim returning to Bloodcreek is key.

Beau reaches over to casually rest his hand on my knee, and I shove his hand away. Just because he gets to be human doesn't mean we're an item. Can't he read between the lines?

Of course, my disregard for him actually makes him chuckle.

"Oh, don't be an idiot." I try nudging Leo's arm with my thumb, but he still doesn't react.

Nothing.

We watch bow-necked egrets hunting fish and marshes that pool over every lowland along the way. Hay and reeds that jostle in the intermittent breeze.

I look to the traces of blood still smeared across the side of Leo's face. I wish he'd just let me *talk* about the gift he gave.

I wish he'd reach over and scoop up my hand—like he did when we were driving to the cemetery—but even then, he was thinking of sacrificing himself to Tess to keep us safe.

I make sure Beau's actually keeping his hands on the steering wheel before tugging out my cell with stiff arms to text Maggie. My thumbs jerk a little too clumsily over the screen.

We're about a hundred miles out of the city, I text her.

I stare at the phone, but she doesn't send a reply. It may be an hour or two till she gets back to me. She and Mr. Harris are covering our tracks, making sure no witch doctors or Blurred Ones are following behind us. Neither's been successful in convincing Raylan to return to Missouri. I imagine he's still doing everything he can to locate Eva, still in the vicinity.

How must he feel, to know Eva killed Tess, his only remaining family? But she was doing what I had to do when I killed Dad: protecting *her* loved ones. Is this how the enemy will beat us? By turning us against each other all in the name of saving friends and family?

Goliath-sized oak trees line the highway, and their leaves twinge with magic, proving Mr. Harris is closer than I originally believed. Trailers squat over riverbanks, and another sea of yellow hay rolls in the wind like a tidal wave.

Insects mark the windshield, warning that we could get

hurt—more than we have already. Our future's never been so fragile nor more bleak. We're headed home, where I'm going to have to explain to Mom why Eva isn't with me.

As my stomach twists and contorts into knots, I can't help feeling like we're heading the wrong way. But we haven't come this far just to forget we are worthy of freeing Eva from the Despairity.

We are capable of beating the Blurred Ones and witch doctors.

We'll get my sister. We will find a way.

THE END

If you enjoyed SLEEP, DON'T FRET, would you please do us a HUGE favor and write a review? Our goal is to qualify for a BookBub to help with our marketing efforts, which means we need to get 50 or so reviews. We would REALLY appreciate it. Even one line helps. You can leave a review at websites like Amazon, Goodreads, Kobo, iBooks, or any other book review site or retailer online. We are a small independent publisher and honest, positive reviews can majorly help us compete with the Big Dawgs. Thank you!

ACKNOWLEDGMENTS

Thanks for not laughing when I, Cammie, say I sort of wrote a couple of books. Mary, thanks for writing the other half. You're a really good writer and an all right person.

Travis, thanks for having more faith in us than we could possibly ever measure up to. I never would have tried without you.

Tamara, thank you for editing for us yet again, and Janet, thank you so much for proofreading for us!

Everyone who has a desire for our "Edgy, Clean" fiction, thank you. Let's keep this going.

To those who have messed up family lives like our characters, you can do this. Our Father in Heaven loves you and knows you can, too.

DISCUSSION QUESTIONS

1. Eva was faced with a pretty difficult decision when Tess said she wanted to kill Knox permanently. If you were Eva, would you have listened to Maggie, or gone along with Tess?

2. A "worldview" is a particular philosophy of life. In what ways has Frost's worldview changed from book one to book two, and how have her behaviors matched that?

3. Leo told Beau, "I know what you are." Why do you think Leo didn't explain Beau's identity to Frost?

4. Raylan's faced with a terrible dilemma when he finds Leo locked up: side with Eva, or support his sister. Why do you think it took him so long to stand up to Tess?

5. While researching Sleep, Don't Fret, the authors visited New Orleans, including going to the Metairie Cemetery, eating beignets, staying at a beach house, and floating the bayou. Which scene came alive the most for you? Why do you think that was?

6. According to Frost, Eva said witch doctor magic was real but counterfeit. How might that be possible?

7. Some people are proponents of mercy, others justice. With Maggie's care for injured squirrels and cats, she advocates for mercy. Tess, however, prefers justice, as she wants *all* Blurred Ones to die permanently. Why do you think each character has this viewpoint?

8. Both Beau and Eva's characters provide humor when the other characters can't find it in them to joke around. Compare and contrast the type of humor each character uses and why both might be needed.

9. Considering what Leo did to Raylan's parents, do you still feel like he deserves to be born and loved by Frost? Why or why not?

10. The Despairity have been biding their time and observing the hunters' troubles for a while. Did you expect them to be the ultimate villains at the end of the book?

ABOUT THE AUTHORS

Mary Gray balances dark and twisty plots with faith-based messages. Some of her best ideas come when she's lurking in the woods, experimenting with frightening foods, or pushing her kids on the tire swing. She is a contributor to The Faithful Creative Magazine, a co-owner of Monster Ivy, and the membership chair of Indie Author Hub.

Cammie Larsen loves all things creative, especially something that tells a fantastic story. She's doing what she can to bring more beauty and insight to the world while building her own life's story. For now, that includes helping run Monster Ivy Publishing, volunteering at her local church, and hanging out near and far with her hubs, kid, and two giant dogs. She's an editor, graphic designer, and contributor to The Faithful Creative Magazine.

To learn more about our publishing company, please visit:
monsterivy.com

ALSO BY THE AUTHOR(S)

HUSH, NOW FORGET - two sisters team up with a pair of hottie hunters to unveil the truth about the Blurred Ones and what they really are.

OUR SWEET GUILLOTINE - a young executioner falls for the daughter of a woman he had to kill...

HER DARK FANTASY: A PREQUEL TO OUR SWEET GUILLOTINE - A short story prequel to French Revolution-era novel, OUR SWEET GUILLOTINE. Young Tempeste witnesses an executioner break apart her mother's feet in an attempt to extract a confession.

THE DOLLHOUSE ASYLUM - a group of teenagers are granted asylum from the apocalypse, only to be forced to reenact some of the most famous, tragic literary couples... or die.

THE DEVILS YOU MEET ON CHRISTMAS DAY - a short story anthology about the outliers, the murderers, the misunderstood, and the forgotten.

HOW TO WRITE FAITH-BASED MESSAGES FOR A SECULAR MARKET - for secular writers who hope to incorporate messages of hope and faith.

HOW TO WRITE CLEAN YET SCINTILLATING ROMANCE - bodice rippers are some of the most lucrative books in the industry. So what if you write books that aren't as steamy?

HOW TO WRITE DARK AND TWISTY BOOKS TO SHOWCASE THE LIGHT - in this brief nonfiction booklet, Mary discusses a psychological and scriptural basis for tackling darker books, some of her favorite techniques for mastering the craft, and how to show the strength of God's light.